Silver Moo

CW00922467

HAVE A
OF 93 GREAT NOVELS
OF
EROTIC DOMINATION

If you like one you will probably like the rest

A NEW TITLE EVERY MONTH

All titles in print are now available from:
www.onlinebookshop.com

Silver Moon Readers Service
109 A Roundhay Road
Leeds
LS8 5AJ
United Kingdom

Electronic editions of all Silver Moon titles can be found at:
www.adultbookshops.com

If you like one of our books you will probably like them all!

If you want to be on our confidential mailing list for our free 20 page
booklet of extracts from past and forthcoming monthly titles write to:-

Silver Moon Reader Services
109A Roundhay Road
Leeds
LS8 5AJ
United Kingdom

http://www.adultbookshops.com

or leave details on our 24hr UK answerphone
08700 10 90 60
International access code then +44 08700 10 90 60

New authors welcome
Please send submissions to
Silver Moon Books Ltd.
PO Box 5663
Nottingham
NG3 6PJ
or
editor@electronicbookshops.com

Amber in Chains first published 2002 Silver Moon Books
ISBN 1-903687-17-9
copyright Francine Whittaker
The right of Francine Whittaker to be identified as the author of this book has been asserted in
accordance with Section 77 and 78 of the Copyrights and Patents Act 1988

AMBER IN CHAINS
by
FRANCINE WHITTAKER

For Martin, with thanks to
Sean O'Kane and Falconer Bridges
for their invaluable assistance.

Also by Francine Whittaker
The Connoisseur
Mistress Blackheart
Punishment Bound

CHAPTER ONE

Josh always felt more at home here at The Lodge than he did back at his own place. Here, in this Neo Gothic country house, set in parklands to rival those of his own nearest neighbours, the blue-blooded Oakley-Deans who still clung on to their much diluted, fading heritage, one could unwind and forget. Here, where the smell of the leather upholstered chairs and sofas mingled with the smell of wax polish and cigars, all underscored with the highly erotic scent of female arousal, there was warmth and congeniality. Not only that, but the Housegirls had a certain pride in their submission, and such a willingness to endure everything that their Masters asked of them that a man could think himself in Heaven.

Yet here in this underground cell, a place of correction that Josh hadn't visited for almost three years, the images of the last time inevitably came back to him. This time it was an entirely different girl who was suspended from the ceiling and whom he had the pleasure of thrashing. She was a Housegirl named... oh, Elke or something, he wasn't really sure and anyway, her name was of little consequence to him. She was one of the new intake, a pretty enough thing with chestnut hair. Her strong back and thighs were already decorated with an arrangement of scorching red stripes.

She was uncomfortably suspended by her wrists in the centre of the room, from long chains which dangled from heavy rings sunk into two lengths of metal attached to the ceiling. Cleverly designed, these could be slowly rotated and locked into position, thus increasing or decreasing the space between the rings. For the present, chains also dangled downward from her wrists, and were attached to her ankles so that she was effectively sitting in mid-air with her arms and legs several feet apart.

Now, as on that previous occasion, he decided to concentrate on the girl's breasts, from which hung metal weights, dangling prettily on the end of three inch chains and held in place by crocodile clips. The way her face contorted when he had clipped them in place confirmed the pain they engendered. Taking aim, he brought the crop down with a savage Crack! which produced a rather satisfying but misplaced welt. He followed it up with several more strikes in quick succession as he admired the juicy swell of her breasts, their nipples grossly distorted by the weights.

Lust tightened his balls. He raised the whip once more, then lowered it again; the positioning of her arms and thighs rather hindered his aim. It was clear that a man of lesser skill would probably miss his target entirely. As it was, even though Josh counted himself among the best in the business, several of his strikes had gone astray and he had made rather a dog's dinner of her arms, not to mention her belly and thighs. Still, it was of no consequence since she was a Housegirl and thus expected to suffer. Even so, he couldn't help but admire the way the girl still refused to make even the slightest sound of protest.

He replaced the crop in the rack and selected a whip with twelve thin, leather strands.

All those years ago, it had been his own slave who had undergone the ruthlessness of his lust. Vulnerable, dark haired and petite, she was irreplaceable. So why did his search go on when, for the most part, he was content? He had a different woman to go home to these days, an Eastern beauty who, if things went according to plan would, tomorrow evening and in the days which followed, help him to clinch a particularly sweet deal.

But now his passion was ignited by his own cruel hand and the helplessness of the magnificent Elke. Naked and displayed in the same lewd manner as his own slave had been, the details of that other time blurred with the present as he set about repeating the incident with uncanny accuracy.

The room then, as now, was different from many of the others inasmuch as it had floor to ceiling mirrors on three of the four walls, the door being discernible only by its handle.

The fourth wall housed the pulley system and various implements of correction. These were contained in specially designed racks, below a barred window set high in the wall. Thus Elke's torment was reflected and she was able to watch the terrible strikes coming as Josh plied the lash with gusto. In addition, she could see her own reactions as, forbidden to orgasm, her soft, open mouth wailed silently.

As before, Josh now dispensed with the chains which hung from Elke's wrists restraints and connected her ankles. Striving to make her position as uncomfortable as possible, he set about fastening her ankles directly to her wrists and tossed the redundant chains aside. Then, operating the machinery, he moved the ceiling rings in an outward curve, which had the effect of pulling her arms further apart. He took enormous pleasure in the knowledge that with her legs held open so, what he liked to think of as cunt-splittingly wide, she must be in dire agony. Taking up his former position, he renewed his onslaught on the meaty globes of her breasts, admiring the fiery lines which so enhanced their appearance.

On reaching this stage on that previous occasion, he had told his slave "Nearly done." Now, as before, with nothing more than a casual flick of his wrist, he slashed further red stripes across the Housegirl's luscious, tormented breasts. As always, he welcomed the feelings he always had while at The Lodge… casual, carefree and privileged to be a member of what was probably the most exclusive club in the whole of the British Isles.

The Lodge, with its opulence and atmospheric splendour, was as high-class an establishment as one could imagine. He remembered how otherworldly it had seemed to him during those first days of his membership. Though he had been delighted to discover that he could still play snooker, albeit in more luxurious surroundings than he had ever been used to. And at The Lodge the side bets weren't for such mundane things as who could down six cans of lager quickest, but were more along the lines of how far a Housegirl could run, pulling

6

a man in a cart behind her. He recalled the first time he had witnessed the glorious spectacle, when the owner of the establishment, John Carpenter, had taken him to watch the 'ponies' being prepared for a race. That was the afternoon when Josh's love affair with the ponies had begun, an affair which had lasted through to the present day.

He strolled over to the wall to operate the pulley, raising the suspended Elke another foot or so. Then, clutching the whip tightly, he positioned himself some distance behind her and braced himself. He watched as beads of sweat trickled lazily between her shoulders and down her back. He noticed how her puckered little hole quivered and tightened in terror, and decided to keep her waiting just for the sheer hell of it.

Suddenly he let fly, cracking the whip across her back time and time again, until he heard a protracted whimper.

"How do you feel about me now, bitch?" he rasped as he drew the first globule of blood, and felt only mildly guilty about speaking to her in a manner frowned upon at this exclusive club. It was a habit he had tried, with little success, to curb.

"I'm happy to serve you, Master Cordell," she told him between sobs.

If the truth be known, he had a very high regard indeed for the girls who serviced the members, allowing themselves to be whipped, fucked and habitually tortured. Dedicated to SM, this wonderful institution provided girls who willingly gave themselves up to pain and humiliation. One place where one could enjoy such amusement at its best was the common room, where the members were at liberty to use any of the Housegirls present. Josh's only problem, during the early days of his membership, had been what to do with the girl once you had taken your pick from what was probably one of the finest stables of Housegirls on the planet.

Eventually, he grew weary of lashing Elke's back and moved round to stand in front of her. This time there was no waiting and he flicked the twelve vicious strips of leather up

7

between her legs, spreading fiery paths along her dewy, vulnerable, shaven slit. Such was the expertise with which he plied the whip that he caught her entire mound and lower belly with one flick, with the added bonus of striking the soft flesh of her inner thighs at the same time. He stood back to admire his handiwork; scarlet weals had been raised instantly, fanning out attractively across her tender flesh.

"Very nice," he complimented coolly, before adding with a slight upward curl of his permanently sneering lips, "a touch more here should do it." His masterful fingers skimmed over the angry lines of fire which decorated her inner thigh, "and here," he told her, touching his fingers to the other thigh. Then he retook his position and, narrowing his eyes for better concentration, took aim.

Once again, white-hot agony spread over her vulva and thighs, just catching her belly. Again and again his feral lust drove him on until, jerking helplessly in her bonds, Elke finally gave in to the brutality and screamed, not a short, sharp shriek but a long, howling sound which erupted from deep inside.

The flogging continued until hot tears flowed down her pretty face and her noise became unbearable. Then, with more displeasure than pity, Josh lowered the pulley and released her. Trying to keep a rein on his irritation, he reminded himself that as a new girl she probably wasn't used to such a severe onslaught. She was so weak that he had to support her as they crossed the room to the small wooden table set against the wall, between the two racks of corrective instruments. He sat her on the hard, wooden chair and attached her ankles to bolts set in the floor. Then, with a feeling of déjà vu, he joined her wrist restraints together and pulled her arms forward, attaching her hands to a heavy ring in the middle of the table.

He drew a cigar from his breast pocket as he repeated the words he had said to his own slave so long ago, "I'll send someone for you." He fumbled in his pocket for his cigar cutter. Fuck! He had left it in his room. As he bit down across the end of his Corona, he recalled that on that previous occasion, as he had observed his slave's frail and maltreated body, he had added, "I'm going back to my room now for a shower. Afterwards, I'm off to try my luck at the gaming tables." Then he had left her alone, to be collected by one of the Russian twins who kept an eye on things. And later, as the rules dictated, she had been available to service other Lodge members. He lit his cigar and drew on it… ahhh! How proud he had been to witness three men abuse her terribly in the common room. His love for her had grown stronger. Safe in the knowledge that she was his, would always be his and, as his lovingly obedient wife, would continue to receive such brutal treatment from him as long as they both lived, he had been overjoyed by her degradation.

Of course, as he had left the holding room three years ago, he couldn't possibly have known that within days tragedy would strike. Now, as the aromatic smoke curled upward, he wondered for the umpteenth time if he had known that their holiday would become headline news when the avalanche struck, would his treatment of her have been any different? Somehow he doubted it.

He blew smoke across Elke's face. She coughed, and he concentrated his attention on the lacerations to the skin of her back. He had been so wrapped up in his memories that he had made a bit of a mess of the new Housegirl and she was in no fit state to service the members tomorrow. He shrugged his shoulders. He would just have to stump up the cash for what would probably be a hefty fine.

***

Amber's throat dried up with fear, which communicated itself to the rest of her body as a heat of arousal which clutched at her insides. This wasn't the first time that her sexuality had landed her in trouble, and she doubted it would be the last.

Don balled his fist between her shoulder blades as he

9

steered her through the crowded bar of The Swan toward the side door. The easy going, smooth tones had all but gone from his voice as he hissed in her ear.

"Remember Sweetheart, I'm not the kind of guy to mess with. I eat tarts like you for breakfast."

She swallowed hard. What she had wanted was excitement. Except now she wasn't altogether sure whether he was playing or if it was all for real. Paradoxically, she rather hoped it was the latter. All the same, she was desperately scared that it might be. He wasn't just some guy she had met in the pub she reminded herself; Don was a villain and something of a legend around the seedier parts of London.

With a heavy hand on her shoulder, he stayed her at the door. Leaning past her, he yanked it open.

"When we get outside, let me go first." Once again she felt the fist in her back. "I'll check if the law's about. If the coast is clear, I'll leg it to the van. Got it?"

She knew she was trembling. "Got it," she whispered.

She waited a second while he checked, then followed at a more leisurely pace. Once she had left the smoky atmosphere of The Swan behind and breathed in the muggy evening air, she acknowledged with trembling anticipation what she had known all along; she was turned on by the prospect of danger. Her insides were aflame.

A slow smile curved her lips as she breezed along towards him.

"Hurry up and get in," Don growled back at her. He wrenched open the passenger door of the dirty, blue Escort van, impatient as always at being kept waiting. "Get a frigging move on, Jane!"

Jane… that's what he called her, but it wasn't her name. She hadn't set out to lie. However, with the kind of company she kept nowadays it was more judicious not to tell the complete truth. She understood perfectly that if any one of her shady lovers, or even work colleagues, were to discover that she was in reality Amber Jane Oakley-Dean and second in line

10

to a vast fortune, the shit would really fly! And if the press were to get wind of her double life, she would probably be cut out of Mummy's will… if she hadn't been already!

Not that she really cared, Amber thought as she eased herself into the front seat. She was enjoying herself far too much. She had good friends… no, mates, she corrected herself, a good job and a whole new identity to go with it. Like her real name, she only used her upper-class accent when she went home to visit, dropped in for a board meeting at the family business or socialized among her own kind. Oh, and when she was angry.

From time to time she used a poky flat that she rented but she would hate to actually live there among the junkies and prostitutes who thought they owned the streets and it would be a pity to give up her SW1 flat permanently. She clicked on her seat belt at the same time as Don slammed her door. Besides, she rather enjoyed her champagne lifestyle. No, she would just have to be careful and make sure that no one discovered her secret life.

She glanced across at Don as he manoeuvred himself into the seat beside her. Already her voracious pussy was pulsing. She knew she was in disreputable company. He only had to look at her the way he was looking at her now and she broke out in a sweat. Except fear wasn't the only thing that made her tremble.

"You wait 'till I get you back to that piddling little flat of yours." He slammed his own door and started the engine. He didn't look at her as he reversed at twice the acceptable speed, then roared away with the engine protesting. "I'll make you sorry you were born."

Driving one-handed, his other hand grasped the top of her jean-clad thigh, his bruising fingers gripping so hard through the heavy material that she squealed.

"I like that in a woman," he gave an unsavoury laugh, "I could get used to the sound of you screaming."

He groped roughly at her crotch as he took a corner at

11

sixty, narrowly missing a motorbike. Again she cried out, though from the near miss or from pain she was unable to tell.

"By the time I'm finished with you tonight, that cunt of yours is going to be so sore that you'll think it's been set on fire. No fooling around tonight, you fucking prick teaser, you're going to do exactly what you're told. Got it?"

Amber smiled in the dark.

Far away and in very different circumstances another girl was also doing exactly what she was told.

***

The beautiful young woman of Arabic extraction stood obediently with her head bowed, beside the heavy oak sideboard where the latest software from Cordell Dynamic International was displayed on the monitor of the latest of the Cordell computer packages. With perfect timing, a message came through on the Cordell Fax 'n' Fone, causing all eyes to momentarily focus on the product rather than the girl.

In his relaxed manner, Joshua Cordell unfastened the top button of his black silk shirt as he turned his own attention to Saskia. Already her sweet pussy would be pulsing with desire. Moist and warm, it would be hungry for him. For that very reason he had refrained from using her for the past week; he wanted her fresh, ripe and willing for his guests, so that she would be all the more tempting as a… perhaps bribe was too strong a word, he mused, his mind still hovering around last night's pleasures at The Lodge.

Josh flicked his eyes around the long, oak refectory table that had in the past graced the Grand Hall of High Briar on the neighbouring land. As the eleven men turned their attention away from the hardware and partook of his hospitality as Dougie, Josh's "butler" poured the claret, his sneer almost broke into a smile. Less than ten years ago, not one of them would have given the "young upstart from the council estate" the time of day. These days, any one of those same men would

12

go to a great deal of trouble to obtain his signature on a contract. They would offer him all kinds of inducements, some of them more appealing than others. One of the eleven had already offered free flights to Paris for all key members of his workforce, while another had offered him shares.

He knew also that at this moment, contracts were as far from their minds as the mating habits of the Mongolian flea; the only thing any of them could think of right now was how they could get to fuck his woman. And that had been Josh's primary reason for inviting the men. Business was business, and he had a few perks of his own on offer. Only the right man would obtain his signature, the most lucrative deal, and thus gain the right to fuck the lovely Saskia.

And right now, that man was probably none other than Reynard Smith of Beevis and Smetherton, who had hardly taken his lecherous eyes off the dusky-skinned Saskia throughout the entire meal.

Once again Josh turned his eyes in her direction. Her nipples were standing out like hard, brown bullets. She would give herself completely if he were to command it, except Josh had no intention of allowing anyone to discover how completely she would surrender herself until the deal was done. However, that could be days, even weeks away, since what he was after was an exclusive deal to re-equip a whole company not only with computers and software, but all the other paraphernalia for the modern working environment, such as copiers, scanners plus microfilm technology for record retention and archiving. Obviously, he would prefer to do business with one of the larger companies like Beevis and Smetherton, although Lockbridge and Dooley were expanding fast and had influential contacts. Dooley himself was here tonight, seated rather cleverly, Josh thought, beside Reynard Smith.

Josh reckoned that all he had to do was keep them gagging for Saskia and with a slight nod of his head, he commanded her to display her charms for his guests.

13

Tall and elegant in the trappings of her subjugation, Saskia dutifully stepped forward and began to sashay slowly around the table. She wore a spiked, black leather band like an Indian squaw across her forehead. It buckled tightly behind her head and was further decorated at the front with a short chain which hung in a loop and rested across the bridge of her nose. Keeping her dark, kohl-lined eyes focussed on the floor, she swayed her shapely hips erotically as she glided barefoot around the table.

As she drew alongside Reynard Smith, the fifty-eight year old reached out with the intention of hooking a finger through the ring of her wide leather collar to pull her head closer to his own, but not sure if it was permitted, he withdrew it again. Instead, Smith glanced down at the viciously spiked cuffs which joined her hands together in front. He took her elbow and had her stand between himself and the slightly younger, ruddy-faced Dooley seated on his right, who immediately stroked his fingers over the design burned into the flesh of Saskia's appetisingly smooth and otherwise unblemished backside.

"Gentlemen," Josh's voice remained perfectly level, "perhaps before we discuss business over brandy and cigars, you'd like to sample the girl? Please feel free," he directed his words toward Smith, "to try her breasts."

Reynard Smith needed no further encouragement and gingerly took her dark nipples between finger and thumb, taking care not to catch himself on the spikes which protruded from the black leather strap beneath her breasts. This lethal binding was joined to two further straps, thankfully spikeless, which crossed her collarbones and fastened behind her back.

"What about her cunt?" Smith asked throatily as he rolled and pinched the hard nipples enthusiastically.

"She enjoys a good frigging, so by all means finger her cunt or anus, or perhaps you'd like to ram a dildo up her backside? It makes her scream, I'm afraid, but there's no need to worry… my staff are well used to that by now. Or maybe

14

you'd like to lick her out? Blow jobs are out of the question though, and she's not available for fucking until…"

"After the brandy?" Dooley, who already had his forefinger buried up to the knuckle in Saskia's rectum, asked hopefully.

"It's a thumbs down on that one," Josh told him as he watched Saskia squirm. "I thought it'd be a rather nice touch if I were to save that pleasure for the one amongst you who comes up with the best terms." He paused as groans of disappointment rumbled round the table. "Better by far to seal the deal with a fuck rather than the traditional handshake!" He paused again, this time for laughter. "Once the deal is done, the 'winner' will be invited back here for a whole weekend, and will be free to use the girl in any, I repeat any way, he wishes."

Josh noticed Reynard Smith swallow hard. He noticed also how one of Smith's hands probed at Saskia's pussy while the other slipped beneath the table. The quick movements of his arm betrayed his energetic wanking to everyone present, especially Saskia, who flicked her tongue over her lips in a tantalizing gesture which implied she was eager to fellate him.

Josh smiled inwardly, already having a pretty good idea of who would be fucking his woman. He was of a mind to make the old lecher wait a bit, and decided there and then to keep him dangling on a line for as long as possible. He thought cynically that the longer Smith gagged to shag the bitch, the sweeter the deal. Of course, it could go the other way and he could lose the deal completely. However, his personal fortune was already vast and it wouldn't do any real harm.

"Don't be too disheartened, Gentlemen, the night is still young. I've no idea, of course, of your personal feelings concerning SM practices, but for those of you who feel inclined to inflict a little pain, you're welcome to make use of the pincers."

He indicated several wicked-looking pieces of equipment which hung on the wall behind him. Made of wrought iron and dating from more barbarous times, their name was self-explanatory. They ranged in size from a pair with handles of about two and half feet down to the smallest pair which always reminded Josh of modern, stainless steel pliers used for the extraction of teeth. He had found the instruments, along with a few other devices of unknown origin, in the cellar when he had acquired the property. He had used the pincers often on his wife. But now she was gone it was the lovely Saskia who bore the brunt of his sadistic tendencies when he wasn't at The Lodge.

"The pincers have many uses," Josh enthused. And it was with deep satisfaction and a rising heat in his balls that he noted the way Saskia flinched as she recalled for herself their many uses. With his own cock pressing determinedly at the front of his trousers, he explained to his guests the applications along with the drawbacks of the various devices.

"I find the largest pair a bit cumbersome; one has to use both hands, but they're ideal for grabbing a woman round the waist. I usually go for the next size down. When the pincers tighten around her tit, she's got little choice but to come when commanded. Though I should warn you that they're particularly heavy and tend to cause the user wrist pain if applied for too long at a time. My personal favourite is the smallest pair, apple-fucking-pie-sweet for twisting nipples and yanking cunt lips. But I leave you to make up your own minds."

Josh drew his eyebrows together in a knotted frown. From where he sat, he could see clearly that it was Saskia herself, and not the men, who flouted the rules. For a moment he watched the unfolding scene with irritation. Looking Reynard Smith directly in the face Saskia smiled archly and, with Dooley's finger still embedded deep in her anus, she sank to her knees.

In a movement taut with rage, Josh scraped back his chair. With his mood suddenly as black as his clothes, he strode around the table. He was just in time to catch Saskia in the act of taking the huge, curved cock of Reynard Smith into the warm cavity of her soft, pliant mouth, despite the vicious spikes around her forehead and under her breasts, which were already digging into Smith's legs.

Josh's hand shot out. "Bitch!" He grabbed a fistful of hair, dragging her up just in time to avoid doing Smith an injury, not to mention giving him the forbidden pleasure and cocking-up Josh's whole scheme. He yanked her to her feet.

Dooley withdrew his finger from her rectum so roughly that she cried out.

"Hurt, did it?" Josh asked sneeringly. "Well, I know something that's going to hurt a fucking lot more. Get over the horse, now!"

He hauled her across the room and flung her towards the corner where a Victorian rocking horse, grey and complete with white mane and tail, stood mounted on its wooden frame. She climbed up and, resting her feet on the frame, obediently took up the required position. Leaning over it to present her bottom, she adjusted her pose carefully so that her stomach rested on the saddle and the spikes beneath her breasts were well out of harm's way.

"What's going on, Cordell?" one of the men asked.

"She's going to be punished," Josh strode purposefully across to the rocking horse, with lust burning his balls as surely as fury burned his brain, "for her disobedience." He strapped Saskia's shapely ankles to the frame, then walked round to the other side. As she was taller than the woman for whom he had first fitted the straps, he attached her elbows to the frame instead of her wrists. He selected a crop from the half dozen displayed in the wall rack behind him, then made a point of treading on her long hair which pooled on the floor before moving off and returning to the opposite side.

"So, who wants to begin?" he proffered the crop to the startled men. "Come on, surely one of you wants to start? After all, it's not every day that you're given the opportunity to give the rump of a beautiful woman a good thrashing."

No one seemed willing to be the first to set about the

17

temptingly delicious backside. And so it was that Josh himself laid down the first vivid stripe. He pulled back his arm a second time, then let fly in a full-throttled assault on Saskia's gloriously quivering bottom. Each time he swiped a swathe of pain across her dusky-toned skin, the horse jerked on its springs under the force, until Saskia was yowling in agony.

Eventually, Reynard Smith broke ranks. As he came closer, Josh stemmed his own enthusiasm and offered the crop to his guest. Nervously, Smith accepted it with a look of disbelief in his eyes and a lecherous grin on his lips. As Josh stepped back out of harm's way and the other men crowded round for a better view, Smith brought the crop down in a feverish fit of stinging blows.

CHAPTER TWO

At the top of a house in one of the seedier side streets of London, Don, the latest in Amber's string of lovers, followed her into the small kitchen. Already her insides were a mishmash of quivering anticipation. Ever since she had oh-so-casually mentioned her fantasies in The Swan, she had been so hot for it that her nipples were sending messages of blistering arousal to her rapacious quim. All she had to do now was wait for him to make his demands. She swung round as he approached.

"So, you lusty bitch, you reckon you're up for a bit of pain?" Don drew his lips back from his teeth in that easy, disarming smile which would bring a flutter to any woman's heart. Although not tall by most people's standards, he would have been considerably taller than her mere five feet had she not been wearing high heels.

Amber's pussy, wet and pulsating, was so ravenous she thought she would die. She bit into her bottom lip to stop herself from voicing her own demands. No, if she was going to do this, she was going to do it right. Tonight she would be as submissive as she knew how. She stifled a giggle. It would be a struggle; although she had tried more than once, she had never been truly submissive in her life. But the fantasies which had dogged her since her late teens flared up in her mind like a fever.

He raked his hand through his unkempt mass of fair hair. "If it's domination you're after, then I'm your man."

Eager-eyed and with barely restrained lust, his gaze swept across Amber's small boned features. He tugged his shirt free from the waistband of his faded jeans and she watched as his long, deceitful fingers began to undo the buttons. She had seen those fingers at work before; comfortingly embracing a pretty, young casualty of theft earlier in the evening, at the exact moment he handed notes across The Swan's bar for consoling drinks... with money he had lifted from the victim's own purse.

just seconds beforehand.

Until now, Amber had known exactly what she was doing; she could hardly claim ignorance since it was with full knowledge of his reputation that she had entered into their relationship. She was no fool, yet like countless others before her she had been seduced, not only by the sincerity of his voice, his blue eyes and rugged jaw-line but also by the roguish nature of the man. His unspoken promise of danger tore at her otherwise law-abiding temperament.

Her lips curved into a teasing smile as she thought of all the women, the young and not so young, who had been beguiled by the excitement of fucking with a criminal. Except for Amber it was more than that, for she wasn't just any woman and, on this occasion, it was herself and not Don who was doing the conning. If he had even the slightest idea that he was just her "bit of rough", there would be hell to pay.

"See this, you little tart?" his hand closed around the significant bulge in his jeans. "It's been up real classy women… much better than you, sweetheart."

Somehow, she very much doubted it, but then he had no idea of her true identity. And she was in no hurry to tell him. She watched as he masturbated through the heavy denim.

"This is the dick that fucked its way round Monaco one summer, fucking all the rich bitches. Then it buggered a certain heiress on her yacht. And this…" he held up his hand, "is the palm that tanned the arse of a real live duchess. If it's punishment you want, then you've come to the right man," he bragged chillingly.

Always the conman, she thought. His words didn't impress her since she had been fucked by a duke herself more than once. Only the prospect of that hand making contact with her own backside held any interest for her. She wet her lips, watching with mounting fervour as he shrugged out of his shirt and tossed it casually across the kitchen to land on the lounge floor of the cramped flat.

Even in these surroundings her need outweighed the

20

danger. This was hardly the side of town in which she had ever expected to live, but how could she possibly invite Don back to her other, considerably more up-market flat? It would just be putting temptation in his way. He would have the place turned over by one of his cronies as soon as her back was turned.

"Get naked, bitch," the light in Don's eyes danced as he curled his top lip in a menacing snarl, "or I'll rip the clothes from your back."

Trembling with excitement, Amber tugged her multi-striped T-shirt over her head. Standing with her back to the sink and with her jeans still snuggling her figure tightly, she reached behind her back. For a moment she faltered before unhooking her bra as, too late she realized her mistake… what if he were to notice it was made of the finest satin that money could buy?

Oh, to hell with it, she thought crossly. What did a man know about underwear anyway? He wouldn't have the slightest idea whether it came from the most exclusive shop in Paris, as indeed it had, or from the local street market. Smilingly, she unhitched the offending garment. Holding it between thumb and forefinger, she extended her arm and let it fall to the stiletto-pocked, linoleum floor and did a sexy little wiggle.

Her breasts bounced a couple of times before settling. If the truth be known she had always been rather proud of them and, though she would be the first to admit they weren't perfect globes, they were basically round and a considerable handful by any man's standards. Strictly speaking she supposed they were just a tad too heavy for her petite frame, though they were malleable enough to titillate the most discerning lover, besides giving her a considerable cleavage when contained. With this in mind she gathered them in her small palms and directed them invitingly towards Don, who now stood stark naked before her.

He reached out a hand and struck her cheek, so hard that

she cried out.

"Don't piss around with me, girl! I told you, I'm not interested in prick teasers, so just get the fucking jeans off!"

As her hand flew to cup her reddened, stinging cheek, her vaginal muscles clenched. Ripples of pure warmth had her almost panting as her violet eyes were drawn inexorably to his crotch. His penis was already twice its normal length and announced by its very erectness as it twitched appreciatively that he was very interested indeed, whatever he might claim to the contrary.

"If you don't do as you're told, you common little whore, I'll come over there and make you."

Despite his warning... no... because of it, she swayed her hips slowly, treating him to a highly sensual display as she moved in time to the music in her head. With the thumb of one hand tucked into the waistband, she began to draw the zip downward as slowly as she was able with the other hand. Bending from the waist so that her enticing breasts started jiggling again, she slithered the heavy denim down her bare legs. She disentangled her high heels and stepped out of the jeans, throwing them aside with a flourish. Okay, so it wasn't exactly submissive, but it sure as hell was fun! she excused herself. Besides, she wanted him to punish her, so it made sense to give him cause.

Smiling like the fox that has just had chicken for breakfast, she straightened up. Apart from her black shoes, she stood naked before him. Her skin, once described by a lover as having the hue and lustre of a pearl, trembled in a most attractive display of fear. Or was it lust? At first, even Amber couldn't decide. When her long nipples, surrounded by wide, knobbly areolae, swelled and hardened into peachy tips, she knew it was the latter.

Once again swaying provocatively, she rested one hand on her hip, letting her other hand stray to the dense, black thicket at the apex of her thighs and combed her fingers lightly through the tight curls.

In a moment he was beside her. His hand shot out and he grasped the back of her neck tightly.

"You want it? Then you're sure as hell going to get it!"

His fingers dug into her flesh as he marched her a few steps, then with a roughness she had considered him incapable of he threw her face down across the small kitchen table. With her petite feet planted on the floor, her backside was nicely presented.

"I'll tan that pert little arse of yours so hard you won't be able to sit down for a month."

With that, his flattened hand came down across her buttocks with a loud Slap! which took her breath away. Reflex made her jerk; yet instead of shrieking out a complaint she exhaled on a whistle between her teeth. Her skin welcomed the unbelievable heat which spread outward across her behind, and she savoured the stinging with a smile.

His hand, heavy and long-fingered, came down again and again in a flurry of excitement and she found herself biting into her lip to stop herself from crying out. She drew in her breath and imagined she was a slave being chastised by her strict Master. And in her mind, her voice quaked as she begged for forgiveness for some misdeed. "P… please My Lord… forgive this poor slave…"

"You got any rope?"

Rudely brought back to reality by Don's voice, she was flummoxed by the question. Frowning, she raised her head to look at him.

Immediately she felt his hand on the back of her head as he pushed it back down again.

"Just answer the question."

"It's not something I keep around the place. Why?"

"Ever been tied up?"

"Of course not!" she lied, telling herself that the other experiments didn't count. And then a frisson of alarm shook her to the core as she realized how vulnerable she would be if he were to tie her up. Fully aware for the first time that, on this

23

occasion, she was playing with fire, she almost called the game off. Don was a thief and a conman, a criminal of uncertain temper, she knew that, but then something stronger than alarm had her trembling.

"Don't move." There was a thuggish side to his character that, until now, he had kept from her. "I'll be right back."

Well, if she was going to do this, she might as well do it right, she thought with a kittenish smile. With her head pressed down onto the second-hand table, she listened as he marched off into the cramped lounge. She heard him snatch her set of keys from where she had left them. Uncertain what was in his mind, nevertheless the very idea that it could be dangerous was sending pulses of arousal straight to her sex. As she lay with her breasts flattened against the tabletop, she could feel every beat of her heart as it reverberated against the melamine top.

Obediently, she waited… and waited. It seemed an age before he came back but when he returned he had a length of thick, orange nylon rope with him.

"Towing rope," he said by way of explanation as he slipped his hands beneath her belly. "I always keep it in the van in case of emergencies. Besides, you never know in my line of work when a bit of rope will come in handy." He eased it around her waist and tied it with a couple of inflexible, complex knots in the hollow of her back.

"Ouch!"

"Shut it!" He reached across to the kitchen utensil jar and extracted a pair of scissors. After cutting the rope, he tied her hands together behind her back. "You never know when a bit of rope will come in handy," he repeated, "like when my mate and me did a job at a Post Office last year. There was a real pretty little thing behind the counter. I gave her the old come-on look and talked my way into the back room. My mate followed me," once again he slid his hand beneath her belly.

Amber trembled as his skin made contact with her own and for the first time she realized she was sweating. He attached the end of the rope to the front, then inched it downward

24

between her belly and the table.

"My mate tied her to the chair, real tight. Just to make it more interesting, I opened her legs and tied rope round her ankles. Then while I hitched one bit of rope to a coat hook on one wall, my made tied the other to a cupboard door on the other side."

In her imagination, Amber could see the girl, frightened and vulnerable, except in her mind it was Amber herself and not the unknown girl who sat helpless before the two men.

"She looked so cute it was all we could do to keep our cocks in our pants, but there was work to do." With one hand he opened the puffy, elongated outer lips of her sex and placed the thick rope between them, holding them apart and grazing them terribly as he yanked it upward.

"Aarrgh!"

"You wanted pain," he told her as he threaded it along the crease between her buttocks. He tied it with another couple of knots to her hands, ensuring that they were resting in the small of her back. "I've wanted to tie a girl up ever since."

He stepped back, and used a knife to cut the flex from her toaster, severing the plug from the other end. Then he swung it in the air and brought it down with a surprisingly sharp sting across her taut, well-proportioned, quivering bottom.

"Ooooow!"

"I told you to shut it. If I'm going to dominate you, you'll have to learn to take a lot more than a bloody flex. Stick your arse in the air."

The rope chafed shockingly as she adjusted her stance so that her bottom was proffered more prominently. The tight little rosebud which nestled between her buttocks sealed even tighter.

If she could have seen his face the glazing over of his eyes would have frightened her as he set about her bottom with gusto. It did hurt, though not so badly that she was unable to stand it; already she was craving punishment from something more substantial.

25

And then it wasn't the flex any more, but the back of a wooden spoon that assailed her bottom with a loud, delicious Smack! Smack! that jerked her body against the table with such force that the table inched its way across the small room. Still the blows came down, surprisingly painful given the absurdity of the implement. She bit into her lip so hard to stifle her shouts of protest that she tasted blood. The impact increased as he put more force behind each swing, pushing the table ever forward until it came to a shuddering halt as it hit the wall.

Tensing under the increased discomfort, she guessed that, in spite of his bragging, this was the first time he had hit a woman. As the blows continued to fall, she couldn't help but thrill at the prospect of facing her family tomorrow. How it would scandalize their outdated, upper-class sensibilities to know that, as she sat through all the courses served by uniformed servants, her backside was a mass of bruises.

However, what Amber couldn't possibly know was that soon her two worlds would collide with devastating consequences. Nor could she have known that, just a few miles West of her own family's estate in rural Buckinghamshire, the other young woman was about to undergo a different, more extreme kind of punishment.

***

Captivating in her nakedness, Saskia's lithe body glistened with gem-like droplets of perspiration. Bound by thick rope to the purpose built frame, her feet were held several inches apart by more rope tied round her ankles, which would leave deep plaited imprints in her soft flesh, and attached to heavy rings sunk into the base of the structure. She was also secured by yet more rope which had been wound over her shoulders and beneath her arms, cutting into her armpits, ensuring that her shoulders would carry the tracks like straps of an invisible dress. As if that weren't enough, a further rope tied about her waist meant she was unable to pull back from the frame and she would, for a short time at least, wear an imprint like a belt.

Her long, black hair was plastered to her beautiful wet, contorted face as tears and sweat mingled. The mascara and kohl she habitually wore had turned into black rivers which spilled down her cheeks, giving her such a look of desperate helplessness that a man couldn't fail but be moved by her pathetic vulnerability.

And Joshua Cordell was most definitely moved, and laid into her with even more vigour. Dressed in his customary black, his silk shirt bore the evidence of his exertion in the form of wet patches which spread outward from his armpits. His enthusiasm for wielding the whip and his undoubted mastery of the art had been gained over several years, and now he kept his Byronic gaze fixed on the trembling, sensual body before him. Her flaring hips and long legs were only matched in perfection by the firm generosity of her uptilting breasts.

Her cries echoed eerily like the sound of a wolf howling at the moon as the terrible cat-o'-nine-tails splayed out savagely across her strong back, adding to the series of raised, reddened lines which already spanned her dusky skin and the red criss-crossing from the crop. And as each explosion of fire detonated across her sensuous form, the force of each strike jerked her tethered body against the unyielding frame.

The focal point of the red-bricked cellar, and the structure to which she was tied, was known as the "ladders" and had the appearance of being just that, a collection of four ladders. Individually, they were a foot wide with rungs placed at intervals of ten inches and, like most of the other equipment in the room, constructed from shiny black metal. One ladder stood upright with another fixed to it at the top, at an angle of about forty-five degrees, so that it looked as if it had been propped up against the first. The structure was high enough to allow a fairly tall man to walk beneath it without stooping. Both frames stood on flared, square bases, bolted to the floor. Each base had two large, metal rings attached, one at either

27

side of the ladder. A further refinement, in the form of two shorter ladders, was attached to the upright to form a cross. These were placed at what was shoulder height for the five feet eight beauty, so that when her hands were tied to it, her arms were held in an unbroken, horizontal line from wrist to wrist.

With her head turned sideways, Saskia's jawbone was pressed hard against the cold metal. Her breasts with their dark brown nipples jutted provocatively through a gap and could be easily reached. Even so Josh's curved brows momentarily forged into a frown as his mind replayed the image of the woman for whom the contraption had originally been designed. She had been several inches shorter than the delectable Saskia and the cross bars had been level with the top of her head so that her arms used to be raised. That had produced an exquisite tautness of the arms which sadly, he had found difficult, if not impossible, to replicate with the Eastern beauty.

On the other hand, Saskia did present him with a particularly agreeable illustration of vulnerability and sexual subjugation. And though his preferences had always been for shorter girls who, in his experience, seemed to exude a natural submissiveness which he put down to their lack of stature, on the whole he was pleased with his acquisition. Her ability to endure everything he meted out still left a lot to be desired, but that would come in time.

After one particularly ferocious blow, Josh lowered the devilish implement and came round to confront her. He felt the sperm heating his tightening balls as his lustful, brooding gaze took in her degradation; rarely had she looked as ravishing as she did now. Had the ropes been removed, she would have crumpled to the floor.

His cock throbbed hotly. Standing beside her, he dragged a few strands of hair from her open, whimpering mouth. He had always had a fondness for black hair and Saskia's, long and straight was, unlike that of the only woman whom he had ever really cared for, natural. He remembered now how he had made his wife have her hair coloured raven black, when they had returned from their honeymoon. And how he had repeatedly flayed the skin from her back if she dared to leave it so long between visits to the salon that her blonde roots began to appear.

He reached out and stroked the column of Saskia's elegant neck with the back of his hand.

"We're nearly done," his concern had more to do with the onset of an ache in his arm than the ferocity with which he had just flogged her. He held her dark, faltering gaze until her enslaved state forced her to lower hers. "It was a foolish lapse on your part, one which I hope won't occur again. That come-on look in your eye and your mouth straying to my dinner guest's prick was most definitely not acceptable behaviour! In future when I have guests, unless I command otherwise you'll act the perfect hostess... obedient, elegant, friendly yet passive, but not the brainless, foreign whore. Is that clear?"

Without hesitation, she answered in the accent he found rather appealing.

"Yes, Master."

"Good girl."

He kissed her cheek lightly, then retook his position slightly behind her. As the uncharacteristic moment of tenderness passed, he pulled back his arm, then continued the flogging with renewed vigour, taking care to lay the vicious lashes across the snake motif which had been burned deep into her flesh by a previous owner. His sneering lips almost smiled when he thought of the delicious droplets of honey which he knew would be leaking from her clutching quim.

With practiced ease, he maintained his rhythm and never let up the thrashing as he undid his fly. He extracted his stiff, heated penis then, as the very last strike fell away, he shoved his rod of iron between her welcoming labia, pounding into her with such force that her bruised and beaten body hammered painfully against the metal frame.

CHAPTER THREE

All through dinner with the family, Amber's desire had been smouldering in her loins. Every now and then, she had caught one of the men looking at her and her breath had snagged in her throat. From time to time, she had thrown one of them a crumb in the form of a lascivious smile or flirtatious glance from her unusual violet eyes.

When eventually the men excused themselves from the table to take brandy and cigars in the recently renovated, nineteenth century drawing room, Amber also excused herself. If there was one thing that she had grown to hate over the years, it was the women's upper-crust gossip once the men had withdrawn. It was far preferable to listen to the girls in the office of Beevis and Smetherton where, by substituting the name Jane for Amber, she worked as an assistant to one of the directors. She was hardly "one of the girls" though so far she had done a pretty good job of convincing her work colleagues that she came from a background similar to their own. The trick was never letting the family get wind of her everyday life.

However, there was only thing that really concerned her as she left the comfort of the elegant dining room and passed through the French windows into the gardens beyond, and that thing was the hunger between her legs. There were times when she was tempted to fool around with the staff, like in days gone by, but today her sights were set higher; today she needed someone of her own class, someone who understood her needs. The question was… was her brother-in-law really the ideal candidate, or was there someone she had yet to meet who had more experience?

The warm breeze of evening stirred her sleek, jet-black, bob hair-do. The feathered layers and long fringe gave her a sexy look which won her many admiring glances. It wasn't conceit on her part which acknowledged her good looks, just plain honesty. And even she would have to admit that there wasn't much of that in her life these days!

As she slung her bag over her shoulder, it was all she could do to keep from running down the steps to the gravel path, except she knew the family would be watching. She also knew that her sister, Harriet, and their mother would be discussing her dress sense and pulled a face as, out loud, she mimicked her elder sibling.

"The girl thinks of no one but herself. She's a disgrace. Her bare midriff put me right off my Fillets au Poivre! And that top was almost see-through. Really! Her skirt's so short you can almost see her knickers!"

Amber grinned mischievously… well you could have… if she had been wearing any.

With a furnace of lust between her legs, she set off through the Formal Gardens. High Briar had once been a grand country estate. These days it still stubbornly refused to open to the public more than twice a week, and would continue to do so for as long as her late Daddy's company was still making money from other people's investments. Dear Daddy… he would be horrified if he were alive to witness her — she smiled as she mentally struggled for the right words — disgraceful behaviour of late.

She knew she was treading on thin ice. If the press were to get wind of her double life, it would destroy Mummy. Mother and daughter had never had much in common. Nonetheless, in her own way, Amber loved her and would never knowingly hurt her… except for that one time when, as a vivacious eighteen year old, she had deliberately set out to wreck her mother's latest relationship.

Well, it hadn't seemed fair. He had been far too young for Mummy and besides, Mummy had already had two husbands at the time and Amber hadn't had a good fuck for over three months, not since the chauffeur had been caught with his cock up her pussy in the rose garden.

Poor Mummy had been devastated when she had attempted to retire to her bedroom with a headache and discovered her intended already ensconced there with her younger daughter.

But Amber had justified the whole thing to herself with the knowledge that it was she who had probably saved Mummy from a lifetime of unhappiness. After all, if the guy could tie Amber's wrists together behind her back and take Mummy's own riding crop to her backside, just think what he could have done to poor Mummy, who had always lived such a sheltered, decent life.

Back then, in Amber's young mind, she had done her mother a huge favour, though now she could see her motives for what they really were… unspeakable envy and an all-consuming lust. Even now the memory of the crop cutting across her flesh brought her out in goosebumps. There hadn't been a great deal of force behind his strikes, nor had it been a prolonged session — Mummy had seen to that. Nevertheless, he had opened her young mind to all kinds of possibilities and set off the fantasies which filled her head, fantasies which were still largely unfulfilled.

A shudder ran from her neck downward as once again, the spectre of the press rose up before her. She knew that, despite her own sassy image, she would never cope with the humiliation of having the details of her life splashed over the tabloids. Disappointment and heartache she could deal with, she always bounced back, but humiliation? Never! So why was she constantly putting everything at risk?

The sad truth of the matter was that at twenty four she was, had always been, a bored little rich girl.

The thin, red fabric of her mini skirt stretched across her backside as she walked, and she wondered what the family would think if they were to see the big, purple bruises on her bottom. She had only one regret; the hiding by Don the Con, as he was affectionately though not inventively known, had left no more than a few token bruises despite his enthusiasm. She couldn't fault him in bed; the previous night had turned into one of hot lust. It was just that, as with most of his big schemes, Don had bottled out half way through the domination session, untying her just as things were getting interesting.

Even so, she had come so deliciously that she knew she just had to have more of the same. All she had to do was find the right man.

***

Sitting on a bundle of rags with her knees tucked beneath her and her hands chained in her lap, Saskia backed up against the wall to which she was secured. The heavy linked chain seemed to jangle in time with her breathing as Dougie approached, with a keener than usual look of contempt in his one good eye.

"You stinking little cat!"

Dougie Ward, Joshua's handyman-cum-caretaker and confidant, took off his cap and threw it across the cellar as he approached the trembling Saskia. A one time window cleaner and former warehouse man, he had slipped into his present role with relative ease when made redundant. Willing to take on almost anything Josh asked of him, he and his wife ran the household and took care of Josh's every day needs. Now, as Jailer and self-appointed torturer, he looked down at Saskia's shivering form.

"I heard you wet yourself. You wait 'till the Master hears about it! And make no mistake, he will hear about it. My missis can't wait to tell him." His eyes, even the semi-blind one, twinkled as he laughed. He turned back the cuff of his checked shirtsleeve and glanced at his watch. "By my reckoning we've got another hour or so before he gets back from his run. Now, what shall we do to pass the time? And remember, I'm not so old that I can't give a girl a good shagging! And you know already that I'm pretty handy with the birch. Next time your Master goes away, I'll show you what I can do with that bullwhip he's got tucked away in his bedroom."

He flicked his eyes around the harshly lit cellar at the various metal contraptions before turning his attention to the array of whips, paddles, crops and canes, all neatly arranged in

33

racks on the far wall. Shaking his head as he realized that any new stripes would be only too easy for Josh to spot, he turned round and made his way back across the cellar to the metal locker in the corner. Taking a bundle of keys from the pocket of his brown workaday cords, he glanced over his shoulder at the trembling girl as he proceeded to unlock it. It only took a few seconds for him to locate all the equipment he had in mind then, leaving the locker door open, with the various bits and pieces in his arms he trooped back across the cellar towards the by now snivelling Saskia.

"Now don't you go telling anyone."

He dropped the gear on the hard stone floor and yanked her head up by her hair. Her eyes widened when he retrieved the first item and forced her mouth open. He shoved the black ball gag in her mouth and fastened it behind her head.

"The Master trusts me, see… known him since he was a nipper."

He crouched down and, without unfastening the chain from her collar made her lie flat on her stomach and placed her tethered hands behind her head. Next he looped a length of chain with clips at either end around her ankle and fastened it to itself, using the slack to drag her leg upward. He clipped it to the rope which bound her hands, then repeated the process with the other leg. He stepped back to admire his work.

"You love a good fucking, don't you, girlie? Even now you want a great dick up that cunt of yours. So try this!"

Without bothering with any form of lubrication, he thrust a wide-girthed dildo up her vagina, chuckling to himself as she moaned her protests against the hardness of the ball gag. He came round to stand in front of her so that she could see him, unzipped his cords and wrested his rigid organ from his underpants.

"That's it, girlie, you keep your eyes fixed on my prick." He wrapped his fist tightly around his penis and began to masturbate himself wildly, all the time keeping his eyes fixed on her. "I was there last night and saw exactly what kind of dirty, foreign alley cat you are. You just love it, don't you? Well, you pissing, filthy whore, lets see how you like this!"

With that, he fountained a hot stream of viscous semen over her face and hair.

***

Amber barely glanced at the regimented rows of blooms as she made her way to the rendezvous point, nor at the perfectly manicured Dwarf Box which lined the route as she swept down the pathway between them. Hotly aroused, if she didn't hurry herself she would be so frustrated by the time she arrived that her body would give out on her and refuse to co-operate. Patience had never been one of her strong points, and the demands of her body were making her tetchy.

Her brother-in-law wasn't the first guy with whom she had had rough sex and neither was Don. But her body's needs to be totally dominated had never been fulfilled by any of the men she knew, and she was beginning to wonder if there was anyone out there in the world who would know how to deal with her. According to the girls at work, there was a whole "scene" of submission and domination, though they all swore they hadn't been tempted to investigate themselves. Amber, of course, had no desire to experience anything too drastic, and had no intention of becoming a sex slave. It was just that, well, the bloody fantasies wouldn't go away. Besides, she doubted that such enslaved women existed anywhere other than in the over-active imaginations of writers. And even if they did and it was possible to become enslaved, how did one go about such things?

She kept her eyes focussed on the distant fields, a jealously guarded conservation area where wild poppies and cornflowers bloomed in glorious abundance, separating High Briar from the neighbouring land. Since childhood she had hankered after the riotous wildness of the forbidden beyond, rather than the restrictive safety of the familiar.

35

It was the same with men. Why settle for the security of a decent, loving relationship when she could enjoy what she thought of as the occasional fuck 'n' wallop with her brother-in-law? If she was lucky, perhaps seeing the bruises inflicted by Don the Con would incite him to use more force this time, though she doubted Sinclair would have the backbone. He might well be something of a legend on the Polo field and a financial wizard to boot, but when it came to games of domination, as with all the men she knew, it was a case of his eagerness outweighing his competence. Still, it was better than nothing.

Merely thinking about such games was having its usual effect, and she could feel juices gathering inside her channel; she would probably be leaking by the time she arrived. With each step her pulses quickened. Sinclair was a handsome man and, as she had told him long ago, he was pretty hot in the sack. However, the whole marriage thing wasn't for her and she had never regretted her decision to remain single. It was just that she needed him in the basest of ways.

She turned left. She would be out of sight of the house once she passed beneath the arch of the Walled Garden and headed off toward the lake from where, on a clear day, one could just make out the outline of what local historians claimed was a ruined priory. Pre-dating the monastery that had been built on the other side of the valley only to be destroyed during the reformation, the remains had always held a fascination for her. Secretly, she had always envied the extraordinary ruins which graced their neighbours' land, land which had once belonged to her own family for generations. As a child she had made up stories about imaginary debauched monks, who had once lived there. It had long been her ambition to explore the site and wander among the fallen masonry. Sadly, the two families had never seen eye to eye so it was a wish that had never been granted. She had hoped things would change when the owner died and the place was sold, but no such luck. Now, bathed in the last of the evening sunshine, the place seemed even more mysterious and inviting than ever.

When she finally arrived at the lake, Sinclair was lounging against the statue of Venus. Dressed impeccably as always, with the arrogance born of a man of his standing, he eased himself away as she approached. Tall, lean faced with an angular jaw, Sinclair was a man with sex appeal.

"You took your time. Do you want to get caught?"

She smiled. "Why? Don't you?"

"Don't be so bloody stupid."

He clasped her hand in his and hurried her the rest of the way. It was a shame, she thought, that Mummy's third husband had insisted on the removal of the maze, though in all honesty it had become a mite tired and threadbare. Family tradition had it that it had been the breeding ground for many an illicit romance through the centuries. It was even rumoured that Amber herself had been conceived there in a moment of passion with a visiting diplomat, and that she wasn't Daddy's child at all. There was no proof, of course, and thankfully Mummy had remained stubbornly silent on the matter, though it hadn't escaped anyone's notice that Amber's looks favoured neither side of the family. The attractive, pearly tone of her skin and unusual eyes had always set her apart from her forebears, as had her ebony hair and petite stature.

Sinclair led her across the lawn down to the shelter of the trees which overlooked the seventeenth century fountain, still in dire need of restoration.

"Why do you have to draw so much attention to yourself, Amber? You're an embarrassment. You could at least have worn a bra. That scrap of material you call a top doesn't leave much to the imagination. Your mother's new husband, Lawrence, didn't know where to look!"

She laughed, and dropped her more usual, cultured tones to impersonate one of the girls from the office.

" 'Course he did, the same place as you. Hubby number four got a fucking great stiffy when he saw my tits. I bet he nearly creamed his pants when he watched my nipples go

37

hard." And her long, fleshy nipples were going hard again right now. She dropped the act to continue, "Judging by the bulge in his trousers, I'd say it's obvious what Mummy sees in this one."

"There's no need to be crude, Amber. You're not a common whore so don't try to act like one." He pointed to the stone seat and issued instructions which were curiously at odds with his previous statement. "Lie down and open your legs."

"If I'm not a whore, what gives you the right to treat me like one?" Flashing her legs at him as she sat down she swung them up onto the seat, making sure he got a good view of her black-fleeced mound. "How's that for an eyeful?" she taunted, then added, "shall I take my clothes off first or are you in too much of a hurry?"

"Just take off your top."

She fiddled for a moment with the shoestring straps, then took hold of the hem of the flimsy lace, bandeau top and dragged it off over her head. As always, she heard Sinclair's intake of breath as her pearly, peach-tipped breasts were revealed. Hastily, he unzipped his trousers. As they dropped around his ankles, he plucked his cock from his Calvin Klein underpants. Hindered by his tailored trousers, he swung himself on top of her. He placed a hand on her collarbone to push her down, then seized her juicy, naked breasts, squeezing them hard.

"Don't make a sound, or someone will hear us," he warned, tugging at her fleshy, extended nipples.

"You could always gag me," she suggested, hopefully.

"Be quiet, or I'll put you over my knee like last time."

She wet her lips with the tip of her tongue and her pussy twitched in anticipation.

He removed one hand from her breast and used it to guide his penis into her ever-moistening channel. As his passion increased, so did the speed with which he pumped in and out. Amber raised her hips and thrusting upward, matched his rhythm stroke for stroke, sure in the knowledge that she gave him a better fuck than her sister did.

And even as he drove into her, she remembered fondly their last encounter a little over a month ago at her flat, not the one she used to entertain the likes of Don but the up-market flat where she received family and friends of her own kind. On that occasion he had whacked her hard with the back of her antique, tortoiseshell hairbrush, and she had had one of the fiercest orgasms of her life, eclipsed only by the one she had experienced last night at Don's hands.

"You're such a beast," she told him now in a raised, taunting voice she hoped would do the trick and produce the much fantasised gag. "Ooooh! You're hurting me!" she added for good measure.

"I told you to shut up."

"Then make me."

In a clumsy movement, he withdrew his cock and struggled to regain his feet. He caught her wrist and made her stand beside him, then sat down on the seat. He pulled her closer, then down over his knees.

Now we're getting somewhere, she thought as his hand came down sharply across her buttocks, pounding her flesh and sending a flood of warmth over her already bruised and tenderised skin.

"Looks like someone's been here before me," he said, bringing his hand down heavily.

"Ouch!" she cried in genuine pain. This was more like it!

Again he struck her, and again, each time heavier than the last until her bottom was a blaze of pain. And it was pain, hot, glorious pain that had a weird way of sending her over the top with desire. The more his hand stung, the more she wanted, even as she cried out. She should tell him to stop, she knew she should, but oh! Not yet!

There was a pause as Sinclair reached behind him, and she heard a Snap! as he broke a branch from one of the trees. He denuded it of leaves, then brought it down in a line of stinging pain across her burning, bruised behind.

Again he swiped the branch before swapping it into his left hand and jabbing two fingers inside her dewy pussy with the other. Thrusting them in and out as, somewhat awkwardly, he struck her again, though being right handed there was less force behind the blows than either of them would have liked.

Nevertheless, as the blows continued to fall, she felt the delicious clenching of her sex muscles. She moaned as her excitement grew, biting on her bottom lip but failing to stifle the scream which broke free and announced her orgasm to the world. And not just once, as for the first time in her life she came twice in quick succession as he continued to frig and beat her simultaneously.

***

Having left Saskia alone in the cellar since her flogging the previous evening, Josh thought it only right that he pay her a visit. After all, apart from the water last night, and the bread and honey his sparkly-eyed housekeeper had taken down around midday, the girl had had nothing to eat. She was probably famished. Still, it served her right. While he didn't object entirely to her giving herself to his dinner guests, indeed, he often encouraged it, as his property it certainly wasn't up to her to decide when and to whom.

With this in mind, he headed for the kitchen. He had the mother of all thirsts to quench and only a glass of Alice Ward's homemade Mint Fruit Fizz would do.

He unzipped the top of his black tracksuit to reveal his tanned chest. His black suede jogging shoes made no sound on the quarry tiled floor as he entered the kitchen, yet even with her back to him, his housekeeper knew he was there.

"Did you enjoy your run?"

"Yes. It's a wonderful evening."

He took a glass from the cupboard then ambled over to the fridge. He poured himself the longed-for drink, then used his forearm to clear away the dirty crockery on the worktop. Like a small boy, he hoisted himself up and settled himself on the edge to drink, all the while thinking of the way Saskia's body had looked when he had last seen her.

Her lovely face, streaked with mascara and puffy from so many tears having been shed, had looked all the more beautiful as, still bound to the ladders and almost unconscious, Saskia had hung limply in her bonds with Josh's semen dripping down the inside of her thighs. The red criss-crossing across her back had been a sight to make any man's cock squirm in his pants, though those across her rounded bottom with its snake brand had given him an extra thrill.

"A lovely evening," he repeated as he came out of his reverie, then added, "why don't you make yourself a cup of tea and go and sit outside?"

"And who's going to do this lot?" Alice turned and with a sweeping movement which took in the whole of the kitchen, drew his attention to the chores still to be done. "The floor's not been washed today, thanks to the girl being out of service."

"I know you miss her company around the place," he flicked his head to dislodge the hank of tawny hair which fell over his eye, "but she has to be punished."

"Miss her company?" Alice's laugh was a chuckle which crinkled her face. "Miss seeing that lazy little whore on her hands and knees more like! With my legs, I can't get down there anymore and, to give the girl her due, she's pretty good with the bucket and cloth."

Always a stickler for things being done her way, Alice had discarded the mop long ago. And when Saskia had been made to take over the job, along with other menial chores befitting her lack of status in the household, Alice had made no allowances; the girl cleaned the floor the old fashioned way. And there was a lot of floor to cover. It was a large room, modernised and fitted out in oak when he had first acquired the property less than five years ago. It hadn't entirely lost the Olde Worlde charm that had first attracted him to the place, though it seemed to Josh that when the old had been ripped out

41

to make way for the new, it had lost its heart. He was only thankful that he hadn't applied the same ruthless destruction to the rest of the house.

Alice was only now beginning the washing up from the meal two hours ago. Sometimes, Josh wondered if it was all too much for her. On the other hand, he considered it best not to broach the subject of the dishwasher which stood idle. It had been installed along with all the other requirements his wife had insisted upon, but his stubborn housekeeper refused to use it, pointing out that she had, "my Dougie to give me a hand," not that her husband was in evidence on that particular evening.

"Where's Dougie? I've got a little job for him."

"Oh, he's just popped down to the cellar."

"How was she when you looked in on her?" Josh asked after Saskia as casually as if he were enquiring after the health of a distant neighbour.

"Tired. You shouldn't have left her tied to that frame all night. It's not surprising she wet herself." Alice shook her head as she admonished him gently. "Whatever she'd done, she didn't deserve that."

"She wet herself? I hope you gave her a thrashing."

"Of course not! She had had quite enough from the look of her back. I took her down and helped her over to her bed."

It always amused Josh when Alice referred to the bundle of rags as a bed, just as she called the bucket in the corner of the cellar a toilet and the slave collar around Saskia's swan-like throat a choker. She even called the cold water tap that Josh had had plumbed into the wall about half way up a shower. The girl had her own room, of course, but he had to guard against her getting above herself.

"I sat with her while she ate a bite and drank a mug of coffee," she continued, "then told her to lie down and, when I left after cleaning the place up a bit, she was sound asleep."

Relieved that she was okay yet at the same time irritated that his wishes hadn't been carried out to the full, he

42

admonished his housekeeper gently. "You really are too soft on her." The permanent sneer which warped his mouth seemed more pronounced tonight. "Still, I suppose it won't have done any harm this time. I hope you remembered to chain her."

"Of course I did! I'm not stupid, just concerned for her well-being… and yours. I'd never forgive myself if she were to escape and you had to go through all that loneliness again."

Now it was Josh's turn to shake his head as the old wound was opened yet again. Nevertheless, he managed a smile. "There's really no need. I wouldn't let her come to any real harm, but she must learn her place. As for escaping… she knows where she's well off." He drained his glass and plonked it down beside the dirty dishes. He walked silently across the room, took a clean plate from the rack then returned to the fridge, from where he removed a couple of drumsticks. He arranged them on the plate with a sausage roll and a lettuce leaf. He imagined the girl in the cellar, naked and shivering as she lay chained to the wall, and he felt his cock stiffen.

"I'll go and look in on her. By the way, when you see Dougie, tell him to come and find me."

With that, he made his way to the cellar. He unlocked the insignificant, paperback-sized, red cupboard on the wall and selected a key from a miscellany of others. He descended the few stairs down to the heavy oak door which led to the cellar, unlocked it and made a mental note to tell Dougie to oil the hinge as the door creaked open. He flicked the switch that flooded the cellar in harsh white light rather than light his preferred candles in the wall sconces. He breezed down the narrow stone steps, stopping half way down to sit for a moment to watch the sleeping figure.

She was lying with her face turned toward him. Someone had cleaned up her face and washed her hair. Still wet, it clung to her naked skin. Curled up with her knees tucked under her chin to keep warm, she was a picture of feminine vulnerability, so erotically beautiful that it tugged at something deep inside. It also tugged at his penis, which responded by swelling.

Balancing the plate on his fingertips, he rose to his feet and continued down the steps and tiptoed towards her. For one brief moment he was almost moved to compassion; she was so deep in sleep it seemed a pity to wake her. Except she hadn't been brought here to sleep, she had been brought here to be punished and to give him pleasure, and pleasure was exactly what he had in mind right now.

Slowly, he extended his leg with the intention of waking her gently, using the toe of his jogging shoe. He changed his mind at the very last moment and with a swift movement kicked her knees.

"Ooowww!"

"Get up!"

In a second she was kneeling with her back straight, her rope-bound hands in her lap. Chained to the wall by her collar, her breasts trembled visibly. It was too much for him and again his foot came out, but instead of kicking her breast he lifted it threateningly with his foot. He held it there for a moment while she trembled in anticipation of the expected blow, then let it bounce back into position as he withdrew his foot again.

Without taking his eyes off her, he placed the plate on the floor, then stood before her once more.

"Stand up."

She was on her feet in an instant, head bowed.

"Turn around. I want to see your back."

Slowly, she turned round to face the wall. She flinched as he touched his fingers to the countless raw marks inscribed across her back and buttocks.

"Very nice, very nice indeed." With a firm hand on her shoulder, he turned her round to face him again and pushed her back down to her knees. Without a trace of the concern which had prompted his visit he told her, "You know what to do, so get on with it."

She leaned forward and reached for the waistband of his tracksuit bottoms with her tethered hands. It only took a moment for her to ease them down and withdraw his hot, pulsing cock. Hard and erect, it quivered visibly as she lowered her head. She opened her mouth and, with the gentleness of an angel, took the shiny glans between her lips.

"Make me come, bitch." He grabbed the back of her head and forced her to take his rod further into her mouth. "And when you've swallowed every last drop, you can have your supper."

Whether it was her greediness for his thick fluid or for the chicken drumsticks he would never know, but it only took a few exquisite, cock-sucking moments before he was shooting his seed deep into her open throat.

***

As Sinclair tidied himself, Amber stood before him, wriggled back into her top and put her hand inside to re-arrange each breast more comfortably. Withdrawing it again after giving each nipple a sly pinch, she smoothed down her short, creased skirt, retrieved her bag and slung it over her shoulder.

"Take this," she delved into her bag and extracted her gold, roller ball pen and embossed notebook. She scribbled an address, ripped out the page and with a flourish handed it to him.

"What's this?"

"The address of my flat."

"Don't be absurd!" He glared at the paper as if it would jump up and bite him. "What are you playing at, Amber? You live in Knightsbridge, not in this sleazy part of town. You do know this is where all the low-life, like prostitutes and petty criminals rule the streets?"

"If you want to continue our little affair..." she tapped the address with her finger, then swung round and headed off up the pathway. She stopped and, with the pretence of removing a stone from her high, hand made, Italian shoes, she bent down to present him with a last glimpse of her darkly swollen pussy lips. She straightened up and, without looking back, she called,

"I'm afraid you'll have to bite the bullet and come to this 'sleazy part of town.' Ring me on my mobile first to let me know you're coming."

"Amber! Where are you going? You can't leave it like this. And you can't go back in the house in that state! One look at you and they'll know you've been up to something."

"Which is why I'm going home. Make my excuses." She laughed, then lied mischievously, "Tell them I'm seeing a paying client!"

CHAPTER FOUR

With her life separated into two neat halves, Amber saw little possibility of trouble. Slipping between the two personalities gave her few headaches, though it hadn't escaped her notice that of late she was beginning to sound more like Jane Dean than her true self even in her head. Jane worked hard at the office and played even harder, while Amber Jane Oakley-Dean paid the occasional visit to the board meetings of the family business and ate at the top London restaurants. And though Amber played hard too, with her well-to-do friends at the casinos and expensive night-clubs, the only real thing the two identities had in common was their enjoyment of sexual indulgence.

As the weeks passed she spent less time with her family and friends of her own class. She knew that she was in the very privileged position of having a life of luxury to fall back on if she came to grief and, whenever things got tough, it was the life to which she was born that she returned to as it tugged relentlessly at her willpower. It wasn't easy being rich... and bored!

What she needed was something to really spice things up.

The only blot on Amber's particular landscape was her fifty-something, lecherous boss, one Reynard Smith. During the few months that she had been with the company, there had been little let up in his pursuit of her; if anything it was getting worse. Now, trapped in the lift with him because it had stopped between two floors, his spiny, yellow-tipped fingers left her cold as they groped ham-fistedly. With his pores oozing the smell of stale cigarettes, he backed her into the corner and wormed his way beneath her short skirt. Shocked to discover that she wasn't wearing panties he clamped his probing digits over her hairy mound. Even her love of sex in potentially public places couldn't overcome her revulsion and she twisted, struggled and protested as best she could.

At that moment the lift started to move again and he barely

had time to snatch his hand away before it came to a shuddering halt at the next floor. As the doors slid back he threatened, "I will have you, Ms. Dean."

"Not if I can help it," she told him as she made her escape. The trouble was that she simply didn't fancy the guy. She was unable to put her finger on what it was exactly that she found so distasteful, but she thought the man completely obnoxious. She told herself it wasn't his fault that he had a nose like an anteater, though that in itself didn't explain the intensity with which she disliked him. Besides, such a flimsy argument had never stopped her from flirting before.

It probably had more to do with his attitudes. It was impossible to believe that in the twenty-first century his outdated, chauvinistic views were tolerated within such a prestigious company. He seemed to regard all the women who worked in his department as lesser beings and considered their purpose in being there only as titillation and a means to satisfy his sexual urges. Quite frankly, Amber could never understand why the guy hadn't ended up in court long ago.

***

It was Joshua Cordell's second stay at The Lodge in as many months, and the days blurred into one glorious week of hedonism. Spoilt for choice, Josh divided his time between the excellent tennis courts, both hard courts and grass, the swimming pool and the Housegirls who provided him with pleasures of the flesh. And then there were the delights of the common room, where every evening one was at liberty to use any of the girls present in any way one wished. Since all the girls were trained by the Lodge's redoubtable Madame Stalevsky to withstand a high degree of suffering obediently and without complaint, this usually entailed some breed of restraint for the girls as well as a damn good thrashing, to which they all submitted willingly.

And then there were the ponies. On one particularly bright

48

morning, Josh requested a girl to be harnessed between the shafts of the lightweight, two-wheeled pony-cart. There were two kinds of carts available here, the trap which seated two people and needed two ponies to pull it, or the more favoured sulky, which seated only one and could easily be pulled by one pony. As usual, Josh chose the latter.

The girl, who's name he could never recall, had flowing hair the colour of polished mahogany and good, surprisingly muscular thighs for one so elegant. As they set off down the track from the stables with the narrow-waisted girl prancing along nicely, past the eighteen hole golf course toward the lake, he noticed that several of the members had been thinking along similar lines and consequently, quite a few girls found themselves between shafts that morning. All were alluringly naked and barefoot. It was a special delight to observe the manner in which the different sized breasts jiggled as the ponies trotted along at a leisurely pace, Josh reflected.

A gust of wind caught his pony's hair, tossing the strands about her head like the multiple thongs of an ill-wielded scourge. Josh's perennially sneering lips twitched at the corners as he flicked the one, narrow strand of the leather whip across her back, searing her skin with a vivid stripe. It was all well and good trotting along as if one had all the time in the world, but he always enjoyed the spectacle of a pony with the wind in her hair and scarlet lines rising across her back as one urged her to increase her speed. Besides, it wasn't as if he were a heavyweight; a girl of her stamina and training should have no trouble galloping along with the sulky behind her. He pulled back his arm and, aiming for a spot slightly above the first line, he brought the whip down a second time. Congratulating himself on his accuracy, he admired the two red streaks across her flesh, so close they almost touched.

He had seen the ponies race once or twice along a set course, and it had given him great pleasure and a rigid cock to watch how the girls strained with the exertion as each put her heart into crossing the line first. Sometimes money changed

49

hands though often it was purely the reputations of the participating Lodge members that were at stake.

Josh turned his pony to the left, taking care not to pull too roughly on the bit; a damaged mouth would be unable to perform even an adequate blowjob, let alone the exceptional service expected of a Housegirl. And this particular girl had exceptionally skilled lips. Soft and compliant, they felt like a satin-gloved hand when they closed around a thick rod of male flesh, while her tongue was recognized as one of the most accomplished and was thus always in demand.

Josh and his pony left the track and set off along one of the tarmac roads which crossed the extensive grounds.

As the morning wore on, he decided to reserve the girl for use that night. This was easily done; any girl reserved in this way was required to wear a disc at her throat which denoted the room of the member in question. This didn't, however, exclude her from her normal duties or use by other members in the common room.

His pony was nearing her optimum speed now. The velvety globes of her buttocks, bearing the fading purple weals of an earlier beating, wobbled enticingly as her feet pounded against the tarmac. Josh was so impressed by the erotic sight of her that he brought the whip down with a loud Crack! across her back, making her strive even harder. And such was the heated effect on him that he whipped her in earnest for the next mile, inscribing her flesh with angry scarlet lines and occasionally drawing small droplets of blood. Any whimpers or howls she made, if in fact she made any sound at all, were carried away by the breeze and therefore didn't detract from the serenity of the parklands as they sped on.

Josh spent a very pleasant morning indeed, bringing the pony out in an attractive sweat which made her glowing, skin glisten as she raced along. The grounds here in Berkshire were at their best at this time of year and he wanted to make the most of them before he returned home.

At last the pony was flagging, and if he were to avoid her

falling down in a pathetic heap he would have to let up. Reluctantly, he pulled on the reins and slowed her to a gentle trot. Without speaking to her he returned her to the stables, where she would be properly cared for. And, sweating himself from the exertion, he went for his habitual swim.

It turned into a blisteringly hot day and, after lunch, Josh joined some of the other members for a round of golf. This was made more interesting by the champagne they took with them, as well as a rather interesting side bet.

Isaiah Camberwell had brought his own slave, a girl named Isabella, to The Lodge with him. This was permitted, providing the girl was available for use by the other members. So it was that the delightful Isabella had been used extensively in the common room the previous evening by one of the new members.

He was someone Josh hadn't had much to do with as yet, though by all accounts he was a solid enough character. By the name of Gascoigne, he was, like several other members, something in the city. At any rate, he wielded the crop and drove the ponies with expertise, which were pretty good credentials in a place like The Lodge. Rumour had it that he had recently married a fortune. It was of no consequence to Josh, who had a hard-earned fortune of his own.

At any rate, Gascoigne had taken Isabella to his room, where she had been quite severely maltreated. She had been returned to her Master after breakfast and allowed to sleep for the rest of the morning. Then she was ordered by her Master to accompany the seven golfers, one of whom was Gascoigne himself.

"I must say," Gascoigne addressed Camberwell as the men assembled outside the club house, "she is most agreeable."

The two men conversed as casually as if they were discussing a favourite hound before the hunt. "I'm glad you found her to your liking."

"She has fine bone structure and her carriage is excellent."

"Thank you. And I was most taken by the fetching pattern

51

you inscribed, most intricate. You have a very sure hand, Gascoigne."

Isabella was duly stripped naked so that the sight of her abused, luscious body could be enjoyed by the seven men, as well as anyone else who happened to be playing golf that hot afternoon. And it was indeed a sight to behold. Her breasts, as well as being lacerated by the lash, sported bruises of varying colour intensity caused in the main by the application of assorted breast clamps and clips. Her thighs and bottom bore bruises along with several, purplish, randomly placed lines as did the swell of her belly. And, of course, her back was decorated with the intricate, latticework design within a rectangle which Camberwell had so admired.

After Josh and his companions had all congratulated Gascoigne on his artistry, Camberwell continued, "I trust she lived up to your own exacting standards in all other aspects." He landed a hefty slap across her rump. "She is a particularly hardy creature."

Gascoigne frowned. "She moves well under the lash, I'll grant you that, Camberwell, though I would disagree on her hardiness. In fact, I think you should address the matter with some urgency."

Camberwell was visibly offended. "Why so?"

"Pardon my mentioning it, but she seems to have a tendency to faint after a couple of dozen strikes."

"Faint?" Camberwell was shocked. "You must be mistaken!"

"I know some men find it attractive but personally I can't abide the habit. It took several seconds before she regained her senses enough for me to begin again and rather impaired my enjoyment."

"I can assure you she has never fainted under the lash before. Perhaps it was a little warm in your room? Of course, we could put her to the test."

Thus the wager was born. Such was Camberwell's faith in Isabella's ability to take anything meted out to her that he bet his opponents she was strong enough to undergo certain ordeals and still remain fresh at the end of the afternoon. And so it was that, while acting as her Master's caddy, pulling a heavy trolley full of golf clubs around, she was to keep up with the men while trotting barefoot.

"I say," one of the seven suggested, "wouldn't it be more interesting if her ankles were shackled?"

This was agreed and someone produced a fifteen inch chain which was duly fitted, joining her ankles together and making walking a chore for the girl. Still with a point to prove, Camberwell decreed that she should receive three strokes of the lash anywhere on her body from each of the seven men, taking it in turns, at every hole. Further, she would still be on her feet to endure a breast beating from each of them on returning to the clubhouse.

And she would do all this Camberwell said, without refreshment, screaming, or even climaxing.

At first, things went well. Though under normal circumstances the chain would have prevented her from matching the men's strides, luckily for her they spent rather a lot of time discussing business and making deals, which necessitated their slowing their own pace. And despite her maltreatment of the previous night she took her beatings well, including the enthusiastic application of the whip wielded by Josh which resulted in the design across her back receiving additional lines which slashed agonizingly across, diagonally from her left shoulder.

Unfortunately and probably due to the onset of some malaise, Isabella didn't continue to live up to her Master's expectations. Not only did the unfortunate girl collapse in a heap and have to be helped to her feet at the thirteenth hole, but she screamed so loudly that a complaint was later made by their fellow golfers, who claimed their games had been seriously affected. As it was considered bad form to disrupt any other member's game, all seven men were later fined. And not only that. Poor Isabella failed miserably in her attempt to hold back her climax while undergoing the breast beatings.

Having lost the wager, Camberwell was obliged by his honour as a Gentleman to keep his end of the bargain. As a result, Isabella was handed over to service each one of the men in which ever orifice they chose before they returned to the house for drinks in the bar and Isabella was taken to one of the punishment cells.

Josh meanwhile returned to his room and awaited the arrival of the nameless girl who had been his pony. This room was one of Josh's particular favourites, with a spectacular view to the South East of the extensive parklands which surrounded the secluded country house. From this floor on a fine day one could see for miles. Yet unseen from the nearest road, The Lodge was unknown to anyone, except for the very select and relatively few members.

Like much of the house though by no means all, the walls of this room were oak panelled. The four-poster bed had a green coverlet which, heavily embroidered in gold to match the canopy, added to the timelessness of the room. Josh always preferred the rooms with the more traditional bedding to those with the duvets favoured by some of the other members. And in this respect as in so many others, the establishment catered for its rich, powerful patrons, endeavouring to make their rooms as comfortable, and their stay as enjoyable, as possible.

Though Josh didn't claim to be an expert on antiques and fine art, he knew enough to recognize that the paintings, furniture and soft furnishings were authentic antiques. The candlesticks were solid silver, though it wouldn't have mattered in the slightest if they were copies since once the candles were lit, the effect was hauntingly magical whatever the age of the candlesticks.

When the girl arrived, at the precise time he had ordered, Josh sat in an easy chair and watched as she stripped off the long, low cut satin dress all the girls were required to wear. He never failed to admire the design which incorporated a slit at the back through which the girls' charms could be fondled

54

discreetly… or not as the occasion dictated. Strictly speaking, it was against Madame Stalevsky's rules to fondle the girls while they went about their more mundane duties. However, it was a rule that, as far as the members were concerned, was made to be broken.

On first becoming a member a few years earlier, it hadn't taken Josh long to discover the way round what was an inconvenience. All one had to do was pay either Ivan or his twin brother Yuri, the two mute, Russians twins who kept an eye on things, a nominal fine and the "offended" girl would be given a quick beating which, quite frankly, was very often the desired result by all concerned. He had put his theory to the test many times and had once had a bet with a couple of other members as to how many times each of them could cause a Housegirl to be flogged for undergoing "a fondle" during the space of twenty-four hours. Of course, the paltry fines had been worth every penny and, though he and his companion had actually lost the bet to a visiting minor Royal, the event had engendered much interest.

Josh came out of his reverie to see that the Housegirl was completely naked, save for her hold-up stockings and high heels. He concentrated his attention for a moment on her firm, bell-shaped breasts with their hard, flushed nuggets.

"I see someone's handled your tits a bit roughly since I returned you to the stables," he observed, noticing the puncture wounds where this morning there had been none. Not that that interfered with his enjoyment in any way; he had always rather admired the lingering evidence of breast torture, though he preferred to inflict it himself.

"What are you waiting for? Get on the bed. You know how I want you."

"Yes, Master Cordell."

Her voice was as soft and warm as her yielding flesh, and without a hint of malice for the scurrilous way in which he had treated her earlier in the day. The girls were trained to obey without question, give their Masters complete satisfaction and were trained to take a great deal of pain and suffering. So it was that however much the girl was made to suffer at Josh's hands he could be sure that she would never show him anything other than willing obedience. Pain and degradation were viewed as badges of office among the girls who were often guilty of showing off their injuries to each other as if they were gold stars of excellence.

He made her lie face down on the bed and bound her wrists and ankles to the sturdy, barley twist bedposts using leather restraints and thick, nylon cord which Josh had commanded she bring with her. Heat rose in his balls, for she looked especially appetising as she lay spread-eagled on the coverlet, bearing the angry weals and broken skin from their earlier encounter.

He studied the grace of her sensuously abused form with its soft sheen of moisture and his penis throbbed. It was all he could do to refrain from ripping his clothes off and pouncing on her. But no, he thought, let her wait. In his long experience, he had proved time and time again that the longer a girl was forced to ponder the vagaries of her fate, the more profound the pleasure for himself.

He knew she would be aware of her vulnerability and that added to his own arousal. He was no barbarian but it was his belief that a woman should give herself mind, body and soul to her Master, and should be grateful to be the source of his pleasure. He swallowed hard, gave in to temptation and began to strip off, willing himself to take his time. Slowly, he removed his black jacket. Smiling inwardly, he hung it over the back of the chair and began to unfasten the buttons of his black shirt.

She whimpered, pulling against her bonds as she wriggled prettily in an effort to encourage him. He smiled at her impatient agitation. With as much self-control as he could muster he undressed, folded his clothes carefully and piled them on the chair. When he was completely naked, he strolled casually across the room. Then his self-control cracked and in a moment he had climbed up onto the bed and was kneeling with his legs inside hers. With another slight whimper, she raised her head and turned to look at him.

"Lie still!" he ordered. All the same, he rather enjoyed her writhings, causing his arrogant, impressive cock to project upward from his groin.

With no thought for the girl's well-being, he didn't bother with lubrication as he plunged his iron rod in into her tight little bottom hole. Despite her thorough training, the shock and pain of it caused a shrill scream to escape her lips and Josh met with some resistance. And then she must have brought to bear all her schooling in the matter of relaxing her muscles because suddenly there was no resistance, allowing him to work past her sphincter. It was with a frenzied passion that he drove deep into her rectum, fucking her for all he was worth and driving her body into the lavishly embroidered bedcover and deep mattress.

While this girl was no stranger to him, having made use of her many times before, he had to admit that this time was especially agreeable. Ever since other members had witnessed her this morning between the shafts, displaying her grace and stamina as she sped through the grounds and pulling the sulky seemingly without effort, she had been much in demand. If he hadn't had the good sense to reserve her early, he would have lost her. In his opinion, there was something most attractive about a girl who had been put to use in such a way, and the liberal use of the whip across her shoulders to spur her on this morning had made her all the more desirable.

Moaning and writhing, she squealed charmingly, stoking the fire in his balls and pumping the spunk up his penis. He could hold back no longer. With a yell that came from deep inside, he filled her with jet after jet of his thick semen until he had emptied the entire contents of his balls deep into her tight little hole.

All at once he reached under him and with a loud Smack! brought his hand down across the meat of her backside as beneath him she tensed, on the verge of coming herself.

"Oh no you don't! You know better than that! I'll have to report your lax conduct to Madame."

It went without saying that it was no idle threat, and he felt her tremble beneath him. All the girls were afraid of the woman who trained them. Russian, long legged and muscular, Madame Stalevsky had a free hand when training the girls and her methods remained a closely guarded secret. Yet strangely, there was adoration there too; he had glimpsed it many times in the eyes of girls when taken away by Madame for correction.

So great was the girl's need to climax that her body was racked by sobs.

"What's up with you?" he demanded. He had given her a hard time of it today but that was what she was here for. "It's no good blubbering every time you're forbidden to come. Keep it up, and I'll really give you something to cry about." He pulled out of her so roughly that she had to bite into the bedcover to stifle her scream. "Where's your respect? What do you say?"

Once again her training took over and her response was immediate, spoken politely and clearly in deferential tones.

"Thank you for using me and bestowing the gift of your seed, Master Cordell."

He leaned along the length of her body with his steely abdomen pressing into the hollow of her back. He unfastened her wrists and eased himself off her. Standing midway along the bed with his back towards her, he gave the command, not caring that her tethered ankles would make obeying awkward.

"Show your appreciation."

Slowly, she raised herself onto her elbows and, with her legs still securely held apart, twisted her torso uncomfortably to drag herself closer to him, until her head was mere inches from his buttocks. When she was in position he pressed his backside hard against her face. Without waiting for further commands she began to lick at his anus, poking the tip of her tongue inside the tight rim. He gasped as he felt her curled, hot tongue paying the homage due. Heated and wet as it worked its way so far inside that her nose was pushed sideways against him, her accomplished tongue soon rekindled his lust. With a backward thrust of his hips, he rammed against her face so hard that her tongue was driven so far inside him that it must have felt to her as if it were being torn from her mouth.

Having reinforced his supremacy over her, he strode away arrogantly, so abruptly that she was left with her debased tongue lolling. He turned around and with a look of disdain crossing his brooding features, looked down on his idea of a perfect woman... sensually abused, degraded and unquestionably compliant. Then dragging her roughly into her former position he retied her wrists to the bedposts.

"I haven't done with you yet."

He had chosen a particularly flexible cane for tonight's entertainment, and now he braced himself, ready to thrash her delightful rump. He took a steadying breath then brought the cane down in a flurry of swipes and in a few moments a myriad angry, scarlet stripes covered her fleshy backside to compliment the delightful pattern he had scored across her back earlier in the day. However, it would be unwise, he reminded himself, to deliver too many more as there would be a fine to pay if she were too weak or damaged to be serviced the following day. His mouth quirked at the corner as he recalled his fine had been quite hefty on the last occasion. Besides, it was rather frowned upon to disturb the other members at this time of night.

***

With her hands tied in front of her, Amber balanced on her shoulders on her sofa. She lay face up, her legs dangled over the back and the blood pounded in her temples. Standing behind the sofa, Sinclair's trim stomach was pressed up against it. He held her slim but sensuously flared hips firmly as she tried to adjust her position, putting the weight of her thighs on his shoulders.

In her mind she saw herself tied to a post with her hands cuffed behind her back, wearing a real blindfold of black velvet, not this ineffectual scrap of material which allowed her to see Sinclair's head bobbing as his slurping became more urgent. His tongue pushed deep into her tight, moist channel and she let out the obligatory moan that she knew always turned him on.

It would be a lie not to admit that she was turned on herself, notwithstanding the fact that the exciting, pulsing need was engendered more from her fantasies than the actualities. There was a hollow feeling inside which seemed to imply that something was missing, even as her throbbing need grew and became more gripping. Terrifying wantonness swirled over her as the shameful truth dawned; she was beginning to outgrow Sinclair and no matter how hard he tried, he would never be able to satisfy her fast evolving needs. And it was very clear to her now that those needs included pain.

She again allowed herself to sink into the fantasy and the image in her head of the unknown, shadowy man raising a whip. In response to her fantasy, she whimpered and began to struggle and in her imaginings was unable to shield herself from the blow…

All at once the image dissolved and she came back to reality with the knowledge that her struggling hadn't been entirely in her head and she had unwittingly managed to loosen her bonds. Her hands were no longer tied, and she reached one slender arm upward and clutched at the top edge of the sofa to steady herself while the nimble fingers of her free hand closed tightly around her hard nipple. Twirling and pinching, she endeavoured to administer the dose of pain her body cried out for. But it was no good. No matter how hard she squeezed and tugged, she was unable to satisfy her hunger.

Defeated, her hand dropped away and she let out a sigh of regret which Sinclair mistook for rapture. As he glowed with pride at his performance she tried, for his sake more than her own, to live up to his expectations, striving to lose herself in the joy of his hot mouth as it continued with its exploration of her luscious, wet pussy. She wiggled her hips a little and drove her vulva up hard against his mouth. But the spell was broken when she was unable to stifle a giggle as she envisaged the scandal that would break if the affair between Amber Oakley-Dean and her illustrious brother-in-law were ever discovered.

Sinclair's hands broke contact with her hips as they slid round between the sofa's upholstery and the satin soft cheeks of her pert behind. He pinched her buttocks and she gave a little noise of protest. Not a scream exactly… the pressure wasn't hard enough to warrant a full-bodied yell and so she whimpered instead.

Nevertheless, Sinclair did have a particularly wicked tongue, and it wasn't long before her writhings were totally authentic. She let out a series of moans as her muscles stiffened. Again his fingers pinched her bottom, this time hard enough to ensure that tomorrow she would have quite a respectable bruise, and she gave an excited cry. One more delicious second and she would be coming.

Without warning, Sinclair snatched his mouth away and Amber was denied orgasm. Anger spilled out of her in a series of expletives as she angrily tore off the blindfold and scrambled upright.

"What the hell do you think you're playing at, you bastard?"

Her violet eyes bored holes in Sinclair's back as he crossed the lounge to retrieve his whisky from the table where he had left it.

"What did you stop for?" she demanded haughtily. "I was just about to come."

He took a deep swig before answering, then plonked the glass down. "I can't do this any more, Amber."

She turned her attention to his fast deflating cock. "What's got into you, a conscience? Or are you afraid of being caught?

Or maybe it's just that you can't deliver the goods anymore."

"Don't be ridiculous. I'm tired, that's all. Of course I can deliver; I meant that I can't do it any more tonight… it's not you, it's this place." He swung his gaze around the room. The entire flat was a hotchpotch of primary colours; yellow sofa and curtains, red chair and lampshade, blue carpet and green tablecloth covering the scratched, gate leg dining table. A decor any further removed from her luxury flat in Knightsbridge, with its thick carpets, predominantly oyster colour scheme, and furniture of the finest in modern design, to say nothing of the under-floor heating, was hard to imagine.

"When will you get some kind of colour scheme worked out? If you must have this secret little hideaway, you could at least buy some decent furniture," he said accusingly. "I'm really not happy about your living in this part of town; it's hardly ideal for a woman of your standing. And besides, I find such surroundings very off-putting."

"You mean you can only do it when surrounded by chandeliers and wood panelling? I'm sorry this place doesn't meet with your requirements but the other flat is hardly ideal for the company I've been keeping. They'd turn the place over as soon as look at it."

"You'll bring disgrace on the family, Amber. Look at you, living like a pauper."

Contemplating her as if he were suddenly seeing her for the first time, he said sneeringly, "Thank God I saw through you and married Harriet."

Amber felt the beginnings of real fury stirring in her depths. What the hell was it to do with him how she lived? And as for disgracing the family, well! She had more guts in her little toe than the rest of them put together, she fumed, and more sense of fun than her whimpering sister Harriet.

"At least I get to see a bit of life, not that pale substitute the rest of you are so fond of. And don't you ever forget that it was I who turned you down, not the other way round. As for the furniture…" she would never have chosen the odd assortment herself because, despite her attempts to play at being poor, she still delighted in beautiful things and would have loved to have surrounded herself with elegant furniture. But the flat had been "fully furnished" when she had moved in and, if she was still intent on continuing with her charade, it wouldn't be wise to go splashing money around. "It's probably escaped your notice, but the real world is full of vibrant colours."

Amber rose from the sofa and stomped across the floor to the eighties wall unit, another item which had seen better days. She pulled down the flap of the drinks compartment and poured herself a whisky. How she hated the stuff, she thought as she knocked it back.

"Why don't you just go? Oh, and Sinclair…" she paused, staring him straight in the eye, "don't bother coming back unless you can do the business."

CHAPTER FIVE

After work one evening, the imagined delights of wallowing in a luxurious bath with a glass of champagne to dispel the tension was just too strong for Amber. Since this was out of the question at her rented flat, she returned to her SW1 home. The luxury flat on the third floor of the Knightsbridge building boasted glorious views over Hyde Park and the Serpentine. And at this time of the year, an evening on her balcony was one of the more acceptable pleasures.

As she stepped from the lift, her heart plummeted to her high heels; her mother's new husband was just closing the door of her flat. She stopped in her tracks and watched as he came along the thickly carpeted hallway towards her.

"Hello, Amber." His wide mouth broke into the smile of a snake charmer. He stopped in front of her and blocked her path.

Fearing something dreadful had happened, her voice carried more than a hint of panic as she asked, "Is something wrong, Lawrence? I saw you leaving my flat."

"No, nothing's wrong. I've been looking for you. I borrowed your Mother's keys. You haven't been down to High Briar for almost two months, you naughty girl. As you and I haven't had a chance to get to know one another I thought I'd stop by." The meaning in his eyes was unmistakable.

Looking down on her diminutive frame, he reached out his hand and skimmed his fingers down the side of her face. She found herself wondering what degenerate part of her warped make up made her act like a complete wanton, because all at once she wanted to get to know him better too, in the basest of ways. Already her upturned face was flushed and she felt his breath warm on her forehead. She shuffled from one dainty foot to the other to try to ease the chaotic hunger between her thighs as her supple, young body cried out for something illicit and forbidden.

Deeply ashamed, she was unable to meet his eyes as a coil

of delicious warmth made itself known in her belly. He backed her up against the wall, and she poked out the tip of her tongue to lick her lips. She knew she should say something but, melting under his gentle fondling, there was nothing she could say. She closed her eyes, pressed her cheek against his palm and paid no heed to anything other than the rigidity of his crotch as he pressed her up against the wall of the chic hallway. As her true nature came to the fore, smilingly she wallowed in the wicked eroticism of it all.

His other hand glided down the side of her neck, then back up again. He splayed his fingers in her hair, then with a firmness of grip which came as a complete contrast to the gentle caress, he gave a sudden tug that made her suck in her breath.

"There are ways to deal with naughty girls, so what pathetic excuses can you come up with to stop me punishing you right here and now?" he jerked her head up sharply by the roots of her hair.

"I... I'm sorry, but I..." She wasn't usually given to stuttering, but he was talking to her with such authority that she mentally shrank several inches in height, inches which she could ill afford to lose either mentally or physically. Only her high heels allowed her head to reach up to his chest. And to make matters worse, she could feel the stirring of his organ as it pressed against her abdomen. Even if he were to take her here and now, she thought wryly, she would have to find a box to stand on! "I have an appointment and I'm... running late. I... ohhhh..." her words trailed to nothing as his hard fingers closed tightly over her breast, squeezing her through the fabric of her blouse. Her heart thumped rapidly as she calculated her chances of getting away.

Regardless, she stood her ground. That sensual part of her that wouldn't be denied shivered beneath his touch while that other, sensible part of her urged her not to fall for another of her mother's husbands. To her shame, her insides began to dissolve as his fingers released her hair and travelled downward towards her chin. He swirled them around the hollow of her throat then increased the pressure, and she knew she was smiling a tad more invitingly than was expedient. Nevertheless, there was a delicious fluttering inside that turned up the arousal flame. There was also a storm brewing in her loins, and an even greater one brewing in her conscience.

She knew her mother had never had much success with men and she had no right to destroy any chance of happiness she might have. Nevertheless, right now Amber wanted Lawrence so badly that it was like a ball of fire inside. He had an aura about him that simply demanded her submission, and she consoled herself with the thought that she wasn't a bad person, simply hungry for the pleasures of the flesh.

She opened her eyes. "Perhaps we can do this another time, Lawrence, when… ohhhh!" her words drifted into a lingering sigh as he released his grip. He took her small hands in his, put them behind her back then took a pair of handcuffs from his pocket. She made no effort to escape as he clipped them over her wrists, telling herself instead that she was helpless. She made no protest when he unfastened the buttons of her blouse. Using a penknife, he cut the straps of her bra before unhooking it and allowing it to fall to the floor.

"My, what long nipples you have," he said as he took one between finger and thumb, then stretched it to its full length. It responded by hardening to a throbbing bullet. He twirled it, gently at first, then pinched it so hard that she whimpered prettily. Her eyelids closed again as she rested her head against the wall, and so she didn't see him dip his hand into his pocket yet again. Only when pain sliced through her left nipple and she cried out did she realize that something was wrong.

Glancing down in horror, she saw that he had clipped a wooden, spring-loaded peg over the tender morsel of flesh. And worse still, his other hand contained three more. He closed a second one over her throbbing right nipple, stopping the blood flow and again making her cry out. He held up the last two pegs for her to see. "Now, where shall I put these?"

Trembling with fear and whimpering with pain more excruciating than anything she had ever felt before, she could hardly believe the whirlwind of lust that swirled around her aching vagina. Again he reached for her malleable orb and, cupping his hand around the underside of her breast, he dug his fingers deep into her flesh. The pain as the act set the terrible peg bobbing up and down was almost unbearable, yet as his pressure increased and his ministrations became rougher, so the wetness of her vagina also increased. Her brain yelled at him to release her and get lost, but oh! the agony was having a strange effect on her and what she really wanted was for him not to go at all. If that meant that she was wicked then she was truly sorry, but the fluttering in her loins was growing stronger by the second. All it would take was for her brain to forget who he was for her to sink into the warmth of the pain which beckoned so invitingly.

All at once, his other hand dived beneath her skirt and, finding that she wasn't wearing panties, it only took a fraction of a heartbeat for his fingers to breach her honeyed entrance. There was nothing gentle about the rapid thrusting in and out as his digits probed deeper. Then, as suddenly as they went in, he withdrew them.

"Slut! You still haven't had enough, have you?"

Amber's breath caught in her throat as she remembered the other two pegs, and her eyes widened in terror. "N… no… please… please Lawrence, not that."

He actually laughed as a blaze of pain burned white-hot when the two pegs closed over her tender, outer lips. Then in an act of real cruelty, he closed both hands over the pegs which now dangled from her pussy and gave them a sharp twist. She screamed so loudly that later she was to wonder why nobody came to her aid. But then, all she could think of was the terrible agony this man was putting her through, and the strange feeling of elation which made her feel drunk.

"Shhh! No screaming. Are you afraid of me, Amber?"

Even with the merging of pain and terror which set her

trembling uncontrollably, she determined never to admit to him how afraid she was. As his hands quit her tormented labia and settled on the pegs which captured her nipples so agonizingly, she realized that all she had to do was raise her leg and kick him in the crotch to make her escape. Yet when she tried to move her legs they stubbornly refused to budge; she was rooted to the spot and completely at his mercy. And then he twisted the pegs, sending brain-numbing pain right to the very root of her. Again she screamed, but still no one came to help her. The agony temporarily brought her to her senses and she became aware through her anguish that at that moment, he was enjoying her pain a whole lot more than she was.

"You see, you are afraid. But I know exactly what you want, Amber. I knew the moment I set eyes on you." His harsh whisper brought her skin out in goosebumps, while his words drove a shard of cold fear straight to her heart... though even now, a hot spear of lust drove pitiless desire through her clitoris. "I recognize the signs of a slut, a slut whose body begs to be maltreated. I can see you now, writhing beneath the lash and screaming out in agony. You know it's what you want."

And then his fingers were inside her again, agitating her so roughly that she thought she would crumple into his arms. And to her shame she knew he was right. She heard the squelching of her own arousal. The dispute wasn't about her arousal but her knowledge that he was her mother's husband.

"It just so happens," he went on, "that I've had a lot of experience with women of your sort. Why don't we go to your apartment so I can show you?"

Amber could see herself too, writhing and panting as he laid into her with a many thonged whip. She heard her voice, faraway and unreal, break the spell.

"Does Mummy know you're here?" she asked stupidly.

"Don't be ridiculous! Besides, what your mother doesn't know won't hurt her. But you're hurting now, aren't you, Amber? You're hurting so much that your whole body is on

68

fire." There was a hint of menace in the pause before he said with chilly emphasis, "And there's so much more where that came from."

Fighting her own demolishing need, she admitted at last that this was wrong; no amount of stoking the fires of her hunger would make it right. She had to get rid of him. She straightened her back, which thrust out her breasts alarmingly and made the pegs wobble again. Then, drawing on the long, illustrious history of her aristocratic forebears for courage, she set her jaw firmly and made her demands in her most haughty voice.

"This has gone far enough. Un-cuff me, Lawrence. I'm not available, now or ever." She eased herself away from the wall. "Go back to Mummy. Let me go, or..."

"Or what?"

"Don't push me," she threatened, "just let me go and I won't mention this."

He gave an arrogant shrug of his shoulders and all four pegs one more final, vicious twist. In response, her double-crossing vagina squelched its delight.

To her surprise, Lawrence took a step sideways and removed the cuffs. "If that's how you feel, so be it. It's your loss; you need to be punished."

"But not by you, never by you."

Relief and regret mingled as he took another step sideways, callously leaving the pegs in place. Drawing in her breath to steady her jittery nerves, she walked past him. With her heart pounding wildly she tossed her head and strode majestically and half naked along the hallway to her flat, inexplicably leaving the pegs in place.

He called after her. "I'll have you one day, you can be sure of it," he warned raspingly, "and you will give yourself to me, willingly."

"Not on your fucking life!" she reiterated venomously, with more confidence than she felt. She knew he was watching her as she halted outside her door. Her fingers shook as she raised the key to the lock. She flicked on the light, knowing it would be impossible to stay here now. Once inside her flat and fearing that he might let himself in later, she closed and bolted the door behind her. She dumped her bag and made her way to the phone, punching in the numbers with one hand while hoiking her skirt up with the other. She slithered two fingers inside her hot, voracious vagina. Her thumb located her unsheathed bud and, still without removing any of the four pegs, she rubbed urgently with her thumb.

"Hi, Don. See you at the flat, in an hour?"

***

Sitting naked on the bed with the equally naked and foxily sensuous Amber across his knees, Don reached down and pinched her already abused, still tender nipple. But sure in the knowledge that it was she who controlled the game, Amber wriggled in token helplessness. Shamelessly she told herself that if it were Lawrence who held her captive her struggle would be authentic. For now there was no mistaking the fact that she was a slave to her desires, and those desires included domination. While Lawrence was by no means responsible for awakening her, he had shown her that her hunger to be punished and… yes, she admitted it now… frightened was more deep-rooted than even she had realized.

Her breasts tightened as fear-tinged arousal, triggered by her earlier encounter, inched its way through her being as she realized that Lawrence had been dangerously serious with his threats. But oh! she had found him so erotically tempting that it had taken great concentration of will on her part to refuse him. She wondered at her sanity; she should be searching for love and tenderness. Only kinky people actively sought out pain… and fear, she admitted shamefully.

"Tonight," Don told her in what she assumed was his 'threatening,' low and growling voice, "we're going to do this properly, with no pissing about from you."

70

Her head was a snarl-up of wild ideas and emotions even as lust lapped at her insides, for although the bruises dished out by Lawrence were more mental than physical, he had left her uncertain about the wisdom of her choices. All she knew for certain was that games were no longer enough.

Yet what was it, exactly, that she did want? She craved sexual excitement from a demanding… at first she hesitated to use the word Master but now it blasted into her brain. The terrifying knowledge that she was actively seeking a demanding Master caused her pussy to juice more freely, and as Don worked two fingers up inside her tight channel, he voiced his delight in a low growl. Nevertheless, she knew he would never make the grade as a Master, for even though he was pretty free with his threats he rarely engendered real fear, not the way that Lawrence had. She thought whimsically that Don, for all his bad-boy antics, had taken to punishing her with the same enthusiasm that a wasp buzzes around a Pimm's in the summer, enthusiastically but afraid to commit.

Nevertheless, her insides were fast becoming a warm miscellany of quivers and tremors of arousal as the various notions flitted through her mind. She lay across Don's knees and ruminated on how delicious her arousal would be if it were linked with fear.

Don twisted his fingers this way and that, and she couldn't help but squeal. His fingers became more demanding and in response, her muscles clenched around them. Mentally, she shrugged her shoulders. Perhaps she shouldn't be too hard on him and at least consider that maybe the fault was hers, and that his ability to truly dominate depended to a greater degree on her ability to submit. It was up to her then, to squash down inside her that part of her that liked to tease; she would have to be willing to relinquish control. Except as much as she fantasised about doing just that, the reality was that she was finding it impossible.

Don thrust his fingers one last time then suddenly withdrew them. That was when she realized he was talking to her.

71

"You wanted domination so you're sure as fuck going to get it. Remember, I'm not some young, brainless la-di-da office type you picked up somewhere, I've got form."

She smiled at his bragging. Maybe his claims were true, but right now they were getting in the way of a seriously good time. She would go right off the boil if he kept up his crowing much longer.

"I'm a dangerous guy to mess around with. Savvy?"

Very probably, she thought wryly, though Lawrence posed more of a mouth-wateringly erotic threat than Don ever could. Still, Don was the best on offer since Lawrence was most definitely off-limits. It was fortunate that Sinclair was still in the wings, for even though she had been so dismissive, she knew he would come running back when his wife refused to play. Besides, if she was really desperate she could always call on one of the servants at High Briar. Except they were all giving her a pretty wide berth since she had been the cause of so many of their number losing their jobs.

Deciding it was up to her to move the game on, she gave another little struggle.

"Y... yes," she bleated in a way she hoped was submissive, "I understand."

"And you're going to do everything I say, right?"

"Right."

Just when she had come to accept that he was all talk and no action, his palm came down in a brutal Slap! across her bottom as he began to lay into her with an impressive display of fast and furious blows.

"This time I brought some 'toys' with me. And I was rooting around the place while you were making coffee," he told her between hard slaps that had him panting and her squealing delightedly, "and I came up with..." there was a pause while he reached behind him, "this!"

"Ooow!" There was one sharp blaze of genuine pain across her taut buttocks which drew a crimson line on either side of the cleft between them. Her clitoris poked free of its hood and began to thrum wildly.

"There! That wasn't so bad, was it?"

Again the slash of pain, then again and again, sweeping thrilling lines of fire across her flesh. Mad she may be but the sensations which assailed her were wholly delicious, sending tinglingly warm, erotic sensations corkscrewing their way from her heated and abused bottom to her breasts. Don set about the task with real enthusiasm. Allowing herself to savour the eroticism of the moment, she tried to ignore the niggling voice in her head which cautioned that her desires could develop into weird compulsions, while another voice alerted her to the fact that the more adventurous her desires became it followed they would outstrip Don's abilities.

Nevertheless, he brought the object down in a series of brutal, fiery lines in a ladder formation, which had Amber yelling one minute and moaning incoherently the next. Her moist sex twitched excitedly as her inflamed bottom became one mass of deliciously hot pain. And then he dealt her another particularly stinging blow.

"Aaarghh!" That one had really hurt. Forgetting her submissive role for a moment she asked accusingly, "What the hell are you using, you bastard?"

He laughed. "Yeah, I'm a bastard all right. It seemed a waste to use a perfectly good bit of bamboo," he tried to swoosh it through the air but the cane was rigid, "for supporting that half-dead houseplant you keep in the lounge, so I nicked it." He set her on her feet with the command, "Fetch the rope."

Annoyed with herself for her lapse, she squared her small shoulders and obediently collected the bundle of orange towrope which she now kept in the cupboard at the bottom of the second-hand wall unit in the cramped lounge. She returned to the bedroom and he snatched it from her hands which trembled excitedly. He had her stand facing the bed with her knees pressed up against it. Then rising to his feet he threw the rope down onto the duvet so that the coil separated into the pre-cut lengths. As she stared down at them, he dragged her hands behind her back and tied them together, causing a knot of pure delight to tighten in her belly. With her pussy beginning to drizzle its sweet juices down the inside of her thighs, she pretended to struggle.

Smack! A patch of fire spread across her bottom cheeks as he used a table tennis bat to great effect as a paddle. In a moment, her quivering cheeks were glowing.

"I sweet talked this out of the hands of a girl at the leisure centre," he told her proudly. A series of brutal, dull Smacks! turned her buttocks into scarlet blotches of heat. Once more she cried out.

"No more yelling! You wanted to play rough, so rough it is." He reached across to the bedside cabinet. "I found these in one of your drawers." Before she had time to make any comment, he rolled two, rather expensive, lace-trimmed handkerchiefs into a ball which he stuffed between her lips. "You're a real surprise. I expected to find a drawer full of knickers, not posh scented sachets and a whole bunch of dainty lace hankies. Getting above yourself, aren't you?" he nodded to the box of tissues on her dressing table. "They not good enough for you now?" he tied a silk scarf across her mouth to keep the hankies in place. Casting the expert eye of a thief over the label, he tut-tutted. "This looks like real expensive stuff. If I didn't know you better, Jane, I'd say you'd been on the rob, too."

She began to tremble visibly, not from fear of what he was about to do to her, nor even from arousal, but from sheer terror that he had discovered her true identity. How could she have been so careless? But if he had found out who she really was, he made no further reference to it and she gave a huge inward sigh of relief as he yanked her to her feet. Using more rope, he drew her legs about eighteen inches apart and tied one ankle to the leg of the bed at its head, before doing the same to the other ankle, tying it to the foot end. He hitched the last piece of rope to her tethered hands and, pulling her arms out tautly

74

behind her, attached it at an angle to the leg of the chest of drawers behind her. Taking care not to trip over the rope, he came and stood beside her.

"I haven't done yet," he informed her. He reached across to the cabinet again then dangled two items in front of her eyes; a pair of exquisite, very long, drop earrings of diamond and ruby, set in gold, sparkled as they caught the light. "Not for pierced ears," he pointed out as he showed her the clips. "I lifted these on my last job but haven't had time to fence them yet."

He unclipped the first earring and let it hover over her left nipple. Behind the gag she held her breath as she anticipated the remembered pain the pegs had caused… pain which didn't materialize since the clip, though strong enough to keep the jewellery in the place for which it was designed, wasn't strong enough to engender anything other than mild discomfort as he closed it over her hardened peak. She couldn't help but notice the sadistic delight that shone in his usually deceitfully-friendly and fraudulently honest blue eyes as he clipped the second one in place.

"Don't they look nice!"

And it was true. Not only did they look stunning as she flicked her eyes downward to her hard, elongated nipples, but they felt good too as the slight movement of her trembling made them swing and brush against the skin below her breasts. Forsaking the bat for the inflexible cane once more, he held it aloft before resuming the beating with renewed vigour.

Unfortunately, her jerking under the renewed onslaught caused the right earring to drop off. Tilting her head back to meet his gaze she noticed for the first time that the sincere smile he employed to hoodwink his victims had turned into an ugly smirk. Fearing his anger, she tried to pull away from him, but the ropes held her fast.

"So, it came off! You know what that means, don't you?" he said, raising the cane again. He brought it down with a Swish! and a dull Thwack! which nevertheless raised a crimson line, this time across the top of her bottom cheeks, just above the valley between them. "Does it hurt?" he mocked, following it up with wild thrashing that set her pearly skin ablaze. "Come on, tell Uncle Don the truth. One nod for yes, two for no."

Hot, dull pain flared through her, warmth flooded her loins and fear swamped her mind, all at the same time as cramps as she had never known assailed her. She wiggled and moaned, her limbs tensed and went rigid. Shutting her eyes against the duel onslaught of the unyielding cane and her muscle cramps, she whimpered and managed a brief, decisive nod of her head.

"Good." The length of rigid cane clattered to the floor. "Now I'm going to fuck you, tart!"

With that, he came to stand behind her again. Then with one hand gripping each sore buttock so hard that white marks appeared over the red patches and horizontal, scarlet lines that adorned her pert backside, he bent at the knees to lower himself into a position whereby he could enter her drizzling, warm pussy more easily. He gave her one final slap across her backside then, without further ado he plunged his iron weapon deep into her clutching, overheated sex.

"You've come already!"

After only four or five of Don's frenzied lunges, she welcomed his seed into her tight, clutching channel.

CHAPTER SIX

After his evening meal, Josh spent a pleasant few hours torturing a Housegirl in one of several dungeons beneath The Lodge. He had hoped to use the brunette, Irena, but she had already been snapped up. And so it was that Josh found himself alone with Elke, the pretty, chestnut haired girl he had abused so badly a couple of months earlier.

Stripped naked apart from her restraints, he couldn't help but notice that she seemed to have gained a couple of pounds. Nothing too drastic, if anything it improved the appearance of her highly sensuous curves. Walking round behind her, he snapped her wrist restraints together, then sank his nails deep into her buttocks. She gave a cry of protest. He did it once more then followed it up by giving her buttocks a swipe with the first instrument which came to hand, a bone handled crop. Afterward, he used her slight weight gain as an excuse to humiliate her and came round to stand in front of her.

"Call yourself a Housegirl?" he said with cool derision, watching delightedly as her face turned crimson and clashed with her hair, "Cowgirl more like! With udders like that," he gave them a both a vicious swipe, knocking them together and then repeating the process to watch them jiggle, "you could keep the whole Lodge in cream for a week. And your rump could feed an army! Since I can't bear to look at you, I'll just have to make up for my disappointment by inflicting as much pain upon that overweight body of yours as it can stand. You might just regain my respect by your suffering. But don't suffer in silence; feel free to scream if it makes you feel better, but you'll receive no sympathy from me."

The dungeons were equipped with all manner of ropes, chains, and whips, as well as a good assortment of stocks and other dungeon furniture with which Josh was well acquainted. And so, after having raised some rather splendid stripes across Elke's torso with the crop while she stood mutely in the centre of the high-ceilinged dungeon, he now hooked her up by her tethered hands, which he had joined in front of her, to one of the chains which hung from special ceiling fixings. He raised her until her feet were a couple of feet from the floor. Lifting her left ankle to waist height in front of her at a right angle to the other leg which dangled freely, he attached a second chain to her ankle restraint and, crossing the expanse of the room, he secured the other end to a hook on the wall. Next he attached a chain to her right ankle and pulled it out behind her, raising that also to waist height so that she was forced to do the splits in mid-air. He fastened this to the opposite wall.

The pain was excruciating and she was barely able to stand the agony as she was rent in two. She was already crying, with her eyes tightly closed and therefore she didn't see him come back across the room nor, thanks to his black suede trainers, did she hear his footfalls. All she could hear above her own wailing was the swishing of a whippy cane as he tested it by cutting it through the air.

Standing in front of her, he pointed the cane toward the floor, then suddenly swung it upward. When the cane struck it was with such force along her tempting slit that she emitted an ear-splitting shriek. Satisfied with how the evening was progressing, Josh sliced cruelly at the inside of her thighs, then returned to the split of her vulva, working them both into a frenzy that ensured the room echoed with blood-curdling screams that befitted a dungeon.

And when he finally left her, alone and in the dark to be collected later, Elke was almost unconscious. In the corridor he passed Gascoigne.

"If you were coming to watch, you're too late." Josh jabbed his thumb over his shoulder. "But she's good for a while longer, providing you douse her down with cold water first."

***

Amber was exhausted, and bathing in a wonderful afterglow

she slept soundly, dreaming of a cruel, dominant Master, a Master who definitely wasn't Don. It was well after midnight when she was awoken by a sharp rap on the door.

"Open up, Miss. Police."

"Just a minute," Amber called warily, her heart pounding in her throat. If the press got hold of this, they would have a field day. It would destroy her mother. "Stay calm," she whispered to herself, "and we might just get through this." After all, Don could probably con his way out of this with his eyes closed. With her finger and thumb squeezing her nipple, bruised from the peg rather than the earring, she turned to Don as he lay beside her.

She had undergone more of a beating at his hands than she would have believed him capable of delivering, and her bottom was still aglow. Nevertheless, all at once she felt curiously let down. It had been wonderful at the time, but she realized that he had released her bonds so soon after his own orgasm that it was as if a "game over" sign had flashed across the screen of the Playstation of her mind.

There was another bang on the door. Without switching on the light she eased herself achingly from the bed. Don stirred, then awoke. Standing naked, she rubbed the burning cheeks of her assaulted backside, then flung back the duvet.

"Open up!" came the voice again, loud and impatient.

"You said they wouldn't come here," she accused, wincing with pain as every movement sent new shivers and pangs of distress... and arousal... through her.

Don flicked the lamp switch. "You think I gave them a fucking invite?"

It was obvious by the following curt "Open up! Police!" that the men outside were losing patience.

"Quickly, Don. Get out of here!"

Not sure which was greater, the excitement which set her heart beating erratically or the fear of the press running the story in the morning, either way her stomach curdled. Her eyes glittered as she tossed Don his trousers and T-shirt.

79

"Take the money and get out!"

Slumping back against the pillow he feigned innocence. He raised his upturned palms and gave an exaggerated shrug of his shoulders. "What money?"

"Miss," came the voice from outside, "I'm going to count to three. One…"

Panic fluttered and grappled at her insides. Don must be guilty of something really serious indeed for the Police to come and arrest him in the middle of the night; obviously he wasn't just a bragging conman after all. She flicked a gaze at him and pondered how harmless he looked. No, she decided, the stories were all in his mind… he was living out his fantasy of being a ruthless villain in the same way that she was leading a double life. Okay, so he liked to brag about the old women he had tricked out of their life savings, and the young couples he had duped into taking out bogus mortgages. But as for burglary… Amber hadn't given it much thought beyond his lifting a few quid here and there.

Her misgivings didn't make sense given how she had sought out his company, but the shame she felt, simply by being in the company of such a callous individual, made her want to curl up and die. The way he preyed on the weak made her feel dirty, tainted by his crimes. Slowly, she became aware that over and above the shame was another feeling, so powerful she could taste it. She wasn't turned on by the danger and bad boy reputation any more. Those very things which had attracted her in the beginning now made her sick. She had never condoned such despicable crimes and had only sought out the company of law-breaking individuals because she had wanted excitement in her life, a counter balance to the glitzy soirees that she had been sickened with and the oh-so-dull men that her standing in polite society obliged her to spend time with.

The hammering on the door echoed around her head, setting all kinds of wild ideas swirling around her brain. What if they broke the door down? What if Don were to hold her

80

hostage?

"Two…"

Absentmindedly, her finger sought out her hard bud as it poked free of its protective hood and she began to rub. She lingered a moment and imagined the humiliation of ending up in court as an accessory to Don's crimes. The very notion made her shudder. It didn't make sense but she was conscious of a rapacious excitement which flared hotly inside; she had always had a high sex drive but this was ridiculous. There was no time to question it now, all she knew was that she felt so horny she was beginning to think she would go insane with need.

As her rubbing grew increasingly rapid her thoughts ran on. What if they weren't the police at all but members of a rival gang? Absurdly, that line of thought set off a delicious quivering in her loins and she let the fantasy continue unchecked. What if they broke in and seduced her? She could see herself now, vulnerable and helpless, completely at the mercy of a gang of men who would no doubt hold her down for each other and take their sadistic pleasure with her.

The growing moistness between her legs was making her uncomfortable. She snatched her hand away and took a deep breath to steady her nerves and try to think more rationally, her fantasies were getting out of control. There were far more important things to be thinking about, such as what if they were the police and discovered her true identity? She glanced at Don.

"I told you to take the money and get out. I know that wad you've got in your rucksack doesn't belong to you. Go, for pity's sake, go!"

"What rucksack?" Ever the conman, he was still playing the innocent.

"The one you've got stashed behind my fridge." Now it was panic that fluttered inside, a panic made all the more keen by the look on Don's face. He was clearly ready to bluff it out. "Just get out, before I decide to let them in and tell them everything I know."

"You don't know anything, you stupid tart."

"Then it won't matter if I let them in, will it?" she swivelled round and took a couple of steps, tripping over the bundle of orange towrope on the floor. Kicking it aside angrily she stormed from the bedroom. Every movement as she headed for the door seemed to jar her bottom, serving as a reminder of her masochistic tendencies and sending wave after wave of erotic warmth through her painful, discoloured flesh. A shiver passed through her and once again she began to masturbate.

"Just coming, Officer," she giggled aloud and wondered if the policeman had any idea how near the mark her statement was.

Suddenly, Don was heading for the kitchen. After a minute of rummaging, he tore back through the lounge, rucksack in one hand and his clothes in the other. He flung the window wide and dived through, his bare backside glowing eerily white in the darkness of the room. Amber heard him clattering down the fire escape and once again giggled aloud, this time imagining how stupid he must look scrambling naked over the back fences. She almost collapsed in a heap of laughter as she imagined him running naked down the narrow alleyways of this part of town, where the local streetwalkers would relieve him of some of his cash.

On the officer's shout of "Three!" she yanked the door open, at the same moment flicking on the light.

"Yes, Officer?" she said sweetly and winked mischievously, thinking how dazed and hot-bollocked they looked as they stared at her petite, nude body.

The younger of the two men cleared his throat. They flashed their ID's and the elder of the men demanded as matter-of-factly as he was able, "Where is he, Miss?"

"Who?" she opened the door wide and stood aside in an invitation to enter, adding belatedly "Do you have a search warrant?" as they entered her flat without answering.

82

She shifted her stance and they followed her into the lounge. She felt the heat in her cheeks as, with mouths agape and eyes staring, the men switched their attention to the two bruised, red-striped splotches that were the globes of her swaying backside. She threw them a coquettish look over her shoulder and gave a self-satisfied smile at the enormous erections which pushed against their trousers.

They pushed past her and with a shout of "The window!" they lunged as best they could across the cramped room.

"Shit! We've lost him!"

"Who?" she repeated prettily.

"Don't give me that, Miss. You know who. We traced him to this address. It's our information that you and Donald Trewin are cohabiting."

"Pardon?" her surprise was genuine. It was true he stayed over occasionally, but she would never have encouraged him to move in. How could she, when part of her life was spent in more luxurious surroundings? Besides, she liked her freedom too much.

"You might as well tell us, Miss. He gave this address to…"

"Then he lied."

"Perhaps you'd like to come down the station and explain your relationship with Mr Trewin?"

She laughed and told them bluntly, "We don't have a relationship. All he comes here for is a fuck."

"That's not all, by the look of you, Miss. Did he assault you? Perhaps you'd like to…"

"No, I wouldn't. It was just…" oh, in for a penny, she thought as she added tartly, "business."

It struck her that they probably believed she was a hooker anyway. After all, the downstairs flat was occupied by someone who advertised as Mistress Josie, and there were enough hollers and hoots emanating from down there every night to more than divert their attention. But oh! What the hell! Concluding that she was in enough trouble already, she saw no harm in adding to it.

"Look, he's not a very good payer," she said, enjoying the fun of deception and thrilling under their scrutiny as they took in her small, sensuously abused form, "but you can take what he left me." Realizing too late that she had stooped to bribery, she tried to extricate herself from the hole she had dug for herself with a gabbled, "Please, don't arrest me. It's my first time."

However, the goddess of mischief had her well and truly under her spell. Refusing to quit, Amber was unable to resist the thrill of cock-teasing one of Her Majesty's officer's of the law. She poked the tip of her tongue out and licked her top lip in a way clearly meant to be provocative. Standing with her weight on one leg and her hand poised delicately on her hip, she winked a second time as she mimicked a friend's husky tones and invited, "You know there'll always be a welcome for you here, Detecti…"

A movement at the door, which still stood wide open, alerted all three. Amber and the two policemen swung round. To Amber's horror, Sinclair stood in the doorway. She had known he would be back but now wasn't the most fortuitous of moments.

"Sir!" The policeman looked flustered. He paused for a moment, then said hurriedly, "I'm sorry, Sir. I had no idea that you knew the young lady."

"I drop in occasionally when I've had a late meeting in Town." Sinclair smiled his sincerest smile for the Policemen, the one he kept for TV presenters who regularly quizzed him on the economy. As one of the directors of her late Daddy's company, he was considered something of an expert and had even been granted a knighthood the previous year. "Perhaps it would be better for all concerned if it remained our secret. Did you know I play squash with your superiors?"

Amber hardly had time to close the door behind the two, hurriedly departing men before Sinclair had grabbed her from behind. He took in the abused state of her bottom and the

84

fading imprints on her wrists and ankles from the ropes.

"What the hell's happened to you? Who's done this to you?"

"Why? Surely you're not jealous? You're not the only guy who likes to play rough."

With his hands either side of her trim waist, he spun her round to face him and cast a hungry glance over her too-heavy breasts. When his hands closed tightly around them she was conscious that his grip paled into insignificance when measured against that of Lawrence, who would probably be the yardstick by which she would measure all future encounters, and she was aware now that Sinclair didn't measure up at all. No matter how hard he squeezed, his touch would never again be enough.

"I don't want to know what's been going on here," his fingers flicked over her long, slightly discoloured nipples; "just make sure you keep it under wraps. If news of your sordid little life were to get out…"

"It won't. I'm too careful. Look, are you going to stand there complaining or have you something more interesting in mind?" already her juicing, tight pussy was clutching in anticipation.

Forsaking her left breast, he dipped his hand in his pocket. She drew in a breath of genuine surprise when he withdrew it again and dangled a pair of handcuffs in front of her face. As a hot tide of wantonness swept over her, she just stopped herself from asking if he had borrowed them from Lawrence. Without being told to she stretched out her arms towards him and allowed him to clip her hands together. With a thrilling warmth glowing in her belly and an increasing drizzle of moisture down the inside of her thighs, she gave him a sideways look from beneath her long, black eyelashes.

"This is new." She ran the tip of her tongue over her lips. "Now I feel like a real sex slave."

"Then you'd better start acting like one. Get in the bedroom."

Yet, in spite of everything that had happened, she was unable to quell that part of her that wanted to tease. She was a lost cause, she admitted ruefully, for hard as she tried she found it impossible to immerse herself completely in the role of a submissive. She gave him a flirtatious wink and wondered distractedly if there was some kind of institution one could attend to learn the art of submission. She had to bite into the side of her mouth to keep from giggling at the absurd notion of someone actually giving instructions on how to be subjugated.

She swung her hips provocatively as she walked ahead of him, laughing the low, sexy laugh she knew turned him on. As her glowing backside bobbed temptingly in front of him, she half hoped he would lash out at her. She flung him a backward glance and noticed that he gave the discarded rope, table tennis bat and earrings an odd sort of look as he passed.

"You really ought to lock your jewels away, Amber," he admonished as they reached her bed. He pushed her face down across it, then crossed the small room to the chest of drawers, on which Don had placed the unbending cane. Retrieving it, he came and stationed himself beside the bed.

"Might as well try this." He raised his arm, then laid another stripe of dull pain across her bottom. "How's that for starters?"

***

Josh made his way to the gaming tables where he had a highly successful few hours. It was therefore almost two in the morning when he nipped up to the Lodge's up-to-the-minute IT suite. Much of the equipment was supplied by Cordell Dynamics International, and he was able to conduct a little overseas business after which he contacted Reynard Smith at home, rousing him from his bed. To Josh's delight, Smith was still hot for the lovely Saskia, to which end he had come up with a scheme of his own. Inwardly, Josh laughed at the idea, though on second thoughts it did have merit.

"There's a young woman who works here," Smith told him, "I'm sure she's the perfect person to convince you that you and I can do business together." Having learnt of Josh's weakness for short, dark haired girls he added, "She's not very tall but what she lacks in height she makes up for with the rest of the package. Lusty little thing, by all accounts. I haven't had too many dealings with her myself," he paused for a little laugh, "I'm afraid I haven't acquired the necessary qualifications to bring this little bitch to heel. However, I'm sure she'd be most obliging when dealing with a man of your experience. I'd be only too happy to set up a meeting. You would, of course, be free to take matters into your own hands."

The inference was plain, and Josh found himself listening to Smith's proposal with interest.

***

Things began to go seriously wrong for Amber at work the next day when the rest of the staff had gone home for the night. She had just slipped on her jacket when her phone rang, and she found herself summoned to Reynard Smith's office.

"Close the door, Ms Dean."

Amber had been aware of his watching her all day and now her skin crawled as his gluttonous eyes slithered over her, downward from her sleek, bob hair-do to rest on her too-heavy breasts. Normally when a man looked at her in such a lusting vein she gave him a come-on smile, made a show of her considerable assets and launched into a major cock-taunting offensive. But this guy made her retch. The cloying sweetness of his aftershave coalesced with the smell of stale cigarettes on his breath and was just too much to stomach. Yet even as she determined not to respond to the lascivious glint in his eyes as he sat back in his chair, her nipples betrayed her by stiffening.

Her stomach gave a shuddering lurch as she realized that her breasts were almost completely visible through the white, provocatively transparent blouse, worn over an equally flimsy

87

white bra, and belatedly wished she had worn something more discreet. In an effort to cover herself she pulled the sides of her mustard coloured jacket together. Mindful never to wear designer labels to work for fear of blowing her cover, her skirt suit was nevertheless of the best quality that a girl living on the salary Beevis and Smetherton paid could afford. Three-inch platform sandals, coupled with the shortness of her skirt, had the effect of making her bare legs look longer, their attractive sheen the result of attentive care and expensive lotions.

"Stand there," he told her, pointing with his nicotine stained, spiny finger, "with your hands at your sides." He turned his attention to an unsigned contract lying on his desk, which he folded, slipped into an envelope and sealed.

As directed, she stood behind the chair in front of his desk, feeling as she had done that one time at boarding school when, at seventeen, she and her friend had sneaked out for an evening on the town. Two Policemen had later discovered them, groping with a couple of boys from a local Comprehensive. The next morning the two girls had been called before their Head. And Amber felt now as she had done then, though this time she could think of no reason why she should feel so guilty.

Smith didn't raise his head to look at her but concentrated on cleaning his fingernails with the end of a straightened out paper clip.

"I couldn't help noticing," he said eventually, dropping the clip in the waste paper basket, "that you've been reluctant to sit at your workstation today. I can only assume that you have sustained some kind of injury to your bottom."

Amber's mouth fell open and she gaped stupidly for a full minute. There was no way he could possibly know what had happened last night! Nevertheless, she found herself growing warm and knew that her pearly skin was turning pink.

Smith returned the handkerchief to his pocket, folded his hands on the desk, and decided to put into practice some of the lessons learned from Joshua Cordell before he dispensed with her.

"Remove your jacket," he said sternly. He leaned closer and mentally traced his fingers over her sensuous curves. He felt the swelling of his organ and sighed. She really was an attractive little thing and it would have been nice to keep her on. However, it was out of the question since people had been asking questions about her and the last thing he needed right now was anyone looking too closely at the way he conducted business. Best get shot of her while he had the chance. He consoled himself with the thought that she was merely the means to an altogether more satisfying end. As was often the case these days, it was the lovely Saskia who filled his thoughts and he was well aware that if he was ever going to lay the bitch and do business with Cordell, then drastic measures were called for. With this in mind he had hatched a plan so perfect he had known Cordell would jump at it. He would rather have taken things at his own pace but Cordell's pre-dawn phone call, not to mention a surprise visit from the police this morning, had rather forced his hand.

He waited while Amber hung her jacket over the back of the chair, then told her, "Consider yourself unemployed."

Smith's words hit her like a bolt from the blue and for a moment all she could do was shake her head in disbelief. Wide-eyed with amazement, she struggled to find her voice.

"What did you say?" Gathering her wits at last she met his gaze defiantly and demanded, "Why? You can't do this."

"I feel obliged to dismiss you on the grounds that you're a highly sensual and obviously wanton young woman whose talents could be better employed elsewhere."

"You're joking!"

"Your wholly unsuitable appearance…" Again he looked her over, and she was unsure whether he was referring to her revealing clothes or the evidence of maltreatment they concealed. Once again, she told herself there was no way he could know and listened disbelievingly as he continued to spell out his outrageously sexist and surely illegal reasons.

89

"As I was saying, your appearance lacks the credibility required for a company of our standing. Clients expect to have the facts laid before them by a competent representative, not an empty-headed, bruised and battered nymphomaniac. In short, you're a filthy whore; an insult to public decency."

She could hardly believe that he had the gall to say it while he drooled at the sight of her breasts.

"How dare you! You've no right to speak to me like that."

The way his eyes snaked over her made her feel dirty. The heat of shame swept over her, staining her skin an even deeper pink, as she acknowledged the truth of his words. Yes, she had been fucked and beaten by more than one man, but that didn't make her a whore. The flare of her nostrils betrayed the depth of her anger and she knew she was trembling. But what she failed to recognize was that the cause wasn't entirely anger; even as humiliation made her horny, she flung the words at him.

"You can't sack me just because you don't like my tits!" If he was sacking her anyway, there was nothing to lose and such was her indignation that her workaday pronunciation slipped and was replaced by her more usual, upper class diction. Haughty and proud, she told him exactly what she thought of him.

"You're nothing but a lecherous old hypocrite. I've seen you with your tongue hanging out every time I walk in the room."

"Interesting though the accent is, there's no need to put on airs and graces on my account. I'm fully aware what you are, Ms Dean."

She was so angry that his words failed to register and she continued as before, her cultured tones incompatible with the string of obscenities which fell from her sensuous, glossed lips.

"You shit! There's nothing you'd like more than to get your own filthy frigging mitts on my 'bruised and battered' body. You'd probably like to add a few fucking bruises of your own! But it's not only me you've got the hots for, is it? I've seen your dick bulging when that young girl from accounts walks by."

"There's no need to be crude."

"Okay, sack me, but have the balls to tell the truth. I know what this is really about… you just can't handle the fact that I rejected you. You're pathetic."

Fury at the injustice of it all made her reckless. Curling her small hands into fists she clutched at her blouse and wrenched it open, showering tiny buttons across the room and ripping the seams. She peeled the garment from her body then, standing in front of him with her hard, fleshy nipples testing the see-through bra, she reached behind her back, unhooked it and flung it across the desk at him.

Calmly he removed it from where it had landed on his head, covering one eye.

"Take a good look because it's the only one you're going to get." Oh-oh! Now she had gone too far. She swallowed hard. A shudder ran through her as she realized the impossible situation she had unwittingly put herself in, and the ensuing silence stretched on endlessly as she chewed on her lip stalling for time, working out the best way to extricate herself from the mess.

He arched an eyebrow as he addressed her. "If you insist on flaunting the abused state of your body, then you shouldn't be surprised if people make certain assumptions."

"I didn't flaunt it," she denied hotly, conveniently ignoring the fact that the top half of her body was naked, and asked herself for the umpteenth time how he could possibly know about the previous night's rough games. There were no stripes or bruises on her breasts. Her hand shot out, but in less time than it took for her to make a grab at her jacket he was on his feet and beside her. Lunging frenziedly at her breasts, he locked his spiny fingers over both succulent, unexpectedly heavy orbs, squeezing them as if attempting to extract their juice.

91

"Get off me!"

Flushed with shame, she wanted to curl up and die as her nipples hardened further beneath his marauding hands until they stood out like corks. She squealed as his fingers squeezed and mauled. In an attempt to fight him off, her own fingers closed around his wrists to dislodge his hands, except they merely held on to him instead as that part of her that liked to play SM games quelled the hostility within her. Spirals of something warm and thrilling finally siphoned off her remaining defiance. To her shame she heard herself enquire breathlessly, "What if someone comes in?"

"They won't."

"But the cleaners…" she protested weakly as her hands dropped away.

"Just do as I say." His voice took on a gruff quality as he played out for real the scenario that had swum around in his head since the evening he had spent at Cordell's place. Still with his fingers digging into her heavy breasts, he told her, "When I take my hands away, I want you to take your skirt off. Leave your shoes on."

CHAPTER SEVEN

At the mercy of her own desires, Amber knew she was lost and the moment his fingers released her she unfastened the side zip of her short skirt. She eased the garment erotically down her bare, silky skinned legs, straightened up and stepped out of the skirt which lay around her ankles. She pointed her toe to try and make her shapely leg appear longer as she stretched it out to kick the garment aside. For a moment, she thought he would have a coronary when he realized she wasn't wearing panties and he ogled her black bush as if he had never seen pubic hair before.

Even now, naked in his office with her pulses quickening and lust uncoiling in her belly, she could hardly believe she was doing this. It made little sense when Smith was a man she loathed. While the inner voice of reason told her to run, her brain contended that what she wanted was to stay and submit.

Whatever it was that had come over her, it was more powerful than she could deal with right now and she determined to give it due deliberation once the whole thing was over. But right now it seemed to her that the correct thing to do was to give herself freely.

She dipped her head and centred her attention on her platform sandals. Once she had stopped fighting the inevitable, it was surprising how easy it was to slip into her longed-for submissive role. Smilingly, she shuddered as joyful anticipation set her clitoris pounding. So it was with a jolt of utter confusion that she realized hot tears of shame were trickling lazily down her cheeks, taking mascara with them. She lifted her head slowly and tried to focus on him through misted eyes. Common sense fought for control and she realized she was behaving exactly as the whore he had accused her of being. Torn now between the sensual thrill of submission and acrid shame, heat stained her skin crimson. She could hardly believe that she had let things get so out of hand. Her shoulders slumped as she wondered at her feeble-mindedness; that her search for a Master should steer her into the clutches of the man she despised was almost too much to bear. And that it was Reynard Smith who had been the first man to reduce her to tears for more years than she could remember added to her distress. Trembling, she made a last-ditch effort to extricate herself before she was completely lost, and bent down to retrieve her skirt.

Smith was too quick for her. He snatched it from her, and a gut-churning ripping noise filled the room. He made a bundle of the torn skirt, along with the ruined blouse and unsullied jacket and threw them aside.

"What am I supposed to wear to go home?" she wailed.

"You'll think of something." He retrieved her bra and dropped it in his pocket as a keepsake. His eyes darkened and suddenly she was afraid.

She let out a shrill "Ooow!" as she received a savage, flat-handed slap across her right breast. She backed away. He took a couple of steps to bring him level with her again, then dealt another blow to her left breast, followed by another and another. Cordell was right, he thought; breasts wobble in the most alluring way when dealt the kind of treatment their design incorporated the need for. And this little tart deserved everything she got. He smiled as he dealt her yet another slap with such force behind it that it almost knocked her off balance.

Staggering backward, she flicked her eyes towards the door, measuring the distance between herself and her escape. But he caught hold of her slender arm and his spiny fingers dug in painfully. It was then she knew there was no escape. Trembling as her heart thumped in her chest, her eyes widened fearfully. She felt dizzy with her shifting emotions and all at once it was easier to give in, believe herself a victim of his lust rather than face the truth that he was right and she was nothing other than a bruised and battered whore.

"Put your clothes over there." He pointed to the brown, lidded storage box placed beside the door to his executive bathroom.

Ashen faced, she was unable to sort out or separate the mishmash of conflicting emotions. Frightened and humiliated, despite her loathing for him she found herself wanting to obey. Bending to retrieve her clothes, once again mischief uncurled inside and she was unable to conquer the temptation to tease. She exaggerated the sway of her hips as she walked, as well as the straight-legged way she bent over to present her taut, red striped bottom with its black-and-blue bruises, to perfection. And while Reynard Smith drooled over the sight of her abused backside and engorged labia which protruded invitingly between her pearly thighs, she dutifully piled her clothes on the box.

She swung round to face him and awaited further instructions. They weren't slow in coming. He motioned for her to come and kneel in front of him. Again the swell of shame washed over her, leaving her feeling totally wretched. She had never coped well with humiliation and was at a loss as to how to deal with it as she took up the required position. Staring up at him with her knees tucked beneath her she watched as, with lips together, he made odd movements with his mouth, as if he found the act of swallowing impossible. Then he reached out a hand and gripped her chin. With fingers and thumb digging spitefully into her cheeks, he forced her mouth open and bent towards her. Then he opened his lips and emitted a long stream of spittle which he directed into her gaping mouth.

Her eyes opened wide as his saliva pooled in her mouth, coating her tongue and dripping insidiously down the back of her throat. Horror and disgust did battle within her, even as excitement flared in the depths of her bowels.

"Swallow it!" he commanded, still gripping her cheeks. "Gulp it down."

She shook her head wildly from side to side, retaining the greater part of the foul liquid in her mouth.

"I said swallow it, you fucking little whore!" He squeezed

her cheeks tighter.

Closing her eyes as if she could shut out the humiliation, she had no choice but to do as he commanded. Forcing herself to swallow it down, she emitted a sob. His fingers bit into her hollowed cheeks. Her ordeal was far from over. As she gagged with repulsion, he repeated the process twice more, then brought his anteater nose up close to her face. Stooping, he slid one spiny finger deep inside her sex. Poking and agitating, he drew incoherent moans from her lips. Of its own volition her body responded by thrusting her belly forward, inviting him to violate her with more than a yellow-stained finger. She closed her eyes and her breath came out in ragged gasps, catching in her throat as her muscles tightened around the ecstasy of his hard, probing digit.

"You're wet," he told her unnecessarily.

He worked his finger frenziedly, wringing moans from her inviting lips and almost bringing her to orgasm. With a mocking smile he extracted it again, glistening with her honeydew. He straightened up and shoved his slick digit in her face for her to see before lifting it to his own mouth and sucking it clean.

She was frantic to orgasm and heard herself wail a desperate, "Please! Bring me off. Please!"

What would Cordell do, he asked himself, then smiled as the answer came to him… nothing, the man would do nothing. "No. I'm reliably informed that it's altogether more agreeable when one disallows climax."

"Bastard!"

"Perhaps I am," he answered, looking rather pleased with himself. "Let's see how you do with this." He unzipped his trousers and extracted his cock from his blue-spotted underpants. He grabbed the back of her head and, shoving her face towards his crotch, the swollen head of his cock nudged against her lips, forcing them apart. She trembled, from suppressed fury and… something else she didn't want to admit to right now, except there was no denying it — he might not be the best boss in the world, but he was pretty damn good in the cock department. Burning with lust-tinged shame, she took his tool into the warm recess of her mouth. Gagging as he slammed into her, she realized that even his prick smelled of cigarettes. Yet nothing could quell her fevered lust as her head bobbed to and fro as she fellated him with relish.

Tears stung her eyes and the relentless pounding of his impressive, upward-curving cock made her jaws ache as she flicked her tongue along the length of his shaft. Controlled now by her own lust, tendrils of quivering warmth reached out from her pussy to her breasts. Her long nipples throbbed and her labia parted to admit her own finger. Warm and moist, it welcomed the invasion, at the same moment as Smith pressed her head so tight against him that it pushed her nose sideways. With a strangled cry, he squirted his acrid sperm down her throat.

***

Having brought herself off in Reynard's bathroom before freshening up, Amber took the proffered seat on the other side of his desk. Now that her own needs had been sated, her anger at her sudden and undeserved dismissal returned. She glared at him across his desk. Disregarding the fact that she was still naked, she let rip and once again her fury made her careless and she failed to disguise her upper-class accent.

"Fun's over! Now you can explain to me exactly what all this is about."

"Actually, it's only just beginning. Believe me, you'll be expected to be more obedient than that, young lady."

"Who says so? You? Huh!" she threw back her head and laughed. "How on earth did you find yourself elevated to such a high position within the company when you talk complete and utter rubbish?"

"You think I'm joking? You won't be laughing if things go to plan." He swept the issue aside with a flick of his wrist, folded his hands on the desk and launched into a diatribe. "You've been with this company for six months now, and while your CV is most impressive I've no further use for you in this department. Beevis and Smetherton is a well respected organisation with a highly motivated work force, and I'm afraid that you just don't fit in."

Anxiety stirred in her bowels. Had he checked more thoroughly and discovered that the whole thing was bogus? Well, maybe not the whole thing... the qualifications were real thanks to her boarding school education, though as for her previous work experience... that bit was made up, in the same way that her glowing references were forged. Assuming her deception had been discovered, she had to fight a childish urge to jump up and down, yell and scream. Instead she protested hotly.

"You can't speak to me like that." Deciding to come clean, she realized there was no point in disguising her cultured accent, without realizing that she had stumbled out of it long ago. "Have you any idea at all who I am?"

"I know exactly who you are, Ms Dean, a young woman with the need to advertise her masochistic tendencies to the world. You're also a woman whose proclivity to lie is well known around the office."

Now she was really angry, so angry that she forgot all about owning up.

"How can you say that?"

"The police were here this morning, asking questions. It seems you 'hang out' with the city low-life and criminal classes."

"Oh come on! One mistake?" So that was it... all that garbage about her appearance was just a smoke screen. "How was I to know the guy was a conman? Besides, he's gone and won't be coming back."

"Nevertheless, yours is hardly the image we want to promote here at B and S. There's always trouble of this nature when a young woman enters the work environment, especially one with your lack of morals. I will admit to being surprised when the officers told me of the apparent ease with which you offered your services to them…"

Amber could hardly believe her ears and her words came out as an indignant explosion. "They'd never tell you that!"

"Oh, but they did. It seems you made rather an impression on them, and they made a point of telling me of the delight with which you displayed your abused body, making no effort to hide the weals." He pondered Cordell's suggestion; humiliate the chosen woman at every opportunity. It seemed pretty good advice to him and he decided to do just that. "Having seen the shameful evidence with my own eyes, I feel I must concur with their opinion that you are nothing but a wanton, degenerate whore, who has no business mixing with decent folk." He watched delightedly as her face crumpled but sadly, she didn't cry. "So, once again, it's my sad duty to point out that you have no future with this company. It's a matter of public knowledge that I don't hold with women working since their whole design is for motherhood. However, I've been forced by legislation to employ women and, with the exception of yourself, so far I haven't been disappointed."

"You mean they all submit to your smutty advances and weirdo games for fear of losing their jobs."

"Don't be stupid, Ms Dean. You have intelligence, it's a shame to waste it."

"So what's the problem? How can you say that and still sack me?"

"The problem is twofold. Firstly, I'd rather not have a gangster's moll in this department, and secondly…"

"Gangster's moll? Oh, come on! This isn't Chicago."

"And secondly," he repeated irritably, "as I believe I mentioned earlier, you have talents which could be better used elsewhere. As I see it, your working here is far too distracting and corrupting for the other members of staff."

"Listen, you stupid old fart, women have rights. I could have you up in front of a tribunal, and when they find out…"

Unmoved by her threats he sat back in his chair. "Your employment will be terminated at the end of the week. However, I have one last assignment for you. One which might result in your obtaining employment more suited to your temperament."

Convinced she knew what was coming next, she shuddered. There was no way on God's sweet earth that she would ever give in to his advances again. As far as she was concerned the man was sick. Except if that were the case then, what did that make her for submitting to him in the first place?

"I've been in negotiations with a very important client for some weeks now. You may have heard of him... Joshua Cordell?"

"Can't say that I have." Of course she had heard of him; the whole world had heard of him. But all she could think of right now was how she could turn this situation around and come out on top. So why tell Smith she knew who he was? Besides, she had never actually met him, nor could she recall what he looked like. She had never cared much for the world of business and only attended board meetings of the family business as a way of safeguarding her claim. She shrugged her narrow shoulders. "So what's this assignment? And why me?"

"Because I have a proposition for him which I hope will finally clinch the deal, and you are just the woman to deliver it. I've set up a breakfast meeting for you at his club, The Naismith Club. If you decide to go through with it and I believe it will be in your best interests, I'm sure you'll walk into a far more suitable position."

"I can't meet him there. For your information, the Naismith is a Gentleman's club."

"How behind the times you are. I'm reliably informed that the club does actually allow women on the premises these days." He handed her the sealed envelope containing the contract.

Her mind was a complete jumble of emotions. What game the old lecher was playing now?

"Give him this." He handed over a second sealed envelope, which contained a very different kind of document, and said ominously, "Do exactly as he tells you. Rumour has it that Cordell has rather unusual tastes, and working practices. If we can close the deal with him it will be a real coup for the company. Your... attributes... are perfect for wooing this particular client. If you hit it off with him, and I'm in no doubt that he'll find you very acceptable indeed, he'll probably require further help, in which case he may well suggest that you spend a little time at his place, thrashing out the terms, so to speak." He gave her a leering grin. "Now, I have a wife to go home to. I suggest you go home and get an early night. You've a busy time ahead of you, starting tomorrow morning at the Naismith Club. There's no need for you to return the contract to me as I will be in contact with Cordell myself tomorrow evening. In fact, there's no need for you to ever set foot on these premises again. Once you have delivered the contract you will sever all ties with this company. You will, of course be paid in full and I'm quite certain Mr Cordell will find a suitable position for you."

With an odd sort of chuckle, he left the office, leaving her naked, confused and with a curious sense of elation surging up from her core.

**

It was Josh's last evening at The Lodge and he had made a return trip to the dungeon, where he had tortured a girl on the rack before leaving her in the stocks to be collected later by Madame herself. Afterwards, he joined one of the other members for a delightful evening meal. Together they discussed the merits of the new system whereby one could view the girls who, due to their period or some other inconvenience, were unable to service guests. It was with regret that Josh confessed that he hadn't had the pleasure of checking it out yet.

"My dear chap, you really should make an effort! After all, it's only their vaginas which are out of service. Why don't you pop along tomorrow?"

"I'd love to. Unfortunately, I have to leave tonight. I have rather a heavy work load at the moment."

His companion was sympathetic. "Then no, you won't have an opportunity to view the exhibits this time. Unfortunately, they're only on display between three and four o'clock, in one of the corridors. What a pity."

"I'll make sure I check it out on my next visit."

"You really must, Cordell. There's nothing like tormenting tits when they're in stocks."

Both men laughed, gave a toast to "tortured tits", then adjourned to the bar for cigars and brandy. Afterwards, Josh made his way to the common room, where the activities in the high-ceilinged room were just heating up. He checked his watch. It would be a shame to leave now. Nevertheless, he had a breakfast meeting in London the following morning and there were a few papers to go through tonight in readiness.

Several members, about twenty five in all, were gathered around in small groups in the long, spacious room. Some were standing around discussing the particular merits of this or that whipping bench or frame which wasn't currently in use while examining the vast array of whips, crops and other disciplinary paraphernalia. A few men relaxed on the lavishly upholstered sofas while others sat in the equally luxurious chairs, enjoying a drink as this or that Housegirl, still wearing her satin dress, knelt on the floor while she sucked cock. The whole point of the common room was that any girl, whether wearing a room disc or not, was common to all the men present. And already the magnificent room was filled with the delightful sounds of SM as girls in various stages of undress, gasped, screamed, and wept, all to the accompaniment of the Thwack! and Slap! of leather and cane against soft skin while they were secured over some frame or other.

There was one group whose attention was fixed on one

particular Housegirl, a slender little thing with hair as black as jet, who had just received a remarkably severe flogging. She was most attractively suspended by her wrist restraints from chains hanging from special fixings in the ceiling, rather than from the sparkling chandelier, as on one of Josh's previous visits. Her feet were some three or four feet from the floor. Her pale back was a mesh of vivid red stripes, as were her taut buttocks and soft thighs. The disc at her throat, which denoted the room of the member who had reserved her, glinted as it caught the light. Josh smiled inwardly; he didn't have to look at the disc to know which of the patrons had chosen her.

He raised his heavy-lidded, hazel eyes almost reverentially to the girl, Marietta, her body bathed in a sheen of sweat. It was odd how the members, himself included, treated the girls with cold, humiliating cruelty while at the same time furnishing them mentally if not physically with a respect they rarely gave to women on the outside. It took a very special kind of woman indeed to give herself up to such treatment willingly.

Pushing these thoughts to the back of his mind, Josh calculated that if he were to make it back in time to snatch at least a few hours sleep, he would have to leave within the next half an hour or so. It was only a short journey from Berkshire to Buckinghamshire but, and now he was brutally truthful with himself, he would either have to leave soon or else he would give in to his lust, retain his room for a further week and let the world go on without him.

The men, laughing and congratulating each other, stood by as Yuri, one of the powerfully built Russian twins, quietly freed the girl.

"Good show."

"What a delightful picture."

"I say, Cordell, you're not going to rush off now?"

Josh stood with his fingertips pressed together as he re-considered his situation. Tight lipped, he scanned the faces of the men… yes, there was Masterson waiting for Marietta, the guy's particular favourite, to be released from her bonds so that he could sample her delights in the privacy of his room. There was little or no jealousy among the majority of members, though having a fondness for petite, dark haired girls himself, Josh did feel that Masterson hogged the girl on his visits. Maybe it was time for a bit of friendly rivalry. Josh acknowledged him with a nod of his head then, his mind made up, issued his directive.

"Yuri, take Marietta over to the fireplace. And fetch me that leggy blonde," he indicated an exceptionally tall girl who had just entered the common room, wearing her red satin, floor length gown. "You know how I like them set up."

There was no let up in the activity as the Russian carried the limp and faintly smiling, hard-nippled Marietta across the vast, opulent room. The air was as thick with lust as it was with cigar smoke as Josh took the crop proffered by Gascoigne.

Some of the men went to surround one piece of apparatus where two girls had just been tethered side by side, while another little group followed Josh. On his way to the fireplace, he turned his head to see Alan Masterson settle himself in one of the chairs in the far corner. Slightly behind and to Masterson's right, a five foot, wrought iron candle holder in which six white candles burned, threw an eerie light across that one corner of the room, casting pleasantly ghostly shadows over a naked girl who was draped over a nearby trestle.

Josh and his band of followers continued on to the marble fireplace, where Yuri had prepared the girls in the required manner. The blonde had been stripped naked and placed a few feet in front of the fire where its illumination threw warm, flickering light over the soft contours of female flesh.

On her knees with her legs spread wide and her palms flat against the floor, her back acted as a most acceptable slab on which to lay the petite, sinewy form of Marietta. Stretched along the length of the blonde's back, shoulder to shoulder,

Marietta's arms were pulled down tautly, her wrists tied to the other girl's forearms. Her legs were also splayed wide and tied to the other girl's legs. This method of displaying her had the effect of defining her ribs most attractively and ensuring that her breasts presented themselves exquisitely for punishment. However, being of small stature her legs didn't quite touch the floor.

Josh took up a position whereby he could deliver a good thrashing while his companions stationed themselves to watch. To his delight they were all in agreement that the arrangement of female meat made an exceptionally pretty sight as both girls exposed the glistening slits of their honeydewed quims. Across the room, some of the other members stopped what they were doing and, momentarily forsaking their own captives, crossed the room for a better view. Only Masterson, much to Josh's annoyance, seemed to be unmoved.

Josh raised his arm, dropping it again when his attention was caught by the sounds emanating from the far side of the room, where a few remaining members were far too involved with their own girls to take any interest in Josh's activities. As their floggings became more urgent, the girls couldn't help but scream, for which, of course, they were flogged even harder.

Josh felt the stirring of his penis as it pushed against the fabric of his trousers. There was nothing like the sound of a girl's scream to get the juices flowing, and the sound of the lash cracking across soft, quivering flesh to bring out the animal in a man. Returning to the job in hand, he slid his brooding, lustful gaze over Marietta's torso and once again relished the way her ribs were so clearly outlined. It was to this region he turned his attention.

First, he flicked the leather keeper of the crop over each rib in turn, then repeated the process, this time a little harder as if he were playing a xylophone. He felt his chest tighten as Marietta acknowledged each stinging flick with a moan and the tiniest of jerking movements, which made the girl below her make little grunting noises in response. He swung his eyes to Marietta's face as he continued the process. Her eyes were closed tightly and she was biting into her lower lip to keep from moaning.

Nevertheless, Josh was quick to notice the flush of arousal which stained her cheeks, just as it had when his colleagues had thrashed her earlier. Smiling, he extended his arm and twisted his body slightly, using the tip of the crop to trace a line from the blonde's mound upward, then up along Marietta's slit and upward over her belly before continuing along the valley between her breasts. They were, Josh considered, exactly right for her frame and wobbled delightfully as she tried to steady her breathing. Then, having satisfied himself that she was ready, he took a breath and raised the crop.

There was a whistle as it cut through the air, followed by a most satisfying Thwack! as it struck the underside of her breast, causing a fine spray of perspiration to leap upward and catching the girl beneath off balance. He stood back to allow them both a moment to recover, braced himself, then drew a sharp line of fire across the swell of Marietta's breast. Now he was really getting into his stride and again brought the crop down in a line directly over the first. The next stripe, laid beside the others, was delivered with such force that it succeeded in drawing a startled cry from Marietta's lips, and those of the blonde.

Spurred on by the laughter and cheers from the assemblage of men, to say nothing of the sounds of the flogging across the room, he threw himself into the task with relish. Time after time he lashed her, laying down a series of blazing, scarlet stripes which covered Marietta's breasts in a series of deep, angry red welts. Delightedly he watched as her lovely body jerked under his force, causing the delectable blonde beneath to jerk also.

Engrossed in the task before him, Josh soon forgot the time. Nothing else mattered save the two girls displayed so lewdly and uncomfortably before him, and the red criss-

106

crossing of Marietta's pale skin. He knew he was no barbarian, just as he knew that even if he lived to be a hundred, nothing would give him more pleasure than the cruelty he was able to inflict upon a submissive girl. And, to give both girls their due, they took everything he meted out to them that evening with obedient surrender. Moreover, apart from that one lapse, in complete silence just as all good Housegirls should.

***

It was well past two in the morning when Josh glanced in his mirror and saw the dark shape of The Lodge receding as he drove down the long, tree lined drive toward the gamekeeper's lodge. He was leaving with memories of a lengthy, most agreeable stay. This evening with Marietta had only been one of many high points and already he was looking forward to his next visit, with the prospect of viewing the "out of service" girls in the corridor.

With such delights uppermost in his mind, he put his foot to the floor and headed home, where he had left Saskia in the care of Alice and Dougie. As always, his instructions concerning his woman had been strict, though he was under no illusions that his wishes would be carried out to the letter by any of his staff. For one thing, he very much doubted that his newly acquired stable lad would have the willpower to leave her chained, manacled and untouched while her Master was away. And, even with Alice Ward on the premises, he doubted that Dougie would deliver the prescribed beatings without also taking advantage of Saskia's charms. Josh chuckled knowingly; that would be beyond the call of duty for his old friend!

Saskia… he had often visualised her between the shafts, but luck had always been against him and, whenever he had taken her to The Lodge she had been in such demand that he had been obliged to abandon the idea. Still, perhaps next time.

It was with reluctance that he switched his thoughts from

the pleasures of slaves to the meeting with the young woman tomorrow. In her capacity as a representative for Beevis and Smetherton, Ms Jane Dean was being sent along by Reynard Smith to deliver a new proposal, with herself as the bait. And if the girl turned out to be everything Smith had promised, though he had detected a slight uneasiness in the man's voice, Josh could very well find himself with a new plaything. Of course, once the deal was done and dusted, Josh would be obliged to keep his word and invite Reynard Smith over one weekend. Dammit! he thought resentfully. He disliked the man intensely, but he had promised the use of Saskia, and he was nothing if not a man of his word. It was probably best to have him over straight away, providing the girl was up to standard.

It had been Josh's own idea to meet the girl at The Naismith Club, though now he was having second thoughts. It had lost much of its appeal since it had started to admit women. Not that he had anything against women in general, though in his opinion the only females who had any business in Gentlemen's clubs were those who knew their place and had a useful purpose, such as the well-trained and willing Housegirls at the Lodge. However, he was well aware that not so very long ago his own background would have denied him membership of both clubs. Even now there were some members who regarded his relaxed manner and casual style of dress as not reflecting the desirable image for a Gentleman, regarding them as the hallmark of a man who was nothing but an upstart. He was still considered an impostor by some, a man out of his class who tried to pass himself off as something he most definitely was not. He supposed that he would always be known as the kid from the council estate who had made good.

Joshua Cordell had been fortunate and got into the computer games market at just the right time. Now his company was worth millions; even Hollywood had made considerable use of his animators' expertise. Soon he had branched out into other areas of computer software and bought up a couple of smaller, failing computer businesses. Once branded with the Cordell company logo, the newly acquired subsidiaries had blossomed and things had really taken off. Next, after buying up a couple of High Street outlets, things had gone from strength to strength. Within a few years his company had swallowed up one of the largest names in the computer business and he had diversified into other areas of office equipment. Now he was *the* name in IT technology and a very rich man indeed.

It hadn't taken Josh long to discover the status that wealth gave a man, so that whatever the minority felt about him, there were countless clubs and institutions who were falling over themselves to sign him up as a member.

CHAPTER EIGHT

Considering her ordeal in Smith's office, Amber slept surprisingly well. For the sake of decency she had called on her ingenuity, along with Smith's stapler, and worn the torn skirt home, with her jacket buttoned up to her neck. She had left the tattered blouse behind in Smith's office where no doubt the cleaners had formed their own opinions as to how it had come to be reduced to scrap material. Hopefully it would go some way towards sullying the old goat's reputation.

She rose early to get ready for the meeting with Joshua Cordell and after her shower, she wrapped a towel around her wet hair and smoothed Honeyed Lavender Wishes body lotion, the best part of thirty pounds a bottle, into her pale skin. Passing back through her bedroom, lavishly furnished in oyster and apricot with gilt fittings, she stood before the full-length mirror that graced the wall of her dressing room to check on her bruises. They were still very much in evidence and were now a deep bluey-purple. She smiled as she touched her fingertips to them then giggled aloud. She pondered on what the highly respectable Joshua Cordell would say if he knew that the woman with whom he was going to have breakfast in an hour's time had been repeatedly beaten, for pleasure.

That thought led on to another, one she really didn't want to examine too rigorously right now; she had submitted to the man she most despised. Angry now that she hadn't put up more of a fight, not just to save her modesty but also to save her job, she channelled her anger into briskly rubbing her hair dry. Of course, she could survive perfectly well without the money. And if she was bored, she could always take on a senior role within the family business.

"So what's the problem?" she asked her reflection.

The answer wasn't long in coming. What she really resented was the humiliation of being sacked as casually as if she were merely one of the lazy, so-called "working class" that Mummy frequently complained about, people like High

Briar's ex-employees, who had no real desire to work and preferred to scrounge off society.

All at once she was consumed with an insatiable desire to get even, and with uncharacteristic malevolence she determined to lose Smith his precious deal, though exactly how she was going to do it she had yet to determine. What kind of fool sacked someone and then sent them to an important meeting?

She had one very effective weapon in her armoury, her femininity, and she had no qualms about using it to her advantage. She would sleep with the devil himself if that's what it would take to lose him his all-important deal.

She snatched up her hairdryer and styled her hair into the sleek, simple bob. Next, she applied her make-up, brassy and bold to match her rebellious mood. By clever use of an eyebrow pencil, she was able to thicken her jet brows and extend their length, completely altering their shape. She used two shades of eye-shadow, one a touch darker than her skin tone and the second a deep bluey-purple, "to match the bruises on my bum," she told the mirror, to add emphasis to her unusual violet eyes. She swept the shadow upward at the outer corners, then applied thick black eyeliner to the top eyelids. Once again she swept it upward. She used kohl beneath her eyes and again swept it upward at the outer corners, to give the illusion of a more exotic shape. Afterwards she finished them off with lashings of mascara.

Next, she cleverly blended her blushers to feign high cheekbones. Then she applied lip liner outside the natural shape of her lips and filled it in with deep claret lipstick topped with gloss. This gave her the appearance of having full, sensuously moist lips. Even she had to admit that the effect was stunning, and knew her already good looks were greatly enhanced. Ha! She would knock Mr Big Shot Joshua Cordell dead! After all, she may as well glean some fun from the situation. She smiled. What she really wanted was to make a fool of Smith, and decided that the best way to do it was to drop the pretence of Jane and meet Cordell on equal terms as Amber. After all, she had nothing to lose since she was out of a job anyway.

Now all she had to do was select the right outfit, and she would be able to twist this guy round her little finger, no matter what kind of 'unusual tastes and working practices' Cordell employed.

***

Amber's red leather boots with the ridiculously high stiletto heels clack-clacked up the stone steps to the heavy door of The Naismith. Tight fitting, they laced up the front and reached up to her bare, mid thigh and were totally unsuitable for a place with such a high reputation. Perhaps she should have worn something more decorous since her outfit was eye-catching at the best of times and was now positively outrageous given her surroundings. She had only worn it a couple of times before, to nightclubs with her upper-crust friends.

On pushing open the door and stepping into the large, burgundy carpeted entrance hall, for a moment she almost lost her nerve. The solemn atmosphere was so thick it almost knocked her back. In the same way that High Briar did, it reeked of history and put Amber in mind of stuffed shirts and, worse still, her own forebears. This was exactly the kind of place the Oakley-Deans approved of; out-dated and frequented by dull old men with monotonous voices who got off on The Times crossword, putting the world to rights, politics and after dinner speeches.

It was deathly silent, so silent that she wanted to scream and bring a shattering end to it all. In less time than it had taken to catch her breath, her mood had done a complete switch. She knew that for her to enter this oak-panelled, mausoleum of a place and to conform was to sentence to death that part of her which had only recently begun to live. It would be emotional suicide; there was nothing for it, she had to liven the place up a bit.

Her face lit up as the devil-switch was once again flicked on. Oh, how she loved to knock the stuffing out of the establishment of which, however bored with it all she might be, she was part. Joyful anticipation brought a wicked smile to her lips and set her eyes flashing. It only took a millisecond for her to decide on her course of action. An imitation of a hooker was called for, but not just any hooker, one like Mistress Josie who lived below her hideaway flat. After all, she observed with mischievous zeal, she was dressed for the part.

The red leather skirt, so short it barely covered her bottom, fitted so snugly that every contour of her pert backside was clearly defined. It was obviously clear to the official inside the doorway who peered at her over his spectacles that she wore no knickers beneath it, and she concluded that it was therefore clear to everyone else. She suppressed a giggle and hoped she wouldn't drop her napkin over breakfast; she would have to be extremely careful if she bent down. She wore the matching leather jacket over a very tight, low-cut, strappy white lace top, through which one could see her very expensive, push-up, lace trimmed bra. It had been worth every penny and accentuated her cleavage very nicely, moulding itself so tightly to her breasts which spilt over the top that very little indeed was left to the imagination.

She had only caught sight of Mistress Josie once but if she kept the image of the hooker firmly in her mind it would give her enough material to work with. Smiling, Amber crooked her index finger through the strap of her shoulder bag and slung it in such a way that it hung down her back and knocked against her outlined bottom. She began an open-mouthed chewing motion as though she had a mouth full of gum and rested her other hand, fingers splayed, on her hip. Then, with the exaggerated swaying of her hips in which she excelled, she crossed to the small reception area where another official, who looked as if he should have retired ten years earlier, watched her with suspicion.

113

"I'm here for a business meeting with Joshua Cordell," she said in her commonest, loudest voice as she continued to chew on air.

"Ms Dean." The man visibly shuddered as he appraised her, announcing in low tones, "Mr. Cordell is expecting you. You will find him in the reading room." He indicated a door which stood open on the left of the rectangular entrance hall. With an expression that suggested she had sullied the place by trampling cow dung over the burgundy carpeting, he told her, "Mr Cordell is seated at one of the tables on the right hand side, by the window."

"Thank you," Amber beamed as she chewed, and couldn't resist winking at him as he gave her a derogatory look which implied he knew exactly what kind of business she was in. She was happily aware of both officials watching her as she crossed the hall to stand in the open doorway. However, she was completely unaware of the auburn haired woman who, on entering the hall from an opposite door, also watched her.

"Amber! I hardly recognized you."

Her heart almost thumped to a complete standstill when she heard the woman's voice peal out across the hall. But worse than that, not only did she hear it but it was well-known to her. This was the very last thing she needed, a friend of Mummy's, here — today of all days. Why oh why hadn't she worn something more respectable? But more to the point, how could she explain her presence here? To divulge that she had a business meeting with an important client would be to acknowledge that she had a job... or rather, she didn't since she had been sacked. Trapped in the hall with her secret life on the verge of discovery, there was nothing she could do to avoid the confrontation. It would be too rude and draw now unwanted attention to herself to ignore the woman, or take flight, though the latter seemed increasingly tempting.

Amber stood her ground and smiled politely as the woman, her meticulously styled, auburn hair not quite masking the few grey strands, came and stood beside her.

"Mrs Huntley-Watts…" Amber stopped her bogus chewing and gave the woman her warmest, sincerest smile, wishing the old bat would just drop dead.

"It's not for me to say, darling, but that outfit's rather common for a place like The Naismith," the woman said in a stage-whisper which drew the attention of the men seated nearest to the door in the reading room.

The men gave a collective, 'they should never have opened the doors to women' sort of look before returning to their newspapers.

Amber recovered her bag from over her back and hung it more conventionally over her shoulder. As the elder woman proffered her cheek to be kissed, Amber had an almost uncontrollable urge to tell her to get stuffed. Watched by the eyes of the officials in the hall, she continued to smile sweetly and returned the gesture as briskly as possible. But Millicent Huntley-Watts' next gesture had Amber's eyes widening and her breath coming out between clenched teeth. Was it by accident or design that the woman's hand glided over the tight leather that stretched across Amber's bottom?

"I had no idea you were a member here, Amber." She ran the fingers of her other hand through Amber's hair and ruffled it, brushing her cheek in the process.

"I'm thinking of joining," Amber breathed self-consciously, making it up as she went along. "I'm only here on probation today." Her high heels had given her enough extra inches to be able to meet the woman's gaze eyeball to eyeball, and she wasn't at all sure that she liked what she saw. She had seen that look many times when appraised by men, but never had she seen such lust in the eyes of a woman.

"A word of advice, then." Again the hand swept over her leather-encased backside, then long, tapering fingers very firmly cupped the swell of her right buttock. "While I rather like your outfit," the hand released her and suddenly dived beneath the hem of Amber's skirt, "the majority of members prefer a more conservative style of dress. I'm sure you won't

115

mind my saying, but you look rather like a street walker."

Amber was frozen to the spot. How dare the woman insult her, and worse still, touch her up at the same time. She had never been touched by another woman and the very idea of it had always seemed unnatural, even abhorrent to her. But this was worse than she had ever imagined; this woman was her mother's age!

"I'm sure your mother wouldn't approve of your coming here dressed like this," she bent one knee slightly to gain better access as she inched her hand forward, closing it firmly over Amber's knickerless, heavily thatched mound, "so I won't say anything, dear."

Amber knew she was trembling, and was also aware that her mother's friend knew it, too. The horror of it all was too much to think about right now as the exploring fingers prised open her slit. God help her, she was wet! She wanted to die of shame as the finger slid in easily. Under the gaze of the officials, the woman began frigging her relentlessly, and it was all Amber could do to keep from moaning, either with loathing or… no, it couldn't be pleasure. Yet she knew that even the slightest sound would have the men glancing up from their papers again.

Millicent Huntley-Watts withdrew her hand and held her finger up for Amber to see the glistening juices which coated it, adding to Amber's crushing humiliation. Then she raised it to her own lips, put it in her mouth and made a show of sucking it clean. As Amber felt a shudder pass through her, Millicent gave her a sincere smile that matched the one that Amber had previously given her.

"I must dash, darling," Millicent oozed. "I'm spending the morning here, then meeting your mother in town for a spot of lunch. Of course, I shan't mention that I've seen you, but you can be sure that I'll look forward to seeing you here again soon." She turned to go and Amber felt gnawing apprehension as Millicent added, "Perhaps you and I can lunch together sometime." She continued to smile as she wiggled her fingers

116

in the air in a goodbye gesture and, to Amber's relief, retraced her steps across the hall and back into the room opposite.

In a state of turmoil, Amber tried to focus her mind. It was clear that Mrs Huntley-Watts wanted to keep the whole thing quiet, and why wouldn't she since it could ruin her reputation along with Amber's? Not only that, but the damn woman was married to a high-ranking member of parliament and if the news got out that she was a... a... Amber could hardly bring herself to think the word... dyke, then it would bring shame upon the minister. Yet unsettling as the experience was, Amber knew there could be no redress and that she would just have to put the whole episode behind her and hope she never came across Millicent Huntley-bloody-Watts again in her entire lifetime. And she had no intention of ever setting foot in the Naismith again, once she had screwed up Smith's deal with Cordell.

Cordell... she had almost forgotten about him! And now that she did remember, she was filled with a new horror. What if Cordell had seen the whole thing? This could seriously harm her reputation as a rampant, fuck-friendly heterosexual.

From her location in the doorway, she scoured what portion of the reading room was visible. At last she spotted him. Just as the club official had told her, Joshua Cordell was seated in one of the leather-backed chairs at a small table by the window. On observing him for the first time, she was somewhat taken aback by the erratic beating of her heart; it was probably related to the incident with Millicent a few moments earlier, she persuaded herself.

The sunlight streamed in, snagging his thick, tawny hair with golden highlights which did nothing to soften his hauntingly brooding expression. She couldn't deny that he was handsome and it wasn't beyond the bounds of possibility that a lot of women would go for his dark, sombre look. His well defined brows were heavy and there was a definite sneer to his lips, as if he were mocking the world. He wore his hair swept back from his forehead, just kissing his collar at the back.

She knew she was being ridiculous but even from this distance she felt overwhelmed by his sexuality; it positively oozed from him. Yet she couldn't help but feel there was something deeply disturbing about the way he was dressed impeccably but entirely in black. It was nothing tangible, merely a feeling she had of danger, made worse by the sober atmosphere of the Gentlemen's Club. As a rule she was far from timid, yet as she watched him concentrating on the screen of the laptop resting across his knees she felt like turning tail and fleeing.

She searched her memory for some kind of data regarding him, wishing she had paid more attention to all those press reports. As she scanned her mind files, she recalled that he was in his thirties and was a self-made man with, reputedly, one of the largest fortunes in the country. What she suspected rather than knew was that he was capable of seducing ten women before breakfast. With a regretful shrug of her shoulders, she reminded herself that she wasn't here for her own seduction, rather she was here to seduce him and in so doing get even with Smith.

That set her wondering what chance she actually had against a man like Cordell. Her resolve weakened as shameful images of the way she had submitted to Smith began to replay in her mind, though for the sake of convenience she chose to overlook the minor irritation that she had rather got off on the experience.

Her insides churned with sickly premonitions of risk, while thrilling bolts of anticipation shot through her pussy. Her instincts warned of danger more potent than anything she had encountered before. She told herself she was being ridiculous and her emotions shifted gear again. Lust and dread became indistinguishable. She wanted to dive for cover, except she also wanted to fall to her knees and worship the brooding entrepreneur, as a slave worships a Master.

With a despairing downward glance she cradled her head in her hands and closed her eyes, admonishing herself churlishly.

Was she so perverted that there was nothing else she could think of except her recurring fantasy? She had been caught unawares by the powerful effect he was having on her and all at once it didn't matter whether she got even with Smith or not. But what was of vital importance was that Joshua Cordell not only fancied her but liked her as well. She was dressed to kill, so why was she suddenly so afraid of rejection?

She was borderline crazy, she told herself, hardly daring to breathe, let alone go in and introduce herself. She had never been the kind of girl to chicken out of a thorny predicament, nor was she the timid wallflower type. Normally, she could hold her own with the best of them. She was here to do a job, and that job was to lose Smith the contract. And she was unable to do that by hovering in the doorway. She had to find some way to turn the tables and make Cordell feel as insignificant as she was beginning to feel now. All she had to do was march right up to him and announce her arrival in her sexiest, cock-withering tones. Haughty Amber Oakley-Dean should have no trouble.

She squared her narrow shoulders, held her head high and grasping the moment, took a deep breath as she set off towards him.

***

Josh knew she was there, of course. He had viewed her indecision in the doorway with amusement, without once giving an indication that he had seen her. The incident with Millicent Huntley-Watts hadn't escaped his notice either, and he had watched Amber's reactions closely, trying to gauge her levels of shame and arousal for future reference. Now, with an air of cool detachment which belied the surging heat in his balls he continued working as, without being invited, Amber took the seat across from him. He found the way she placed her bag on the floor and made a show of leaning back in her seat and crossing her legs most entertaining. Her short leather

119

skirt rose up further and afforded him a tempting flash of the naked, pearly flesh above her boot that was hard to ignore.

However, ignore it he did as he scanned the rows of data displayed on the screen before him. Making women wait was something of a speciality with him; both in matters of business and more particularly pleasure. It was his opinion that a woman, especially a sexy piece of skirt like this one, was easier to manipulate once she had been kept on tenterhooks, with her insides quivering with nervous tension.

His fingers continued to move deftly over the keyboard.

Amber found her attention riveted on his hands and tried to imagine what kind of delights his preoccupied digits would engender if they were to skim over her body with such expertise. As if responding to his touch, her nipples hardened and she found her hand straying downward to dip between her hot thighs. She snatched it away again and sat demurely with her hands folded in her lap, hoping he hadn't noticed her indiscretion. If he had, he made no reference.

Still he ignored her and she was astounded by his arrogance. She wasn't used to being snubbed. It was so humiliating! It reminded her of the way Mummy kept the housekeeper waiting when she presented the weekly menu. As Amber's pique increased, it was on the tip of her tongue to tell him exactly what she thought of him, but decided against it on the grounds that he would think he had won. She distracted herself by appraising him while she had the chance.

Up close, she could see that the shirt and tie were silk, the trousers expensively tailored and the shoes Italian. And as for the aftershave… being something of a connoisseur on the matter she inhaled deeply, testing her ability to put a name to it… faintly mossy, a pinch of ginger, musky with a hint of citrus… it had to be Savage Wilderness.

With her hands still folded in her lap, she began to flick one thumbnail over the other. It was either that or drum her fingers on the table as the silence between them dragged on until, with almost theatrical precision, Josh snapped the laptop closed. Placing it beside him on the floor, he finally acknowledged her presence with little more than a suggestion of a smile from his contemptuous lips. He made no move to rise from his seat, nor did he offer to shake her hand.

Her fragile patience was about to bubble over. To try and keep it under control she made a fuss of checking her watch, the jewel encrusted Cartier, not the cheap blue, gimmicky one which she always wore as Jane.

"Jane Dean, I presume." It wasn't a question; he made it sound like an accusation.

She opened her mouth to speak but no words came out and she was aware of her own hesitation. She had already decided to tell him there had been a mistake and that her name was Amber Dean, not Jane. It would be easy enough to convince him that Reynard Smith was a complete imbecile and couldn't be trusted in business. After all, if he couldn't get the names of his employees right, it was doubtful he could be trusted with anything as important as the contract. On the other hand, she had the feeling that to lie to this broodily handsome man was a greater risk than to tell him the truth. Therefore, the wisest course of action would be to take him into her confidence, come clean and own up to what was, in effect, nothing more than a harmless prank. Surely a man like Cordell would understand that she was only pretending to be Jane Dean for a laugh?

When she opened her mouth to speak, there was a provocative curve to her glossed lips. Except the words she spoke in her own, upper-class accent weren't the words she had planned to utter at all.

"Yes, I'm Jane. And you're Joshua Cordell."

"Most people call me Josh." He gave her outfit the once over, and yet again she felt herself shrink several inches under his censorious scrutiny. "The boots would look better with stockings."

Setting her mouth sternly she said haughtily, "I thought we were here to discuss business, not my wardrobe. Not that it's

121

any concern of yours but I've never worn stockings in my life, nor do I wear tights. I've got good legs and I prefer to leave them bare. Besides, this skirt's too short; the stocking tops would show."

"Nevertheless, you'll wear stockings from now on."

Unable to believe the arrogance of the man, she speared him with a blazing, nose-flaring regard and retaliated more hotly than she intended. "Who are you to tell me what I can and can't wear?"

"Someone who has every right. In future, you'll wear only what I tell you or provide for you."

She stood up huffily. "You're mad." She snatched up her bag and was about to march off when he rose to his feet. His arm shot out and grabbed her.

"Sit!"

To some degree side-tracked by his hazel eyes, which met hers with a cool authority which made her mentally shed the extra inches provided by her high heels, she hardly noticed how the seconds ticked by. However, what she did notice was the way his eyes remained on her face a long time, as if he were committing every detail of her elaborately made-up features to memory. The air between them seemed to pulse and crackle with a highly explosive charge that momentarily took Amber's breath away. Disconcerting arrows of desire headed straight for her belly. For the first time in her life she felt as if her ability to flirt had utterly failed her, and it was a real struggle to maintain her current, though somewhat diminished, confidence. But she wasn't about to roll over and die just yet. Once again, she took a deep breath and held her head high.

"I'm not a bloody dog!"

"If I have to repeat myself, Ms Dean, you'll be leaving here with a very sore bottom indeed."

She knew it was just a threat, of course. Shrugging herself free, she pulled a face and plonked herself down, dumped her bag on the floor and kicked it under the table. She wasn't sure what his game was, nor did she want to find out. Angry that they had got off on completely the wrong foot, she tried to keep a rein on her temper and forced a laugh.

"Okay, let's cut the crap and get down to business. I have a busy schedule." Oh, she lied so convincingly these days. How could she leave now when the way he issued his commands set her pulses racing? A fierce throbbing set her quim on fire and already she could feel a moistness between her legs. She would have to excuse herself and go to the Ladies to sort herself out since she had blown her chance to impress him. And that left her little chance of discrediting Smith. Still, the morning had only just begun and maybe there was still time to salvage something from the disaster. In a nervous gesture her hand rubbed her throat.

There was something about the dark way in which he regarded her that made her feel like a mouse cornered by the neighbourhood tom cat. For the first time in her entire life she knew that she, Amber Jane Oakley-Dean, was truly out of her depth. So it came as something of a shock to see her own sizzling arousal reflected in his heavy-lidded eyes. Suddenly feeling very small and vulnerable, she tried to tear her gaze away but her own fascination forbade it. When his hand reached out towards her across the table and grabbed her wrist, she drew in a sharp breath. He uprooted her other arm sharply and dragged it across the table towards him so that she had to rise from her seat and rest her elbow on the polished wood.

"No, Jane, we have business," he corrected as his grip tightened. "Your only business is to satisfy me. I know you don't have any other engagements today, so I suggest that it's you who cuts the crap. You see, you were only promised breakfast but I, on the other hand, was promised much more than that."

She felt the colour drain from her face. When she finally spoke, her words came out as a tremulous whisper.

"What do you have in mind?"

Speaking softly, the bluntness of his words shook her to the core at the same time as he shook her arm. "I intend to fuck the

123

arse off you. Now, we can either do it right here in full view of the other members, for which we'll be thrown out and barred for life, or you can wait for me in the Ladies. This is the last choice you'll ever be asked to make. So, Ms Jane Dean, choose carefully. Which is it to be?"

If he didn't let go he would stop her blood flow. She bit into her bottom lip as if that could ease the discomfort. Her nipples were pushing hard against the insides of her bra and she knew he would see them through the thin fabric of her strappy top. She felt her buttocks tighten. Never had a man made her feel this way before, as if she were completely at his mercy. The tone in which she answered him was almost reverential.

"Can you point me in the direction of the toilets, please?"

CHAPTER NINE

The Ladies toilets were a clichéd concession to womanhood in an otherwise male domain, done out in pink-for-a-girl ceramic tiles. There was the ubiquitous vase of artificial flowers on the windowsill, while a plethora of mirrors catered to the female's need to check her make-up at every given opportunity. Snorting at woman's vanity, Amber checked hers.

Under normal circumstances, she would have felt right at home among the well-dressed, well-heeled women who stood before the mirrors but a feeling of being desperately out of place swept over her. She stepped back as casually as she was able and sauntered towards the cubicles. As if they knew how she was feeling, the women watched her closely in the mirrors, looking her up and down with, 'they let anybody in these days' looks. Then, just as she was about to enter a vacant cubicle, she spotted Millicent Huntley-Watts drying her hands under the warm air. Amber was about to dive inside the cubicle when she realized she was too late; Millicent had spotted her.

The warm air machine switched off. "Ah, Amber. I'm glad I've bumped into you again. I have a little proposition for you."

There was a twittering from the line of women, some of who were probably well acquainted themselves with Millicent's 'propositions.'

Mischievously playing to her audience, Amber chirped breezily, "Sorry, I can't stop for a grope and stroke now. I'm fucking desperate for a piss!" She ducked into the cubicle and slammed the door to a backdrop of gasps and tut-tutting, above which Millicent's voice rang out.

"Oh, the charm of the aristocracy! One has to laugh at their little foibles."

Amber's pulses were pounding like a marching band in her head and her limbs were beginning to tremble. Things could hardly be worse. Her secret life was on the verge of discovery, she had been publicly groped, then defended, by an upper class lesbian. On top of that, she was becoming such a perverted wanton that she was waiting for some stranger to fuck her in the ladies' toilets, with a row of preening women listening outside. She was so ashamed and fearful of discovery that she felt as though her insides had turned to liquid. She pulled down the seat lid and, sitting down heavily, buried her face in her hands. If all she had to do to extricate herself from a potential disaster was get up and walk out, why did she feel trapped?

And then she became aware of another feeling as her ravenous pussy began to pulsate. All at once a joyful effervescence made her want to laugh aloud as, not for the first time, the excitement of sex in a public place gripped her. As always, it was that very fear of being caught in the act which added to her arousal.

She heard the women leave one by one. It seemed an age that she listened to the silence. Impatient by nature, she had never been much good at waiting, and doubts began to surface. Convincing herself that Josh had stood her up, she got to her feet, slowly slid back the bolt and opened the door. Her heart raced as the blood continued to pump excitement through her veins.

It was at that precise moment that Josh entered the cloakroom to be greeted by a haughty, "I think you've made a mistake, Mr Cordell," from the last woman to leave.

"No, no mistake."

Causing a complete and utter blitz on Amber's senses, Josh walked towards her. Demurely, she stepped backward to allow him to enter the small space. There wasn't much room in the cramped cubicle, yet even if they had been on opposite sides of the ballroom at High Briar his presence would have overwhelmed her as surely as it was doing now. She opened her mouth to speak. He raised a finger to his lips.

He closed the door behind him and gestured for her to lift the toilet seat lid. She gave him a puzzled look before obediently turning to do as he asked. Once facing him again, he told her to raise the seat itself. When she had complied, he made her remove her skirt and sit down on the bare porcelain which, once again, she did without question. The porcelain struck cold against her hot thighs as she fidgeted to arrange herself as comfortably as possible on the rim without letting her bottom fall.

Delighted that his guess had been correct and that she wasn't wearing knickers, in his opinion the most inconvenient of devices known to man, Josh's hungry gaze fell on her thick, black pubes which frizzed delightfully over her prominent mound. He didn't utter a word as he began to peel off her leather jacket. Taking no account of its cost he threw it to the floor. Obeying his unspoken command, she raised her slender arms. His hands closed around the hem of her skimpy white top. Painfully slowly and in a way that set her insides trembling, he drew it upward over her head. He dropped it to the floor to land on top of the jacket and kept his eyes on her as she lowered her arms again. Quivering with excitement, she made no protest when he reached behind her back and unhooked her bra.

As he dragged the straps down her arms, his gaze locked onto her breasts. While he considered them far too heavy for her petite frame, he had to fight the desire to fall upon them and bury his head between the two luscious, pearly orbs. Except, they weren't perfect spheres at all and had a tendency to hang slightly to the side. No matter, he conceded as the bra joined the other garments on the floor. Like a connoisseur assessing a new acquisition, he cupped his hands beneath them to gauge their weight, before snatching his hands away to observe their bounce. Mentally he catalogued them as his bright, hazel eyes ravaged the long, fleshy nipples, peachy against the pale skin. Already swollen and desire-hardened, they stood out stiffly from wide, knobbly areolae. He closed his eyes and lightly skimmed his fingers over them, as if reading Braille.

Amber closed her own eyes. Even she was not averse to gentle fondling, and Josh's touch was so light and fluid as his

127

fingers skirted her nipples that it set her whole being aquiver. After having being kept waiting for so long even the slightest touch was as precious as water in the desert, and her need was almost as great, so great she could scarcely control it. Her eyes snapped open to see him watching her face intently. She smiled, and her hands were driven to shaking with lust as she reached out towards his fly.

"No," he whispered tersely, ceasing his gentle caress, "put your hands behind your head."

Stunned by the authority in his voice, without question she interlaced her fingers across the back of her head and wasn't totally unaware of the way her breasts were thrust forward. Bending from the waist, he raised her right leg and rested her foot against his thigh. To her surprise he began to unlace her boot, impatiently plucking at the long lace until he had removed it altogether and she had her first inkling of his intentions. She was used to having her wrists bound but there was something about his coolness as he set her foot back on the floor which frightened her. Her tremulous breath caught in her throat when his exacting hands disentangled her fingers and deftly bound her wrists together.

Her pearly skin deepened to a shame-induced pink as the humiliation of the situation swept over her. Half naked and almost falling down the loo, the fact that it was her own bootlace which tied her somehow made the whole thing more shameful. Her pulses raced with fear and her clitoris joined in the rhythm. It was as if her dreams were coming true, except... except she was never so terribly frightened in the fantasies as she was now. Joshua Cordell was unlike any of the others for this was no game he was playing... this was for real! More frightened than she had ever been, she pleaded for release with her made-up eyes and knew instantly she had made a mistake... this guy got off on women pleading.

As his intense gaze locked onto her pubes once more, some false modesty induced her to close her legs and keep her thighs pressed together.

"Keep them open," the whispered command was issued as he placed a demanding palm on each knee and eased them apart. His hands remained there several seconds longer than necessary. "Don't close them again unless I tell you. Now pee." He was well-pleased by the flare of utter dismay in her eyes.

"What?" she hissed back, "not with you watching!"

Her vulnerability was brought home to her as his hand shot out and struck her cheek with a stingingly vicious blow. Refusing to cry out, she turned her head away, but he merely struck the other cheek.

"Don't question me! Pee, you fucking bitch."

No stranger to bad language herself, somehow his use of it added to her shame, and her fear of disobeying him. Screwing up her eyes against the mortifying humiliation, she bore down and forced herself to eject a long, hot stream of golden urine. Seemingly never ending, the whooshing sound was so loud that she considered praying to die.

"Good girl," he whispered when she finally stopped. "Do as well as that next time and I'll have to think of some way to reward you."

Her head fell back; she closed her eyes and moaned as his praise served only to make her pulverising shame seem a hundred times worse. But almost at once her eyes snapped open again when she heard the rasping of his zip as he unfastened his fly. Joyfully she feasted her eyes on his cock as he held it tightly in his hand, so close that her lips automatically opened to take it into the warmth of her mouth. Oh, to take that wonderful organ into the depths of her throat and suck it into tumescence.

"You're not worthy to take such a specimen between your filthy lips," he hissed as he drew back from her and clasped his own hand tightly around his shaft.

He looked down on her with a snort of derision that made her feel, for the first time in her life, utterly worthless. Then with sudden understanding she realized that it had never been

129

his intention to allow her to fellate him; it was yet another way to humiliate her. Well, if he thought he could make her feel any worse than she did now, he was mistaken.

Except it was Amber who was mistaken as he directed his own scalding stream. Mortified, she sucked in her breath as the hot liquid splashed the skin between the valley of her breasts. Never had she felt as filthy. The stream flowed hotly down her belly to drip from her pubes in golden droplets. Yet she didn't just feel dirty but cheated as well. She consoled herself with the thought that he would allow her to suck him afterward.

Her hopes were dashed again when he relinquished his hold on his cock. His hands shot out and grasped her breasts, squeezing the malleable orbs fiercely. He dug sharp fingernails into her pinkened flesh, then tugged spitefully at the long, fleshy nipples. Then one hand released its grip and snaked downward over her flesh. Stooping slightly, he sought out the entrance to the peachy slit between her legs.

Tugging spitefully at her fleshy, lengthy labials, he whispered, "I've never had a girl with protruding lips before," and delved two fingers deep inside her tight cavern.

Her muscles tightened in appreciation. Her sigh came out as a long, low moan which seemed to echo and swirl from one cubicle to another.

"Quiet!" he ground out as he agitated her heated insides furiously.

It was impossible to keep quiet when she was being forced to endure so much. Humiliation gave way to need as he pushed her ever nearer to climax. Then, with what he considered perfect timing, he withdrew his glistening fingers, leaving her bereft with a greater need than ever to come. She let out a protracted noise from deep in her throat, a noise which was neither human nor animal but something in-between and ethereal.

Straightening up, he tore his hand from her breasts. With a quick movement which could have been lust or anger he grabbed the toilet roll and began to unwind a length of sheets, like an advertisement puppy. He scrunched them up and stuffed them in her mouth. With her hands behind her neck she was unable to remove it and with scared, widened eyes she had no choice other than to submit to whatever indignities he had in store for her. The absorbent paper soaked up the saliva in her mouth; she was so dry she felt as if she would never be able to swallow properly again. She tried to spit it out but to no avail as it clogged her mouth.

Now she felt smaller and more vulnerable than ever. Grabbing her elbow, he yanked her to her feet and her eyes once more locked onto his cock, which now reared up with iron-hard vigour. He spun her round and, with a hand in the hollow of her back, sent her sprawling toward the wall so that her body was bowed over the toilet bowl. Her head crashed against the cistern, almost knocking her senseless. Lust caught in his throat as his eyes homed in on the fading weals and dark bruises decorating her taut bottom. Smith was right, she clearly liked the rough stuff, and had clearly suffered at somebody's hands. He bowed at the knees to facilitate easier penetration, and almost at once she felt the bulbous head of his penis nudging at her entrance. Then, without the tender foreplay enjoyed by lovers he forced his way in, pistoning in and out with such severity she was terrified he would rip her insides. His hands reached round and seized her breasts again, twisting and squeezing her nipples so brutally that she made noises of protest into the improvised gag.

Her humiliation was heightened further and her skin turned an even deeper shade when she heard the concerned voice of a woman drifting from a neighbouring cubicle... not just any voice, but bloody Millicent's.

"Are you all right in there?"

Amber's heart stopped. There was no way to know how long the witch had been there, listening. Amber was convinced she had come back to spy; the old dyke probably got off on eavesdropping on other people's sex lives.

Josh ripped the toilet tissue from Amber's mouth and there

was a tense moment when she tried to find her voice. Still clutching at her breast, warningly he dug his fingers deep into her yielding flesh. She drew in a sharp breath and for a moment was so afraid that she almost called for help. Only it wasn't simply fear plaguing her mind and tangling her insides. She heard herself answer as her body's demands dictated.

"Quite all right, thanks," she said quietly, and immediately the wad was replaced in her mouth. She was rewarded by an extra powerful thrust of his rod which brought hot tears stingingly to her eyes.

Josh's hand quit her left breast. Grabbing a handful of her short hair, he pulled her head back so roughly that again she gave a muffled cry. Scrunching his fingers tightly in the silken strands he gripped tightly. And then he was pumping his hot seed into her, so fiercely she was unable to stop herself whimpering. Her muscles began to contract. Her overdue orgasm hit with the force of a tornado. In her mind, she screamed like a wild thing while in reality she made only a muffled moan into her gag.

A couple of cubicles along, the toilet flushed.

Amber felt dirty. How could she have lowered her standards to such an extent? Self-loathing caused the tears to spill from her brimming eyes as she turned crimson with shame.

Once more Josh yanked the wad from her mouth, then wrenched his cock out of her so roughly that her whole body jerked, resulting in her head banging sharply against the cistern yet again.

"Ouch!"

His hissed "I'll give you 'ouch' if you don't behave," chilled her insides. Still clutching at her hair he dragged her to her feet and spun her round. She looked up into his eyes and saw nothing but contempt. Devastated, she bit back a sob as he untied her hands. They fell limply to her sides as she stood facing him, listening to the sounds of Millicent Huntley-Watts washing, then drying her hands. Only when Josh was sure that

132

the blasted woman had finally gone did he address Amber sneeringly. "Tidy yourself, whore, then meet me at my table."

He draped her bootlace round her neck and then he was gone, leaving her feeling wholly ravaged, humiliated and… no, she wouldn't allow herself to admit to feeling happy. That would make her the weirdest kind of wanton. How could she possibly be happy, she asked herself, when the bastard had pissed on her then practically raped her? She pulled down the toilet seat and lid and plonked herself down again. Anger tangled with her other emotions as she set about re-lacing her boot. At last it was done and she began removing tiny fragments of paper from her tongue. It was only then that she became aware that she was smiling, and acknowledged that the zing had been put back into her life.

***

Over a breakfast of croissants and coffee which Josh ordered for her, he put in a few business calls on his mobile. However, one call in particular caught Amber's attention.

"Tell Alice I'll be bringing the girl home and that she'll be staying." He spoke in authoritative but kindly tones. "See to it that the other one is suitably dressed. Oh, Dougie? Meet me out front with some hardware."

"You're taking a lot for granted," Amber told him as he switched off his phone.

"Don't fool yourself. You know as well as I do that you want to come back with me. I'll put in a call to Smith, informing him that we haven't concluded our business." The tone of his voice suggested it would be pointless to argue. "He'll understand perfectly when I explain we've a few problems to iron out. He'll be delighted that you've agreed to spend the weekend as my guest."

"I haven't agreed."

"But you haven't refused either." His eyes slid over her with a hungry gaze. "Nor will you if you know what's good

133

for you."

The frostily courteous, broodingly sexy and yes, unbelievably chauvinistic Joshua Cordell wasn't a man to be messed with, she could see that now. Plus she had the uncomfortable feeling that Reynard Smith understood far more than he had let on.

"Okay, you win." Somehow she had the feeling he always did. "So, tell me where we're going so I can follow you."

"You'll come in my car."

"What about mine?"

"No problem." He held out his hand for her keys and with an obedience which shocked even her, she handed them over. He summoned one of the Naismith officials with a hand gesture. "See to it that the young lady's car is delivered to my home address." He dropped the keys into the upturned palm of the official, then dipped his hand inside his jacket. Withdrawing an impressive bundle of notes, he peeled off a few without counting them and then slipped them to the official. With the slightest nod of his head the official turned on his heel and Josh returned the bundle to his pocket.

"You think you can buy everything?" Amber asked with a sardonic twist to her glossed lips.

"I don't think, I know."

"Well, you can't buy me!"

"My dear Jane, I don't have to. You've been served up on a plate."

***

"Nice car," she complimented, struggling to keep in character despite her upper-crust accent, and hoping that he wouldn't notice the identical car parked a few bays away. Huh! He wasn't the only one with blacked out windows, she scoffed. She wasn't in the habit of using her Mercedes for work yet today she had done just that instead of using the Fiat. She was beginning to wish she hadn't been so careless.

134

"I'm glad you like it. I've had one or two little extras fitted that you won't find elsewhere."

"Such as?"

"You'll see." He told her to remove her jacket, and it never occurred to her to question his motives. When he held out his hand she gave it to him.

In the brief moments that followed, her thoughts returned to the issue which was beginning to annoy her. With Smith having given her the sack, there was no real reason why she didn't come clean and tell Joshua her true identity. It could only bode well for the future. Besides, with the intimacy she hoped would take place between them, it seemed rather churlish not to mention that she was as rich as he was.

"There's something you should know," she began coyly, fluttering her lashes.

"Shut up and get in the car." He opened the rear door and threw her jacket and bag across to the front seat, then ushered her inside the warm interior.

She blinked up at him questioningly. "I assumed I'd be sitting alongside you."

"A woman should know her place from the outset." He grabbed her arm and roughly thrust her forward, sending her sprawling across the back seat. He grabbed a fistful of her hair and with his hand in the small of her back, sharply yanked her upright.

"Ouch! You're hurting me."

"I'll hurt you a lot more if you don't do as you're told. Get right in. Sit in the middle."

"Okay. Just let go."

When he released his hold she scrambled across to sit in the designated position. She shrugged, guessing he wanted to look up her skirt in the rear view mirror. When she was settled comfortably, he leaned across her, brushing his arm against her breasts in a way that sent shivers darting through her as he fastened her safety belt.

"I'm quite capable of doing it myself."

135

"I'm sure you are, Jane, but this isn't your run-of-the-mill safety belt. You'll notice it has a rather unusual clip." He snapped it closed. "Show me how you'd remove it."

Accepting the challenge, she pushed the safety release. There was slight panic in her voice as it refused to budge. "You should get this thing fixed, Josh. It's dangerous."

"Not at all. It's designed to open automatically on impact. Otherwise, it can only be opened from a switch on the dash." There was reassurance in his voice though no such emotion was evident in his habitually sombre expression as he continued. "Sit up straight." He placed both hands on her booted legs, curled his fingers around them and slid them downward. Clasping each ankle, he adjusted her feet until they were about fifteen inches apart. "Keep them there."

"Why?"

"Don't ask questions, just do it." With that he closed the door.

She felt very vulnerable and unbelievably stupid. While everyone knew something of Cordell's public image no one seemed to know anything of his private life. Yet here she was, trustingly sitting in the back of his car, obeying him as if he had some hold over her.

He slid into the driver's seat and turned the ignition. He flicked a switch, operating arms rests which automatically came down on either side of her, effectively hemming her in. As she rested her arms along their length, the pressure activated some unseen mechanism and before she knew what was happening, wide metal clips snapped closed around her wrists.

"Josh!" Vainly she struggled to wrench her arms free. There was a humming noise and her to horror, corresponding clips sprung up from the floor and clamped tightly around her ankles. Now she was really scared and her voice rose along with her fear. "You bastard! Let me go or I'll scream." Instinct made her struggle but it was no use; she was very effectively imprisoned. "You can't do this... let me go!"

"I make the rules, and I prefer to drive in silence," he told her as the car glided out of its parking bay. "Sit back and be quiet."

"What's the matter with you? Old Smith warned me you had some strange ideas, but this…"

"Is probably exactly what 'old Smith' had planned for you. He's sent you along as a kind of sweetener." The car began to negotiate its way through the London traffic.

"What's that supposed to mean?" she demanded as her violet eyes met his brooding hazel gaze in the mirror.

"He's offered your services as a way of getting me to sign the contract for what he thinks is a rather good deal for his company. Of course, that's not his only reason… I've got something he wants. I suspect what he didn't tell you was that he was recently a dinner guest at my house, where he rather took a shine to my woman."

"You mean you're married?" While his marital status was no concern of hers, in fact she often preferred married men because there was little chance of her getting lumbered with a commitment she didn't want, something about the casual way he referred to his partner set sirens shrieking in her head.

"No, I'm not married."

It never occurred to her to question him further. Instead, she blurted out, "Why aren't I surprised? If you treat all women with such contempt, it's no wonder no one will have you."

The atmosphere inside the car became as dark and menacing as his gaze. Now he was angry.

"Shut up, or I'll have to stop the car and make you."

"Don't tell me you're going to gag me as well," she said on a false laugh. "I'm not surprised you're single. Who in their right mind would marry a weirdo like you? No mentally sound woman would let you fuck them in the toilets either, which says a lot for my sanity."

The hostility shining in his heavy-lidded eyes in the mirror brought her to her senses. She clamped her lips together, deciding it was probably best not to anger him further.

He spent the next few seconds wondering if he was asking too much of her. After all, the girl hadn't had any training and probably had no knowledge of how a slave should behave. All things considered, it would probably be kinder to come down extra hard on her, perhaps carry out his threat. Caught in the perpetual traffic jam that was this part of town, he slipped from the front seat and opened the rear door. He slid in beside her and produced a gag. Not an old piece of cloth but a real one with a black ball attached to a strip of rubber.

"Since you seem unable to understand a simple command, you leave me no option."

She barely had time to gasp in astonishment before he pushed the ball between her lips, ensuring that her jaws were held wide open as it pressed down on her tongue. He fastened the strap behind her head with a metal buckle, then with a twitch of his lips which could have been a smile, he slid from the back seat and retook his place behind the wheel as the traffic began to inch forward again.

"It's time you learnt to obey me as your Master and show me the respect due."

If her mouth hadn't been full she would have laughed at his arrogance. As it was, she had no choice but to sit back quietly and look out of the window as they made their way through the traffic.

He didn't speak to her again but concentrated instead on his driving as they headed out of town. Gagged and unable to move due to her bindings, Amber dared not think too far ahead or dwell on her fate too closely. Nonetheless, as they left the A40 and headed for High Wycombe, Amber grew increasingly restless.

She knew these roads. And then, with the power of a ten-ton truck, realization hit her; she knew where he was taking her. Suddenly the full horror of her own stupidity dawned on her. Joshua Cordell was none other than the Oakley-Dean's neighbour, the millionaire who had bought the land with the

Priory ruins about five years ago. She recalled that he had had a wife then, but there was some talk of her being killed in a skiing accident.

And then she was overcome with a different emotion altogether, namely guilt. She could have bitten off her tongue. No wonder the man looked so morose. Still, that didn't excuse his behaviour. He had no right to imprison her. Except… well, she had got in the car willingly, and she should have smelled a rat long ago. But the question which exploded into her mind and then refused to lie down and die was why the hell had it taken her so long to recognise him as their neighbour?

Because they had never met, she excused herself. Besides, he hadn't recognized her either. Why should he? The Oakley-Deans would never lower themselves to mix with the likes of him, a man with new money who, rumour had it, came from a council estate. Hell! If Mummy could see her now. It wasn't so much that he was holding her captive but that Joshua Cordell was probably as low down the social scale as one could get. Amber's family could trace their roots back to the earliest times, and their wealth stemmed from an ancestor who had found favour with Henry VIII. He had been granted High Briar as payment for services rendered to the King. Mummy would probably find it easier to cope with her daughter's double life than this.

Now she knew she was in trouble, and worse was to come. She had only scratched the surface of how much worse when they skirted High Briar and drove on to Josh's land, and had no way of knowing what kind of torments awaited her.

CHAPTER TEN

The familiar ruins of the old priory and the field where poppies and cornflowers grew weren't visible, Amber noticed, from this side as they drove onto Josh's land. They headed along the strip of pot-holed tarmac which followed the meanderings of the river, which also flowed through High Briar. Travelling between an orchard on one side and an ancient meadow on the other, she immediately fell in love with the wildness of the place, something long since eradicated from her own home, where everything was manicured and seemed somehow artificial. Even in the enclosed environment of the Merc the fragrance of apples wafted in.

Josh couldn't possibly have known that any distress she felt was caused more by her proximity to her ancestral home than the bleakness of her predicament. As far as he was concerned, if ever a girl was made for agonized subservience, it was the delectable Jane Dean. Fettered and helpless, her vulnerability made her even more appetizing than she had been back at the Naismith and sent energizing messages to his phallus. He met her violet gaze in the mirror and impaled her with a cold-hearted stare.

With a hint of amusement it struck him that with her glossy, dark red lips framing the black ball of the gag and her elaborately painted eyes wide open as if in a state of perpetual surprise, she resembled one of those inflatable sex dolls. By the time he had finished with her, she would be as compliant. Of course, in other respects she was very much like a doll... one made of the finest porcelain. Petite and fragile, for the first time he doubted that she had the stamina required to pull a sulky.

Damn the bitch! Disgruntled, as aspirations of using her for one of his favourite pastimes were dashed, he determined that that particular failing would be one of the first things he would address. He put his foot to the floor and directed his anger at the tarmac. Tomorrow, she would accompany him on his daily run.

With a heave of his shoulders he shrugged off his impatience and eased off the pedal. It was glaringly transparent even at this early stage that he would need longer than a weekend to enjoy himself to the full, especially as part of that time would also be given over to entertaining his guest. As the former manor house with its outbuildings came into view, he made up his mind that he would do everything in his power to ensure that Jane Dean would never again be a free woman. The quicker he put her in chains, the better.

***

A particularly splendid horse chestnut, under which Josh parked the car, threw welcome shade across the forecourt. Taking in her surroundings, Amber noticed that on one side a footbridge across the river linked the house with the fields and orchard beyond. On the other side, a wooden fence with five bars bordered a copse-dotted field where horses grazed.

Josh flicked a switch and as if by magic, Amber's seat belt and shackles opened. Unsure what was expected of her she remained in her seat. Curiously, she didn't even attempt to remove the gag.

He unfolded himself languorously from the driver's seat, methodically checking the interior. He took a silver carrying case for his cigars from the glove compartment, extracted a long corona which he slipped into his breast pocket, then returned the case. He straightened up and closed the door. Opening the passenger door, he regarded his prize with casual interest.

Josh caught the sound of crunching gravel coming from the side of the house, "Hi Dougie," he said without looking round.

Amber turned her head to see a man approaching who she took to be an odd job man or gardener. Nearer seventy than sixty, with a flat cap plonked at an angle on his head, he wore a checked shirt with the sleeves rolled up and brown cords. In

141

one hand he carried a large, green metal strong box.

Hot flickers of agitation trilled joyously through her body at the sight of a riding crop in Dougie's other hand, as her mind was overrun with images of herself tied up and cowering under its stinging caress. Engulfed by a wave of hot wantonness, curiously at odds with the cold fingers of dread which gripped her heart, she couldn't help the quivers and tingles that warmed her loins.

Josh reached into the car and clasped a bruisingly tight hand round her neck, then hauled her out onto the forecourt. He guided her across the gravel, halting her a few feet away from the car.

The gurgling of the river gave a deceptively tranquil air to the scene as he grabbed hold of her wrists and pinioned them behind her back. Yanking them upward, with one strong hand he imprisoned them between her shoulder blades.

"Bracelets, Dougie."

"Well, Josh lad, what've you got there?" Dougie set the box on the floor, unlocked it and began rummaging. He handed over the handcuffs with a broad smile.

"A new toy."

"Got a name, has she?"

"Jane. I'm afraid it's going to mean extra work for you. Can you handle two sluts?"

The elder man laughed. "'Course I can! I'm not past it yet. You just line up the girlies, and I'll do the rest!"

Something about the manner in which Josh conversed with the man, more than the actual words, set Amber's teeth on edge; new-moneyed people had no idea how to speak to a menial. Mummy would never treat staff in such a familiar way!

Shame torched her face as Dougie regarded her. While his half-blind eye tried to focus, his good-eyed gaze slid insidiously over her scarlet face, coming to rest on the ball gag.

"Talker, is she?"

"You'd never believe the way she prattles on!"

Gripping her wrists, Josh lowered her arms so that her hands rested on her pert, leather-sheathed bottom. He clicked the metal cuffs closed around her slender wrists, then backed off a few steps to view her as if she had been caught stealing his apples. Dougie stood his ground.

"What do you think, Dougie?"

Tremors shook her body as Dougie's work-callused hand made an exploratory grab at her breast. A shudder of revulsion passed though her as he kneaded her roughly. Alarmingly, her quivering sex began to secrete its sweet juices while her wilful nipples hardened into firm peaks of peachy flesh. She giggled inwardly. Was there no end to her wantonness?

"Not bad, but her tits are a bit heavy for such a skinny thing." Having made his stinging criticisms of what Amber had always considered her best assets, Dougie turned his back on her to take his place beside his employer. "I assume no one will come looking for her?"

From the corner of her eye, Amber flashed a glance in the direction of home. A shiver of dread passed through her; only now did the full impact of her situation finally hit home. No one knew she was here, except Reynard Smith. Somehow she doubted he would do anything to save her. Except she wasn't sure just yet if she actually wanted to be saved.

"Apparently, there's no family or close friends to worry about. She's a nobody, and I can do anything I please to her, starting now."

He hunkered down and retrieved a heavy linked, tarnished steel, industrial chain from the metal box. As he draped one end across Amber's shoulders, she noted that clips had been added to both ends. He pulled it tighter and formed a loop by fastening a clip to one of the links. He took a moment to congratulate himself on the effect of the dirty chain against her soft, pearly skin.

Turning the loop round so that the length of chain dangled down her back, he pulled her wrists upward and used the chain

143

to couple them to the loop. Thus her hands were held in place between her shoulders.

It only took a moment for her to understand the dilemma he had forced upon her; to lower her arms tightened the loop around her throat. Therefore she must endure the discomfort of keeping her hands raised to enjoy the comfort that slackening the loop offered.

Shame forbade her to face the men and she lowered her gaze to the ground. How could she stand so sedately before them while they discussed her as if she were no longer there? She didn't question too closely the strange force which rooted her to the spot, with her upper arms already aching from her weighty, filthy restraints. It wouldn't be so bad if it was a new chain, she thought wistfully. Her persistent fantasies threw shadows across her crushing humiliation and she saw herself in her imagination bound hand and foot with bonds made of the purest gold. The reality was that instead of her bonds making her feel like a highly prized slave to a wealthy sheikh she felt worthless, grubby and at the mercy of a pseudo-Lord and his lecherous retainer.

She shuffled her feet and pressed her thighs together as a trickle of moisture leaked from her ironically voracious quim. Slowly it dawned on her that her very vulnerability was stirring up all kinds of weird, out-of-place emotions; humility alongside worthlessness, gratitude and pleasure. She stood stock still under Josh's dark, mocking gaze and allowed herself to tremble as he addressed her with a cold, derisory regard.

"Listen, my posh-voiced little tart, you're going to have more things done to that peachy-sweet body over the next couple of days than you could ever imagine. And when you leave here... assuming you ever do... you'll be toting a whole fucking lot more bruises than you've arrived with. Did you bring a penknife, Dougie?"

"Sorry Josh, I didn't think. Will these do?" He extracted a pair of red-handled secateurs from his pocket.

"Great. Thanks."

Josh's smirk chilled her marrow as he took the offered pruning tool. Powerless to protect herself, she feared the worst. She had never intended that things should go this far. Never had she felt so terribly vulnerable... so afraid and so... so... disconnected from reality.

Admiring the way her trembling caused her breasts to quake, Josh slipped the cold blades beneath the hem of her lacy top, cutting up the middle to the neck. Afterward he cut through the shoulder straps. "Hope it wasn't expensive," he remarked sneeringly as he plucked the scrap of lace from her body and threw it aside, following it with her bra. Her succulent, ponderous orbs swung freely and then settled.

"They don't hang right..." Dougie observed, "... shaped more like lemons than melons!"

"You're right, they definitely hang to the side," Josh kept his eyes riveted to her juicy breasts, their bullet hard nipples and wide, dark, knobbly areolae. "They're not perfect globes and they're far too weighty for her petite stature. Nevertheless, they bounce well enough." He raised his hand and delivered a loud Smack! which resulted in a scarlet blotch rising across her left breast, which was nevertheless firm enough for it not to knock into her other one. His expression suggested he had been cheated. He turned his attention to the right one and repeated the process with more force, almost knocking her sideways. "Now that's better," he approved as her breasts bounced energetically. "Let's see an action replay."

Tears sprang to her eyes and the secateurs fell to the ground. A frisson of alarm caused her to flick her fear-drenched eyes to those of her abuser and discerned nothing but contempt in their depths. Again he struck her; she scrabbled backward.

Under the watchful gaze of his hired hand, who did nothing to prevent Josh's brutality, he whacked her again. Her long fringe flopped in her eyes as she was sent crashing into the fence. Unable to brush her hair aside, she gave a sideways toss of her head and blinked rapidly in an effort to dislodge the fine strands from her sore, watering eyes.

Grabbing her elbow he hauled her to her feet and threw her sideways, away from the fence. He struck again, "Tits always look better with a bit of added colour," he commented as the red patches spread, and again, finally hitting her backhand. She staggered backward, barely managing to stay upright. Once more she tossed her head to dislodge her hair from her eyes.

He chose that moment to strike out one last time, catching her off guard and sending her sprawling on the ground. Indifferent to her muffled cries against the ball gag as the gravel bit into her flesh, he kicked out at her flanks for no reason other than he could.

Lying inelegantly, even the slightest movement drove the sharp stones into her flesh, scratching her lotion-softened skin painfully.

Josh stood over her and with a mocking gaze told his companion, "My hand stings like fuck."

"I'm not surprised, lad. I can see how red it is from here."

To further impress upon her the insignificance of her pain compared to the importance of his own, Josh made a show of flapping his hand and raising it to his mouth and blowing on it. Bending down, he slipped his fingers under the loop around Amber's neck. He yanked her to her feet then retrieved the secateurs. Pressing his hand against her belly, to her horror he started cutting up the front of her leather skirt.

She mumbled a protest against the ball of the gag. Damn the bastard! she fumed. It was real leather. Okay, so she had the funds to replace it but she was thinking principle here. The ill-fated skirt fell away and landed at her feet.

Josh circled her slowly, inhaling deeply to take in the scent of her femininity. Beneath the overpriced perfume was the more natural, more primitive scent of desire which mingled with his own lust to concoct a volatile brew of depravity. He took in every curve, every sinew of her body, noting the placement of every bruise and weal. He would have preferred to acquire her unmarked but he wouldn't let a little thing like

146

that ruin his enjoyment.

Of course, some girls marked up easier than others and he had yet to find out which category she fell into. Either way, the paleness of her skin made each stripe seem extra vivid; even the faintest impressions would be visible for longer than on his foreign woman's dusky skin. The downside was that he would seldom have a completely spotless surface to work with unless he abstained from beating her for several consecutive days, which was quite out of the question. He would just have to amuse himself elsewhere in between times. It was fortunate that he had Saskia and his beloved SM club.

He dismissed Dougie with a terse, "Leave the crop." Continuing with his appraisal while Dougie set the implement down on the gravel, Josh waited until Dougie had gone before speaking.

"Your muscle tone isn't bad," he told her, surmising that maybe she was more athletic than he had at first thought. He could only assume that she worked out in her lunch hour; it was remiss of Smith not to have mentioned it.

"You're here for one reason only," he said, his even tone nevertheless oozing menace, "so that I can mistreat your body purely for my pleasure. I enjoy sexually abusing women, Jane, it's a hobby of mine."

As she stood naked, save for her red, thigh-high, stiletto boots, his eyes raked over every inch of her pearly nudity. And engulfed by a wave of humiliation, absurdly she noticed every detail as he slid the long cigar from his breast pocket. The corona was at least six inches long with a girth of about an inch. With a slow, deliberate movement he drew his lighter from his trouser pocket. Gold and set with a small diamond in the lower left corner, his initials were engraved in the centre... JWC. Next, he took a gold cutter from the other pocket. She watched him clip the end of the cigar before returning both cutter and lighter to his pocket and couldn't help but wonder what the W stood for.

He slipped the cigar between his cynical lips and drew on it

147

a few times before removing it again. Stepping closer, he blew the grey, aromatic smoke in her face, stinging her already sore, reddened eyes terribly. Unable to cough because of the gag, her face puffed up and turned scarlet.

Her predicament merely added to his amusement and he reached for her crotch. Clutching her vulva tightly, he held the cigar so close that she felt its heat on her pulsating sex. Deciding that even Josh wouldn't be so spiteful as to burn her, terror rose from the pit of her stomach regardless, to mingle with the blistering lust already ensconced there. An insidious warmth flooded her being with an odd sense of pride at the prospect of being punished by this darkly brooding sensualist. As her pulses pounded in her temples her spirit soared, floating somewhere between euphoria and outrage.

Blinking rapidly to clear her vision as excitement surged upward from her tingle-gripped belly, in that second she knew she had found the dark-shadowed figure of her fantasies.

"I'm especially fond of petite, dark haired girls," he told her suddenly, the neutrality of his tone belying the ferocious blaze in his scrotum. His penis throbbed madly and he was experiencing a great deal of discomfort; if he didn't indulge his lust soon he would be in indescribable distress himself. He threw a contemptuous look in her direction and watched her wither before his eyes. If his timing was correct, any minute now he should see the tears start to flow.

"Is the colour of your hair natural?" He raised a questioning brow as he upended the cigar.

Unsure of the relevance of the question she answered it with a hesitant nod of her head. Secretly she gave thanks to whoever really was her father for passing on his genes, overjoyed that her ebony hair made her desirable to the man who poured such disdain upon her. She followed up the thought with a quick prayer that her mother would maintain her silence on the matter and thus safeguard Amber's inheritance. She had grown tired of playing at being poor since the humiliation of being sacked as if she were one of the lower

148

classes. Moreover, she realized now that she should have owned up to Josh at the beginning, for the longer she left it the harder it would be.

Working his delinquent fingers over the folds of her sugar-slicked vulva, he deftly parted her heated labia. While one hand clutched the neck chain possessively, his other hand inserted the unlit end of the cigar inside her hot, juicing channel. To her shame, her ravenous pussy sucked it in, her muscles clenching tightly around it. He continued to shove the cigar upward, until the lighted end burned mere inches from her flushed, delicate petals.

"Smoking can seriously damage your health," he jibed as her eyes widened in alarm, before adding warningly, "no sudden moves or it will fall out."

She altered her stance to exert more pressure on the cigar, squeezing tightly. The only way to ensure it remained in place was to press her thighs together, but that would mean burning her own tender flesh. Curiously, the idea excited her and set pulses throbbing frantically in her clitoris. Her breasts tightened as snippets of lust deflected her outrage. And yet, on a more rational level, she was terribly afraid.

Always keen to observe the spectacle of tears cascading down a tormented woman's cheeks, to Josh's delight Amber's tears broke free in a gushing torrent. Her artistically made-up features became streaked with muddy rivers of mascara and kohl, leaving the bluey-purple of her eye-shadow stark against her paleness. She looked every inch the slut she was about to become. Fuck the bitch! She was driving him crazy.

The hunger to humiliate her at every opportunity fought with the necessity to take it slowly. This was no Lodge Housegirl who had given herself up willingly to a fulfilling life of pain and degradation, he reminded himself. Even so, it was imperative that she understood what was required of her right from the beginning; there would be no slow learning curve for her!

"You've the same rights here as my foreign woman, and

that means you've no rights at all. You're inferior to everyone else. You'll be subservient to all members of staff. Don't bother trying to curry favour with them; your only friends will be shackles and whips, and torture too if I can find the time. You're completely at my mercy, a word which, unfortunately for you, isn't in my vocabulary. You're nothing but an undisciplined whore. As such you can expect nothing but the harshest treatment. My word is law; flout the rules and you'll suffer dearly. Obey me… I'm your Master."

He focussed his attention on the cigar protruding from her slick, elongated labials as she squeezed her muscles to keep it in place. It wasn't so much her disobedience which bothered him, but had more to do with her quarrelsome manner, over-active vocal chords… and playacting.

He had come a long way since his formative years and he had made it alone, with nothing but an interest in technology and gritty determination… and a sizeable loan from a canny bank manager. What he didn't do was set out to deceive by putting on false airs and graces… that posh accent of hers just had to be fake, just as the Cartier on her wrist had to be stolen.

Her tears evaporated and her eyes bulged with terror as she stood with the cigar stuffed up her vagina. What she didn't know was that it had gone out long ago, a fact which Josh felt obliged to keep to himself.

"I'm going to remove the ball now," he told her as he unfastened the gag. "No talking."

In her imagination, she looked up into the adoring eyes of her shadowy Master. And then heat flooded her vulnerable body as she realized she was really here, with Josh, about to live her fantasy for real. Tilting her head, she felt his raw, animal breath heating her forehead. She gave an inward smile and gazed into his eyes. But instead of adoration she saw only the reflection of cruelty.

She wanted this, she really did, except now her senses were overloaded and the maelstrom of emotion dragged her under; her fiery nature took control. As before, her upper class accent seemed at odds with the language which spilt from her glossed lips.

"You're a fucking bastard, Cordell! What gives you the right to treat me like this? Let me go, now!"

Anger flashed across his face. "No talking means no fucking talking!"

She backed up a few paces. For her own good she should stop now, so what drove her to spit the words venomously into his sneering features?

"Listen, face-ache, you'll never be my Master. You're just a jumped-up fucking nobody. Who do you think I am, some kind of bloody numb-brained fool who's just going to let you kick her around without fighting back?"

But she wasn't fighting back, she was trying to provoke him, and enjoying herself into the bargain. If she could get him really mad, he might prove to her just how masterful he could be. She drew in a deep a breath and then let rip. "For your information, you turd-brained tosser, I happen to be…"

"Shut up!" A dark flicker of malevolence crossed his face as he bent down and snatched up the crop. Straightening up, he strode menacingly towards her, thwacking the shaft across his open palm. He speared her with a look so cold and compelling that she almost yielded to his superiority. "Turn round. Get over there by the car and bend over the bonnet."

Oh, she did so want to submit, to be his slave and feel the crop on her backside, but she was having far too much fun! Just a little more goading and the scene would be set.

"This has gone far enough, fart-face! When people realize I'm missing, the place will be crawling with Pol…"

"Shut your fucking mouth, you worthless little bitch! Get over the car, now."

He gave her a shove in the small of her back. She was gripped by an overwhelming desire to obey, yet in spite of her frantically willing her legs to move they stubbornly remained rooted to the spot.

"Move, bitch! I'm not playing games here. I demand

obedience."

As she swivelled round, she couldn't help but relax her muscles and the cigar was ejected.

"You call that obedience?" He felt the pulses in her neck beneath his hard fingers as they clamped around the back. He marched her across to his car, pressing her down across the bonnet. There was a thump as her forehead hit the shiny Merc. "Fucking bitch! If you've dented the bodywork you'll be sorry!"

A blindingly hot pain sliced across her bottom and had her screaming shrilly as he brought the crop down with a satisfying Thwack! across her left buttock. The pain spread outward like ink on blotting paper.

If she could have seen, she would have been amazed at the depth of colour in that one stripe. A more virulent Thwack! drew a vivid scarlet line slightly above the first. She bit into her lip but it didn't prevent her from crying out. Thwack! Thwack! Her screams rose in intensity, the stinging like nothing she had known before. She was in the hands of an expert; all others before him were as inept as a cricketer on a polo field.

Thwack! Now he was really getting into his stride. He struck the right cheek of her deliciously pert bottom with more force than she could bear and she screamed at the top of her lungs. But that only seemed to turn him on more and several frantic Thwacks! followed. God help her, this pain was all too real. And yet…

As fire spread outward across her soft, trembling flesh, now decorated with a series of lines as red as her boots, she was shocked to discover how much the sound of the crop striking her body thrilled her. Anticipation of the next strike engendered such a heady mix of dread and excitement that she thought she would die. She wanted this, had always wanted it, except now her face reddened at the shocking way her pouting pussy expelled glistening juices.

His savagery increased as strike after pitiless strike burned into her quivering flesh, throwing up a fine spray of perspiration. Adjusting his stance, he turned his attention to the spot where her thighs joined the undersides of her bottom, blazing electrifying pain across her exposed, lust-swollen pussy lips which hung temptingly between her legs. Her screams rang out to be carried far and wide by the summer breeze which warmed her back. Each stroke lit up her brain with intense red lights as surely as he laid red stripes across her most tender flesh. And as the blows came faster and stronger, so her screams became shriller. Once again her face was awash with tears. Between sobs that racked her body, she heard her quivering voice pleading for mercy.

"P… p… please, have mercy…"

"The more you scream, the more you get."

True to his word, the strikes kept on coming. Carried away now by the sheer loveliness of the scarlet welts which rose so spectacularly across her pale, quakingly sweet body, he directed his aim across the swell of her rump, either side of the deep cleft of her bottom. In his mind he pictured the intricate design Gascoigne had inscribed upon the lovely Isabella.

Shit! He had just laid that last strike in completely the wrong place and had utterly demolished his own artistry, obliterating the finer details with one foul strike.

Annoyed with himself for his clumsiness, he took it out on Amber, laying into her with a new ferocity which ensured she would keep screaming.

She wished he would gag her again to save her from herself. But there was no such luck as he continued to slash at her mercilessly assaulted backside. Then slowly, the blazing lights in her brain faded and were replaced by a pinky glow, somewhere around the time the pain ceased and became something more tolerable. However, Josh was a skilful practitioner and just when it began to dawn on her that pleasure was taking over and she was heading for the biggest orgasm of her life, he stopped.

The abruptness of her return to earth was as cruel as the

flogging itself. As the pleasure was sharply curtailed, pain re-asserted itself, leaving her breathless, sore and unimaginably frustrated.

The crop clattered to the ground. He stepped aside and leaned against the car with a barked, "Stay there!"

Casually he retrieved the cigar from where it had fallen and placed it between his sneering lips to re-light it. Grabbing a fistful of her hair by the roots, he turned her head to look at him and once again removed the cigar.

Tugging her head back to expose her perfect, vulnerable throat encircled by the tarnished chain, he placed the lighted end of the cigar against the swell of her ravaged backside, and held it there.

Her agonized yowl was like that of an animal caught in a snare. Ahhh, there was nothing like the sight of a woman suffering to enhance the enjoyment of a good cigar, Josh thought.

***

Chains suited her rather well, Josh mused as he rummaged through the metal box. He glanced up at the afternoon sun and knew he had wasted too much time; he really should get the bitch inside. Finding what he was looking for at last, he slammed the box shut and returned to where Amber was still whimpering, slumped over the car. Once more he clenched his fist in her hair, this time pulling her upright before spinning her round to face the house. He was determined to break her in as soon as possible and, even if she turned out to be completely useless as a pony girl, there was no harm in introducing her to the rudimentaries.

"Open your mouth."

Barely had she opened her lips before he shoved the shiny metal bit in her mouth, forcing it back and making her gag. Her mouth was held wide open in a rather unattractive and desperately uncomfortable grimace which bared perfect teeth.

Metal rings were connected to each end of the bit, to which a wide, adjustable leather strap was attached, which he now pulled tightly across the back of her head to hold it in place. Lastly, he clipped the ends of a long chain to the rings to serve as reins.

Unfortunately, having no sulky to attach her to, he would have to follow her on foot as if ploughing a field. He stood some four feet behind her, took up the slack and gave the chain a sharp, jangling jerk.

"Walk on."

For a moment Amber hesitated. Despite the scurrilous treatment he had already dealt her, as well as the bit which felt as if it would permanently damage her jaw, there was no denying her happiness. Feeling now rather as the carefree Amber had felt while playing at being wild, captured Shetland Ponies with her well-to-do school friends as a youngster, she was overjoyed at reliving the experience of being "broken in". Remembering how the games were played, she scraped her booted boot elegantly on the ground three times, tossed her head defiantly so that her short, feathery-styled hair flew up around her head, and whinnied prettily.

Heat flared in her loins. Carried away on a tide of euphoria, in a blatant display of her talent for flirting she set off walking towards the substantial house and exaggerated the swaying of her assaulted backside.

Unable to resist the erotic movements of her abused, naked behind, Josh slashed the crop across her rump as she walked, adding weals to those that would soon be a deep, alluring purple. He jerked the chain sharply, steering her towards the side of the house by pulling harder than necessary on the right side and tugging her mouth spitefully so that she gave a high-pitched squawk of discomfort.

"Trot on."

Obediently she began a rather nice trotting motion on the balls of her feet. That would set her juicy orbs bouncing! And, unsupported by a bra, their weight would be causing

155

something close to pain, he smirked. Of course, the chain around her neck which still imprisoned her hands between her shoulders would be causing her some discomfort also, though his enjoyment of inflicting pain was somewhat marred by the knowledge that the smarting from the burn wasn't that long-lasting.

As they headed down the side of the house towards the kitchen, he momentarily thought of the previous night's entertainment at The Lodge. It warmed a man's heart, to say nothing of his balls, to know you were free to do anything you wanted to a piece of female meat. And the only limit now was his own imagination, he reflected as he pulled Amber up sharply outside the door. He removed the bit and reins, leaving the other chains in place.

It was odd but, now that she was his property, he felt justified in withholding the respect he felt for Housegirls.

CHAPTER ELEVEN

It didn't come easy to a girl with Amber's upbringing to be subservient, but she gave it her best shot. She waited as patiently as she knew how for the moment when Josh would surely take her to his bed and fuck her.

Josh poured himself a drink and seated himself at the table, beside his housekeeper.

"What do you want me to do with her?" Alice's tone suggested she had been lumbered with the orphaned child of a long lost relative.

As before, Josh discussed her as if she were no longer present.

"Obviously she needs cleaning up, but that can be dealt with later. She's to have no home comforts, just agonizing degradation. What I expect to get from her is mind-blowing entertainment and complete servitude."

She hardly noticed his words due to the acute shame she felt under the derisory gaze of his housekeeper. She had never stood naked before another woman before, not even one of her own servants. Her pale, striped and battered flesh burned crimson from her hairline downward, disappearing into the thigh-high boots. As yet unaware of the tall, elegant, dusky skinned maid who stood with her back to the wall, Amber stood silently beside the table in the large kitchen.

Her arms ached hellishly, though she had grown accustomed to the weighty links around her neck. From the corner of her eye she glimpsed her reins hanging on a hook and couldn't help but smile as warm dervishes fluttered in her belly.

Cursing her own wantonness for having brought such ignominy upon her, as well as the wellspring of need that had been uncorked, even now her clitoris thrummed for attention. Her nipples stood out like corks in wine bottles. Absurdly, she was shocked to discover how intense her desire for pain really was as she kept her eyes fixed on the quarry tiles, telling herself she could endure any punishment Josh saw fit to administer.

She wanted desperately to please him and be a true submissive. Yet as much as she wanted to be, had always known she must be, it was going to be tough. She knew her biggest problems would be coping with the crushing humiliations, worse by far than any savagery he could inflict, along with the necessity to keep her flirting in check.

What she chose to overlook, however, was her most intractable trait… her quarrelsome nature.

"Don't you think she blushes nicely, Alice? Easily, too. I'll probably keep her in chains most of the time since they suit her so well."

"Her trembling makes them jingle like a music box," Alice laughed as she scraped back her chair. Circling the new slave, she took in the livid weals and the round burn on her bottom. "I see you've made a start on her already. What do I call her?"

"Jane. Say hello to Mrs Ward, Jane."

Amber eyed the woman through lowered lashes before lifting her make-up smudged face. Though remarkably calm given that she had heard every word spoken with a strange clarity, all that concerned her now was her ability to conduct herself with dignity in front of a servant. Squaring her narrow shoulders, she held her head high and said in her haughtiest voice, "Good afternoon."

"Right little Lady Muck, isn't she?" the housekeeper's face crinkled with amusement as she retook her seat. "You've got your work cut out with this one."

However, Josh saw nothing amusing about the situation. On the contrary, his face darkened. He leapt to his feet, delivering a hearty slap to Amber's face. So angry was he that he failed to take any pleasure from the patch of scarlet which flared instantly across her cheek. His growl was as fierce as that of a streetwise cur.

"I won't stand for this shit. *You're* the subordinate here, not my housekeeper. Address her as Mrs Ward and show her some fucking respect. Try again, and this time I want you to curtsy. You do know how to curtsy?"

Amber's eyes widened in horror. How could she, one of the aristocracy, minor admittedly, be expected to treat a mere housekeeper with deference? It might have been different if she were still playing at being a commoner, but this was totally out of the question. Indignation thudded at the back of her throat as she reminded herself, lest she forget due to the undiluted lust this weird set-up engendered, that she was Amber Jane Oakley-Dean.

"Mr Cordell," she started patronisingly, "there's been some kind of mistake. I think you should know that I'm not Ja…" her voice trailed to nothing when a warning, black look from Josh had her toeing the line with relative ease. She dipped at the knee and, still speaking in her cultured tones, chanted in an altogether more submissive vein, "Pleased to meet you, Mrs Ward."

If she had expected any praise from her Master, she was disappointed.

"Look at you! Lipstick everywhere except on your frigging lips. Is that mascara or tar? I don't care for the blue eye-shadow; you won't wear it again. Do you always hide behind so much war paint? Answer."

The humiliation was more than she could stand and her eyes filled with water. Anger exploded in her brain and fell from her trembling lips as sniping arrogance.

"I won't be spoken to by you or anyone one else in such a manner. And it's your fault I'm in this state. So, Mr Cordell, I suggest you release me and have this… this… person conduct me to the bathroom. I'll take a shower, you can find me some clothes and I'll be out of here as soon as my car turns up."

He linked his fingers through the chain at her throat and pulled her up onto tiptoes. "I said 'answer' not give me a bloody lecture. I'll ask you again, and this time make it a simple 'yes or no, Master.' Do you always hide behind your make-up?"

"Why should I want to hide? You stupid bastard! I'll do my make-up how I like." Her nostrils flared and her eyes blazed with violet defiance. "Call you Master? What do you think I am, some fucking horse that you can dig your heels into for a jolly canter across the fields? What do you want me to do, take the jumps at the local gymkhana? Listen, you arrogant bastard, I'm not scared of you!"

"Then you should be."

With a finger crooked beneath the neck chain he dragged her across the kitchen. For the first time, on her peripheral vision she saw the maid standing near the wall. Afraid to turn her head for a better look, she stared ahead as he took her to the sink, either side of which were cupboards and work surfaces. Absurdly, she noticed too that the window above the sink unit gave a magnificent view over the orchard.

He summoned Saskia with a terse "Whore! Fetch me an apple." Almost at once, she appeared at his side holding out a large green apple. As he snatched it from her, he commanded, "on your knees. You know what to do."

Unhesitatingly, Saskia fell down in front of him and moving gracefully took out his engorged penis. Closing her pink lips around it, she wasted no time. Her head bobbed back and forth as she slurped noisily, seemingly unperturbed by the presence of either the housekeeper or Amber.

"This is my woman, Saskia," he told Amber coolly. "Learn from her. What I demand is obedience without question." He held the apple in front of Amber's mouth, its fragrance serving to remind her that she was thirsty. "Take a bite."

She did as she was bidden, then spat it out with a yelled, "That's a cooking apple!"

"Tough. Take a bite, Jane."

Once again she did as she was asked, pulling a face as she chewed it. Conscious of the young woman on her knees who fellated Josh with such expertise, she felt an unwarranted loathing of his woman. Learn from her? She would rather put a dent in that beautiful face!

160

"Stop daydreaming! Swallow. Take another bite." Once more she bit into the sour flesh, to the sound of ripping fabric as Josh tore a strip from Alice's apron. Using it as a gag to hold the apple in place between Amber's teeth, he tied it behind her head. "You're too lippy by far and I won't stand for it. Fetch the stool, Alice."

Doing as she was bidden, Alice placed the stool in front of the sink unit and perched Amber upon it. He dragged it back slightly, obliging Saskia to move with him. With his hand on Amber's nape he shoved her head forward, forcing her to bend, with her back straight and with her head over the sink.

"What have you got that I can to tie her with?"

Alice immediately produced a ball of kitchen string, which he used to bind Amber's feet to the front legs of the stool, winding it round and round so that she was unable to pull free. Then he tied the string to one of the taps, looped it through her handcuffs, pulled it taut and wound it round the other tap, then stretched it back across to the first tap, completing the triangle. He repeated the process twice more before cutting the string.

Moving sideways, with Saskia shuffling along on her knees with her lips still firmly clamped around his phallus, he tied the string to the handle of the cupboard on the left. He pulled it taut across Amber's back before moving sideways the other way, once again obliging Saskia to do likewise, then wound it round the cupboard handle on the other side. Then the whole process was repeated several more times. When he was satisfied that Amber was secure, he grabbed Saskia's head. He ground her face against his groin, thrusting his cock deep into her throat, but his attention was focussed on the helpless, tethered body of his new slave. He gave a deep, low growl and ejected his seed, forcing Saskia to swallow it down.

When he had finished he snatched his flaccid tool from her mouth, wiped it in her hair and ordered her to return to her former position. Rising to her feet, she obeyed wordlessly while he tucked his penis away.

The thin string bit painfully into Amber's tender flesh

while Josh and Alice stood behind her, discussing her as if her incapacity somehow rendered her invisible.

"How long is she staying?"

"That depends. A couple of days, years… forever… Who knows?"

Two years of maltreatment? The thought should have filled Amber with dread but curiously, far worse was his indifference towards her.

"The same rules apply as always, though I especially don't want her wandering around the place alone. When she needs fresh air and exercise, get one of the men to take her on a lead."

"She got any clothes?"

"Afraid not. I'll have a few things made for her but until then we'll have to make do with what we have lying around. Or I might keep her naked. Which room have you put her in?"

"I wasn't sure what you had in mind, but assumed you'd want the two of them kept apart. I thought the lilac room guest room."

"Okay, but remember, she's not a guest here. Did you fix up the bed?"

"Just as you like it."

"Good." His voice took on a kindly tone which Amber was never to hear directed at herself. "It's a lovely afternoon, Alice. Why don't you treat yourself to a spell in the garden? She can't come to any harm now and Dougie can take her to her room later." Josh leaned forward and reached for the tap.

Amber gave a muffled cry as icy water hit the back of her head. Damn the bastard! Surely it wasn't necessary to turn the tap on?

Behind her, Josh snapped his fingers and she heard Saskia scurry after him as his footsteps receded across the room. The door which led to the rest of the house opened.

"I'll have dinner at the usual time, Alice."

She heard the door close behind him.

The housekeeper took her straw golfing visor from a hook

on her way out of the back door, banging it closed behind her.

***

Left alone for what seemed an age, with the putrid stink from the plughole clogging her throat, Amber wept bitterly. Was this the nightmare that her fantasies had brought her to? Surely there was no pleasure in this, even if she did feel a curious sense of being needed underlying the anguish. Fear clenched the tight vent of her anus and her breathing pattern became more ragged as, too late, she realized this was only the beginning; there would be plenty more where this came from.

The back of her head was numb with cold and only the sound of the water reminded her that it was still flowing. Her jaw ached from having been wedged open by the apple for so long and her narrow bonds cut viciously into her flesh. Not to mention the cramps in her arms engendered from still having her hands chained between her shoulders.

As her body fought to absorb the various torments, she realized her mistake. She had believed she was a real masochist, when what she had really wanted was merely small doses of pain to intensify her arousal, not this kind of cruelty. This was beyond endurance.

***

Without speaking, Alice cut through the various strands of string, making Amber flinch as the housekeeper trailed her fingers over the deep, scored imprints. At last the gag and sour apple were removed.

"Get down."

Alice didn't bother to offer assistance but seated herself at the table, leaving her to struggle painfully. Quiveringly, she stood immobile beside the stool and awaited instructions. They weren't long in coming.

"Stand there." Alice pointed to a spot in front and slightly to one side of her chair. She folded her hands on the tabletop while she waited for Amber to take the designated place. "It's time you and I got a few things straight."

Amber pushed to the back of her mind the mild eroticism of standing naked, save for boots and chains, and slowly crossed the floor to stand sullenly in the nominated spot.

She had had plenty of time to think and one thing she knew for certain was that she didn't like Mrs bloody Ward one little bit. The deprivation of her freedom, to say nothing of her self-respect, had done little to subdue her. On the contrary, she was infuriated. Floundering in her own hatred, the rush of the words as they fell from her lipstick-smeared mouth almost choked her.

"I don't take kindly to being treated like dirt by a self-important servant. You'll get your comeuppance. Now take these chains off and let me out of here."

"Quiet! I'm the one who sees to your welfare as well as beats you," she pointed to the cane hanging on a meat hook over the dishwasher, "so you'd better keep on my good side."

"Hags like you don't have one!"

"As you're about to find out." Alice rose from her seat and took the cane from the meat hook. She whooooshed it through the air a couple of times. "You... over here now and bend over the table."

Hesitantly, but too proud to admit how terrified she was by refusing, Amber shuffled over to where Alice had posted herself at the far end of the table. She bent forward until her breasts were flattened against the tabletop.

Alice ran the fingers of one hand over the newly-delivered raised welts across Amber's buttocks, while holding her down with the other. Then she laid the cane experimentally across Amber's bottom cheeks. She raised it again and then suddenly brought the cane down in a series of rapid blows designed to make Amber shriek. And shriek she did, at the top of her lungs as the housekeeper rained the cutting blows across her bottom... there was nothing erotic about this! Hot tears flowed down her face and puddled on the tabletop.

When she had finished, Alice grabbed Amber by her cuffed wrists and hauled her upright before retaking her seat.

"Now shut up and be a good girl. You must be tired."

For the first time it dawned on her that she was. And with the realization came her slow surrender. All things considered, the balance of power was very much in the housekeeper's favour. As the shame of what had befallen her hit home, she knew she had no choice but to yield to the elder woman. Deciding it would be in her best interests to knuckle down to her new position in life, Amber modified her tone and replaced the haughtiness with a quiet, almost pleading quality.

"Please take these chains off. I promise I won't go wandering about the place. And I'm hardly likely to run off without any clothes."

Alice's face crinkled as she acknowledged Amber's first real attempt at submission. She didn't, however, moderate her own tone as she ran through the rules.

"Restraints can't come off until Josh says so. You're not supposed to speak at all unless you're given permission or asked a specific question. And don't forget to call him Master."

Amber pulled a face. "What's in a name?" she said, thinking of her own. A loud sob shook her shoulders as it escaped from her lips. Shocked that she still had tears left to cry, the effort of holding them back had her trembling uncontrollably.

She was surprised to feel a comforting hand from Alice, which settled on her narrow hip. But comfort was the last thing she wanted… what she did want was to take Josh's magnificent cock in her mouth as Saskia had done. She wanted to be his obedient, unquestioning slave.

She wasn't at all sure she liked the way the housekeeper's hand moved from her hip to slowly glide over her belly. Even worse was the way the fingers plucked at her pubic hair.

"Mrs Ward, p… please don't do that."

"Quiet."

"But… look, I'm not who you all think I am. My name's not even Jane, it's Am…"

"You're not very bright, are you?"

The housekeeper's fingers continued to pluck, then suddenly changed tack and yanked her pubes spitefully, making Amber squeal.

"I said no talking. And it doesn't matter who you are, here you're just another toy."

Despite Alice's normally kindly features, there wasn't a trace of compassion in her sparkling eyes as she appraised her, starting at her crotch and working upward. She prised open Amber's thighs and ran her finger over her hot, delicate folds. Without comment she judged Amber's suitability as a plaything.

The back door swung open and the fingers ceased their probing. Alice's hand returned to the tabletop as Dougie came in.

Amber was sent to stand in the corner with the instructions to stand with her feet apart and head bowed. Alice rose to boil the kettle.

Neither husband nor wife paid Amber any further attention as they discussed her over a cup of coffee. Amber flicked her tongue over her dry, cracked lips. Briefly she thought of asking for a drink, but changed her mind almost at once for fear of Alice taking the cane to her backside again.

At last, Dougie rose to his feet.

"Well, I'd better be getting this one to her room." Positioning himself in front of her, he groped her breasts. "Turn round, girlie."

He unclipped her hands from the neck chain and unfastened one of the cuffs before spinning her round to face into the room again, only to re-cuff her hands in front. Next he attached a long chain with a leather loop at the other end, to the loop around her neck.

"Sorry, Josh's orders," he told her with no remorse at all as he tied a blindfold tightly in place, not a scrap of material like Sinclair had used but a real one which blocked out all light.

She froze as she heard yet more jangling of chains, and Alice quizzing her husband.

"He wants that as well?"

"Hell no!" With a Click! Dougie snapped the cold, metal ankle restraint shut, then did the same with her other leg. "I thought I might as well have a bit of fun while I'm about it." He gave a tug on the lead. "Move!"

It was only when Amber fell to the floor that she discovered there was a chain linking her ankles.

***

Compelled to take small steps by the chain, which was far too short, and the blindfold, Amber was barely able to climb the stairs. She stumbled many times, once falling face down and slithering back down the steps she had clambered up so painstakingly.

She felt Dougie's foot on the back of her neck.

"Don't get up. It's not often I have a girlie fall at my feet. Besides, you'll only fall down again. So while you're there, you may as well do something useful."

She shivered with disgust as she realized what was coming next. She heard the rasping of a zip only a second before she felt the tip of his cock nudging against her lips.

She felt sick. And yet, somehow her blindfold, along with her chains, legitimised the whole thing. She couldn't escape, she was a victim and there was nothing she could do, she told herself, as she opened her eager lips, taking the unseen tool deep into her throat.

Reality was of no consequence as she joyously sucked on Dougie's prick. Denied sight, on the back of her eyelids it was Josh who pressed her nose into his groin; it was Josh who rammed his weapon so hard that she gagged, and it was Josh who spurted thick, creamy liquid down her throat.

"Okay girlie, get a move on!"

Dougie's voice invaded her fantasy with brutal clarity as he hauled her forward by the chain, without giving her time to regain her feet. Instead he dragged her up the stairs on her stomach, and she was compelled to haul herself up by her cuffed hands, using her feet to steady herself as she dragged them behind.

Once again she slipped back, this time almost taking Dougie with her.

He let go of the lead and she continued to slither down an entire flight of stairs, finally coming to a halt in an undignified heap on a small landing.

Dougie took his time coming to assist her. As he slipped his hand beneath the neck chain and hauled her to her feet, she wondered if Josh knew how his supposedly loyal servants treated his... she almost smiled as she thought the word... slaves.

"You useless tart! Get up the stairs, now."

Humiliated and broken, nevertheless there was a curious buzzing of joy in her heart as she made the arduous climb, for she realized for the first time that she was a slave rather than a servant, the lowest of the low. And so it was only right and proper that the staff should treat her as such.

Somehow they made it to the desired floor, by her calculations the third and top storey. Her shackled legs were aching terribly by the time she felt her stilettos sink into carpet. A door opened and she almost lost her balance when Dougie shoved her into the room.

When he removed the blindfold she found herself standing in the middle of a bedroom. Decorated with a pretty shade of lilac silk wallpaper with embossed trailing flowers, it was a light, spacious room, completely dominated by a large double bed with an iron bedstead. Her eyelids took up a rapid flickering to clear her vision as her mouth dropped open in dismay... there were chains lying on top of the bare mattress, one at each corner.

Dougie removed all the chains, uncuffed her hands and removed the chain between her ankles. Free for the first time, she rubbed her wrists to bring the life back into them.

"When your hands are free," he told her, "cross them behind your back."

He closed the door on his way out. There was the grating of a key in the lock. So, she wasn't merely a slave, she was a prisoner as well.

***

After she had showered and washed her hair, Amber's restless gaze took in her surroundings, focussing her attention first on the chains which were anchored one to each corner of the bed. Surely he wasn't going to have her chained up at night?

She glided across the highly polished floor to the French windows which led on to a balcony, one of the later additions to the original house. The black wrought iron railings, about waist height for a taller person, came up to her breastbone. She raised her elbows to support herself and looked out over a stable yard surrounded by outbuildings, with a curious post in the centre of the yard, beside which her car had been parked tantalizingly within view. She smiled bleakly as she wondered what Joshua Cordell would make of the fact that working class Jane Dean drove a luxury motor like his own.

For the first time she actually considered escaping. High Briar lay across the fields to the East. She could easily take one of Josh's horses. Measuring the distance between the balcony and the ground, she concluded that if she were to attempt such a climb without a rope or a ladder she would risk serious injury. And there was little chance of Mrs Ward supplying either. She supposed she could always call on assistance from Saskia. Except that would leave the other girl here alone, with the man who Amber wanted, yes, truly wanted, as her Master. While Amber continued to make do with the likes of Don and Sinclair, Saskia would be fucked,

169

whipped and generally mistreated by Josh. After everything she had been through, that just wasn't fair!

She shrugged her narrow shoulders and returned inside, just as Alice arrived with a hot meal and coffee which she took alone in her room. And when it was dark, Alice returned to light a number of candles which were dotted around the room. Then she had Amber lie face down on the bed, spread-eagled her and chained her.

And so that first night, in the soft heather glow of the room, chained naked to her bed like some kind of criminal, whorls of elation filled her with pride in her new-found subjugation.

CHAPTER TWELVE

Amber hardly slept that first night. Once, she thought she heard a wailing sound coming from the stable yard. Unable to get up to investigate, she lifted her head and lay listening for the sound to come again, but heard nothing other than the unseasonably ferocious wind and heavy rain.

Dwelling a while on her new, dominated position, the only thing which really rankled was the authority of Mrs Ward. It would be easier to stomach, she reasoned, if she were to detach herself completely from reality and surrender herself utterly to the persona of Jane. It wouldn't really be lying since it was who everyone thought she was anyway.

Except paradoxically, she wanted Josh to know who she really was. Surely it would make her subjugation more meaningful if he knew that he, a nobody from the poor side of town, had complete and utter control over a member of the aristocracy. The longing to own up was so strong she could taste it.

Heavy with the trials of the long, extraordinary day, her eyelids closed at last, and she had a couple of hours sleep before Alice woke her at dawn.

***

Amber stood stretching her poor, aching limbs.

"Look at yourself, girl!" Alice grabbed her wrist and flung her towards the full-length mirror. "See what a slave looks like."

Drowsily, Amber did as she was bidden. For a moment she merely watched the reflected rise and fall of her breasts, smiling serenely as her long, fleshy nipples stiffened under her own gaze. But beyond the left-over fuzziness of sleep lay reality, and with a horrified gasp she took in the blue-purple bruises on her breasts. Still, it was to be expected; Josh had given them a bit of a battering.

171

She turned slowly, partly because it hurt to move and partly because of the growing disquiet of confronting her own image. Hesitantly, she turned her back to the mirror and peeked over her shoulder.

Shock made her eyes bulge. To see the evidence of the maltreated slave she had become so clearly defined on her body took her breath away. Then shock gave way to pride in the erotic beauty of her maltreated flesh, before her emotions settled into a warm, comforting glow. Her eyes took in every detail of the intricate network of livid weals patterning her sore behind and saw them as the confirmation of a Master's ownership rather than the inscription of brutality. Her lazy fingertips skimmed reverentially over the welts and multi-coloured bruises, laid over the fading ones delivered by Sinclair, so very long ago it seemed now.

She smiled weakly and fleetingly thought of Lawrence… ah, if he could only see her now! Everything he had said about her was true, God help her, it really was. From now on there would be no more fantasies; this was all too shatteringly real.

Yet with the final acceptance of her status came insurmountable shame, a commodity she had never dealt well with. Her shoulders heaved and she dabbed at her moistening eyes with the back of her hand.

"Go empty your bladder and bowels," Alice instructed tersely. "Take a shower." She shoved Amber towards the en suite with unnecessary roughness. "Be quick about it.

When she emerged a short while later, it was to find an extraordinary array of items on the bed. Holding them up one by one, she would have been amused if she wasn't so astonished.

"I'm not wearing this!" she declared as she regarded the emerald green waspie, a shiny, latex affair which laced up the front and had suspenders attached. "Maybe if it was made of something feminine, satin or silk maybe, but this… this is dreadful!"

"I doubt you'll be wearing if for long."

With a disgruntled snort, Amber examined the stockings. Nothing outrageous there, just ordinary flesh coloured with a wide band of lace at the top. Next were the shoes.

"These are totally out of the question! I don't care if they are a perfect match, I doubt I can walk in them." A mile high, the spiky, ankle-strapped shoes were higher heeled than her own boots. Pulling a face, she evaluated the next item. "What am I supposed to do with this?" Seven inches wide, the strip of matching latex had fastenings at each end. Lastly, she turned her attention to the pile of familiar tarnished chains. "What are these for?"

"You know very well. Your Master is coming to collect you at 9.30, so if you get a move on, you'll have time for breakfast. You'll need your energy, you're going jogging."

"In these?" Pitting her will against that of the housekeeper, she snatched up the shoes and held them aloft in one hand with the waspie in the other. "Dream on!" Flinging them down on the bed in disgust, she exploded in a voice like the one she used to mimic, "I'd rather go frigging naked."

"Behave yourself, Jane and remember what you are. Get over here so I can dress you."

"All right! Keep your hair on." She stomped sulkily around the bed, stopping directly in front of the servant. She placed her feet together and pretended to click her heels. Rolling her eyes heavenward, she raised her arms at her sides and stood like the Angel of the North. "So earn your bloody wages and dress me!"

"Watch your step, my girl. You've already earned a good six lashes."

"Is that right?" Amber jeered. "What for?"

"Talking."

"Oh, and you're going to report me, right?" she trilled sarcastically.

There was an unsavoury smile on Alice's lips as her deceptively kindly face crinkled.

"No, you're going to own up. Now keep quiet or I'll gag

173

you."

It was enough to bring Amber to her senses. She pursed her lips and lowered her eyes as Alice's dextrous fingers laced her into the restrictive waspie, cinching her already slender waist so tight that it somewhat hampered her breathing. Next, she had Amber turn round and cuffed her hands behind her. Snatching up the band of latex, the housekeeper strapped it across Amber's breasts and round her upper arms before fastening it at the back. Next, to Amber's horror, the elder woman delved down the front of the latex band and manipulated Amber's heavy orbs so they blossomed alluringly over the top.

With her arms bound to her body, she felt like a mummy bandaged for the tomb. She drew in a breath before letting it out in a broken sigh of despair. Catching site of herself in the mirror reinforced her sense of vulnerability. And she supposed she did look kind of sexy, in a perverted sort of way.

"Lift your foot."

Balancing precariously on one leg, Amber sent mental darts of hatred to the woman as Alice eased the stocking up her leg before doing the same with the other leg. With a hand on each shoulder she made Amber sit on the bed while she fitted her small feet into the shoes, fastening the ankle straps tightly. Lastly, she fixed the chain round her neck, leaving the end slack to serve as a lead. She gave it a jerk and had Amber follow her down the back stairs to the kitchen.

Alice positioned the new slavegirl beside the dishwasher. She slipped the end of the lead over the meat hook with the cane, leaving enough slack so that Amber could reach the special bottle Dougie had rigged up beside the hook. Similar to the kind of water dispenser one fits in a gerbil cage, at the end of the angled metal tube was a ball which stopped the liquid from escaping. It took her several minutes to work out how to push the ball up the tube with her tongue to release the liquid, but only a millisecond to swallow the woeful amount of juice she actually managed to release.

On the top of the dishwasher was a cereal bowl. But by the time she had sussed out the workings of the bottle, the cereal and milk had turned into a soggy, unappetising mess.

"There's no telling when your next meal will be," Alice told her warningly, "your Master tends to get carried away when he's enjoying himself and completely forgets the time."

Amber wrinkled her nose in disgust before bending to lick up the cereal. Failing to flick up the gloop with her tongue, she ended up with her nose buried in the bowl and making hideous snorting noises as she attempted to eat. With shame she raised her head, horribly aware of the mush around her mouth, down her chin and on the tip of her nose.

Dougie wiped her clean with a rag then took her outside to wait for Josh, closing the door with a shout to his wife, "I'm just off to the stable yard."

His lecherous grin set Amber's heart beating furiously as he looped the end of the chain over a bracket beside the kitchen door. Her trembling as his good eye snaked over her slender, latex encased form set the chains jingling. Powerless to protect herself, she closed her eyes, not daring to object even when his work-roughened hand slipped between her hot thighs, nudging them apart forcefully. Unmannerly, craggy fingers probed at her folds and crevices, prising open her exquisitely developed, protruding lips, sliding them into her tight channel with shameless ease.

"Well, girlie, I can't abide your sideways-hanging tits, but at least you've got a nice tight cunt. Wet, too." He frigged her roughly, jabbing his fingers up to the knuckle inside her. "Keep your mouth shut and your cunt open," he told her as he withdrew his fingers, "Let's see what sort of fuck you are."

Screwing up her eyes, she listened to the slide of his zipper. She held her breath as his cock forced its way in. To her shame, her body welcomed the impropriety as he fucked her, though it wasn't shame engendered by his brutal use of her but had more to do with the underhanded nature of the act, not merely a violation of her body but an abuse of her Master's trust. Yet it was she who felt disloyal.

Even so, she couldn't curb her instincts as she thrust her abdomen towards him, bucking wildly on his penis. Then she felt the thrilling mounting of her climax and welcomed the first spasms joyously.

"That's it, girlie, come for Dougie."

Her muscles spasmed in that pain-like way that had her shrieking, only a second or two before he came. It was only when she felt him withdraw and his semen seep from her that sickening guilt overwhelmed her. Spent, and hanging limply in her bonds, she opened her eyes and saw the threat in his.

"I wouldn't tell Josh if I were you."

With silent menace, he tidied himself before making his way to the stables, leaving her with his sperm glistening on her inner thighs.

There was considerable warmth already in the early morning sun, despite the terrible weather during the night. The latex around her bust was growing uncomfortably warm, as was the waspie.

Someone had opened the kitchen door and she could hear Josh chatting amiably with his housekeeper over coffee. With nothing else to do, she considered how he seemed so at home with his servants in the kitchen and supposed it was natural given that he was from the same class; it simply shouted of his lack of breeding. The thought of drinking coffee with servants was enough to turn her stomach. Sex, of course, was another matter entirely.

Amber closed her eyes and watched the colours changing on the back of her eyelids as the sun beamed down upon her. With her spirit drifting contentedly in the warm serenity, she failed to hear Josh's approach.

Treading softly in his suede running shoes, the first she knew of his presence was his ferocious roar.

"Eyes front!"

With swift obedience she turned to face him. Her eyes sprang open.

176

He was dressed, as he had habitually dressed for many years, in black because he considered it rather added to his image and made him appear all the more intimidating.

Her world shattered when he looked her over with as much passion as one would view the contents of a fishmonger's slab. Already bleak with misery at what she saw as her infidelity, she hung her head and trembled, his coolness serving to add to her distress. Quiveringly, she feared the evidence of her betrayal was all too apparent as it slithered down her legs.

He called for Alice.

"Someone's been at her," he growled accusingly.

"Well, if you will have her left here for the neighbourhood toms, you shouldn't be surprised. Anyway, she's got something to tell you, haven't you, slut?"

Hearing herself referred to in such a derogatory manner set her cheeks aflame. At first, she wasn't sure exactly what the housekeeper was referring to since her guilty secrets were mounting with amazing speed. She inhaled deeply, then took a chance and jumped in with both feet.

"Please, Master, I beg your forgiveness. I've been talking without your express permission."

"Very nicely put, Jane," he complimented without warmth or interest. "I'll punish you later."

Swiftly changing the subject, he pointed out that her shoes were unsuitable, not that her comfort was any of his concern, he told his housekeeper as she bent down to remove them, he just didn't care to see a good pair ruined.

Standing now in her stockinged feet, Amber was a good six inches shorter.

"The ground's absolutely sodden, thanks to that rainstorm last night." He reflected on how fortunate it was that he didn't have a chill this morning, since he had been soaked through while disciplining Saskia in the stable yard last night. "I know you're busy, Alice, but could you go and release Saskia? She's been tied to the whipping post for most of the night. She'll need cleaning up a bit and my houseguest will be arriving shortly."

Amber stood patiently until the housekeeper had gone. When she raised her head she gave Josh a thin smile which he didn't return as he unhooked her lead and removed the chain from her throat, only to replace it with another. Made of a series of metal rings, each three quarters of an inch in diameter and joined together by small links, it fastened with a padlock at the back.

"This is your new slave collar. You'll wear it always," he told her as the padlock clicked shut.

For the first time, she noticed a black canvas bag at his feet. Hefting it up, he looped one strap of the weighty bag round her neck and positioned it to hang over her bound arms. Then he fastened two straps at the bottom across her belly.

"Okay bitch, it's time to start your training."

***

Amber had always considered herself pretty good at athletics at school, and she was pretty sure that under normal circumstances she would have had no trouble keeping up with her Master as he headed off across the fields towards the ruins, following the course of the river. She might not be in such good shape now but it was primarily her bonds and the encumbrance of the bag which prevented her from catching him.

Always possessed of a fanciful imagination, it struck her that from this distance and angle, the ruins resembled the skeletal remains of some giant, reclining beast in a mythical landscape. Its backbone was a structure forty feet in height, with a row of imposing, ten feet high arches along the top.

As they approached it she was really beginning to suffer. Her breasts hurt from the tight binding which did its best to flatten them, and her arms burned achingly. The restrictive waspie felt as it were squeezing her innards up through her body. God help her, her lungs were on fire! She struggled on across the mire, fighting to keep hold of the silken strand that bound her to her desires. Amidst her anguish, she could think of little else but how to win praise from her hard-hearted Master.

Her stockinged feet squelched in the grass. Numb from the cold and caked in mud, they became heavier with each step. Feeling utterly wretched with the mud-spattered stockings clinging uncomfortably to her legs, she was close to collapse. Fearing the consequences of the run more than punishment for speaking, between ragged gasps for breath, she appealed to the compassion she mistakenly believed lay just below his hard exterior.

"I… can't go… on, Master. P… please, let me… stop… before… drop." Sapped of all energy, without waiting for his permission she came to a halt, not far from the river's edge and took in great lungfuls of air.

Heavy browed and hawkish, he turned and retraced his steps, stopping inches from her.

"What's up with you?"

"I'm worn out, and… and my b… boobs are h… hurting like hell. Need… help. Band's too tight… and waspie… tight."

"What do you want me to do about it?" incredulous that she should even consider relief, he told her, "You're a slave now and must learn to accept any treatment dealt you, no matter how uncomfortable or agonizing."

Slowly, her breathing became more regular and her, "What are you trying to do, destroy me?" was spoken in her more normal, haughty manner.

"Far from it. I'm improving your stamina. Now get a move on. We've got a lot to get through." He stood back and with a hand gesture, commanded her to run on ahead.

At a more leisurely pace, he brought up the rear, a most enjoyable place to be when one considered the view of her luscious, stripy bottom, framed by the green suspenders. As he watched her struggling through the ooze, he willed her to slip over. Ah! She would be so adorably humiliated and it occurred to him that perhaps he should have removed the breast binding and waspie after all. Not for any consideration for her well-being, but she would look so blindingly sexy with mud clinging to her pearly, sensuous curves.

***

The mystique of the ruins forbade an exhausted Amber from approaching too closely. Except, it wasn't just mystique, there was a feeling of decadence oozing from the very stones, just as she always knew there would be. She stopped just short of the ruins and rested near an ancient oak and her teenage imaginings of debauched monks came back to her.

Up close, she could see there were several unconnected walls in various states of dilapidation which reminded one of the violent history of the place. It was almost impossible to imagine how it must have looked when complete. Having gazed on the priory for so many years from afar, dreamed of exploring every nook and cranny, to be here now sent tingles of excitement fizzing through her. Except it wasn't only the ruins that had that effect, but also the presence of Josh as he came up behind her.

For no apparent reason he gave her a forceful shove towards the tree.

"Oww!" She stumbled and landed heavily, scraping her face against the bark.

Using the chain collar he yanked her upright with her back towards him and unhitched the bag before steering her a good distance away from the tree, then he un-cuffed her hands. Next, he unfastened the latex band. Stepping back a pace, his gaze zoomed in on her breasts as they swung free from their constraint.

"A guy could really have fun with those luscious tits."

Brought almost to the point of complete exhaustion, nevertheless her nipples hardened into stiff peaks under his stare. Glancing downward, and knowing that he had noticed

180

them too made her sizzling quim twitch and her clitoris throb. Oh, why didn't he just fuck her and be done with it? Except, there was something shamefully erotic about standing here in nothing but a tight waspie and stockings, she thought as he folded the band carefully.

"This is where your education really begins," he joined her hands in front of her. "Now we'll find out what you're really made of. Take off the stockings."

With her cuffed hands she unhitched the suspenders and dragged each mud-splattered stocking down her leg, placing them in his outstretched hand with the green latex band.

"Look at the state of these. Mrs Ward will have something to say on the matter. I'll have to punish you for getting them dirty."

"But it's not my fault!"

"Shut your mouth. You really are the most argumentative bitch."

He grabbed her arm and turned her round so she stood with her slender back towards him. He unfastened the hooks and eyes and removed the waspie, then stood back to admire the sensuous curve of her, as yet unblemished, graceful back.

"Stay put," he commanded as he walked back to the tree and draped the garments over the stout roots. When he returned, he had the bag with him. "On your knees, slut."

"Please, Josh. It's a muddy patch, and…"

"Master," he corrected. There was a resounding Smack! as his hand made contact with her breast, setting it bouncing and raising a scarlet patch to add to the bruises. "And stop fucking arguing!"

With a heavy hand on each shoulder, he pushed her down onto her knees. Standing behind her with his long legs astride hers, he raised his foot and with a muddy trainer between her shoulders gave her a hard shove that drove her face down into the mud. As she lay spluttering, he removed his boot and repeated the order.

"On your knees, now."

181

With a squelching sound, she pulled herself free from the mire.

"I want you on all fours. Arse in the air."

She turned to look at him over her shoulder, spat mud from her mouth and struggled to the required position.

He circled her slowly to take in the erotic view and watched a dollop of mud slither from her face to plop into the pool of slush in which her hands were buried wrist deep. There was so much slime on her face and in her hair that it looked as if she had washed in the stuff. The glistening sludge on her breasts dried hard and cracked before his eyes. Standing behind her once more, he stepped back to view her humiliation in all its splendour. Ah, there was nothing like the sight of a slave on her knees for her Master, and one displayed so provocatively was mouth-wateringly sweet. The tiny rosebud buried deep in the crease between her abused buttocks clenched and unclenched, and her flushed vulva glistened a muddy welcome between her legs.

It only took a moment for Josh to free his mighty erection and position himself for entry. And entry was brutal. Bowing at the knees, he gripped her by the haunches, digging his fingers deep into her flesh and rammed into her, slamming his groin against her backside. Like a wild beast he took what was rightfully his and fucked her with animal lust, without affection or consideration.

"I'm going to fill that cunt of yours to overflowing," he told her as the musky scent of sex filled the air. Against the backdrop of the gurgling river and singing birds he violated her with almost malicious fervour, not caring if her groans were of ecstasy or distress.

"Fucking bitch!" he yelled as he shot his thick, steaming seed deep inside her clutching channel. Then, sensing the closeness of Amber's orgasm, he withdrew. "No, you don't! You're not allowed to come until I give permission," he laughed. "Unfortunately, on this occasion, it's most definitely denied."

Having finished with her, he gave her another shove which again sent her sprawling. Turning his back on her, he tucked his deflated weapon back in his jogging trousers before reaching for the bag. He took out a bottle and helped himself to some of Alice's renowned Mint Fruit Fizz, before re-sealing the bottle and replacing it in the bag.

Not only had he brought Amber's approaching climax to a shuddering halt before it hit, leaving her severely frustrated, but he paid little attention as she again struggled to wrench herself free from the sucking mud.

He slung the bag over his shoulder and made off towards the tree for a much needed rest in the shade.

"Crawl over to the river," he called without looking back. "Clean yourself up. Then run across to the ruins and wait for me."

Turning round to settle himself on the grass with his back resting against the tree, he watched her slime-coated body as it crawled slowly, like some grubby little animal, in the direction of the river.

Humiliated and angry, she hung her head in abject misery. Totally unaware of the lust which still burned in his dark, brooding gaze, she wept bitterly.

CHAPTER THIRTEEN

Obediently, she came and stood before him with lowered eyes. His casual glance took in the twinkling beads of water which evaporated slowly on her petite, mantrap of a body. Two sparkling droplets hung from her nipples like diamonds. There was no doubt about it, hers was a body that begged for attention of the most brutal kind. And she begged so prettily into the bargain.

Grabbing her roughly by the arm, he marched her right up to the ruins, skirting what had once been the main part of the priory and leading her onward to the backbone of the stone beast. He shoved her through an archway, on the other side of which was a narrow, partially intact stairway.

His palm moulded itself around her striped bottom cheek, "Up there, now!" and with fingers digging into her flesh, he gave her an upward shove.

Helpless to do otherwise, she began to ascend the steep, treacherously narrow steps. One slip could prove fatal and she leaned against the wall for support as she climbed ever upward, praying there were no loose stones to facilitate the collapse of the entire structure.

Up and up they went, Josh following with the bag, until they came to the row of arches at the top of the wall. The stairway merged into at a ledge of about sixteen inches which ran behind the arches, and it was along this he made her walk. Terrified of falling and unable to save herself due to her cuffed hands she was too afraid to look down. Instead she held her breath as if that would help her to keep her balance. Cautiously, she began to inch her way along.

At the half way point she came across a wooden, slatted platform which halted her progress. As wide as the ledge itself, it stood about three feet high and four feet long.

"What have you stopped for?" he barked. "Turn round, back up and stand with her calves pressed against the platform."

Manoeuvring carefully, she turned to face him and did as directed. He unslung the bag from his shoulder, set it down on the ledge and rummaged inside.

Frozen with terror and convinced that an accident was about to befall her, she hung her head and screwed her eyes up tightly. She was going to fall, she just knew she was.

Reading her thoughts, he told her cynically, "You won't fall... I'm going to make sure of it. Open your eyes."

She did as she was bidden, and Josh held up two shiny, metal pegs for her to see, each one about two and a half inches long. Her body relaxed and she allowed herself a smile. Well, if he's got nothing worse than clothes pegs, she thought smugly, there's no problem. Excitement effervesced through her as she anticipated the remembered pleasure-pain that pegs engendered.

"They're made from stainless steel," he informed her coolly, "more pleasing to the eye than conventional pegs. There are other differences, too." He pointed out small holes drilled through each of the tail ends. "And this is another difference."

Amber drew in a horrified breath as he opened them to display the four rows of tiny, needle-sharp teeth across their jaws. He brought his hand closer to her right breast, and for a moment the peg hovered over her hard, throbbing nipple. Instinct made her raise her cuffed hands to protect herself but with a quick, rough gesture he pushed them away.

"Aaaarghh!" A blaze of agony sliced through her as he closed the spiteful jaws over the tender peak. "No! I can't stand it!"

Anger flashed in his dark eyes as he dealt a sharp blow to one cheek, then the other.

"Of course you'll stand it, and a whole lot more besides!" He closed his finger and thumb over the peg and twisted her imprisoned nipple viciously.

She shrieked in agony. Hot tears stung her eyes. No, she wouldn't cry again, she just wouldn't! Except the pain was

185

excruciating and her eyes were unable to contain the salty water and the first few drops began their lazy crawl down her flushed cheeks.

She looked so frail and abused, it was all he could do to concentrate. But concentrate he must; there was so much more pain to inflict yet. As he raised a second peg she tried to back off but the platform blocked her escape.

"There's nowhere to run to. You've no choice but to stand here and take it. Long teats like yours were made to be tortured." He snapped the second peg closed over the other nipple.

She screamed again as the vicious teeth punctured her abused flesh.

"Two will do for now. But I've got lots more," he whispered with a villainous twist of his lips.

Then he attached a short, narrow chain to each peg by means of a small clasp passed through the holes, thus joining her breasts together. Next, he hung a heavy, diamond shaped metal weight from the middle link of the chain and her nipples were pulled grotesquely but oh-so-sweetly out of shape. He gave her the once over, dwelling a while on her agony, and her nipples which were already sporting an attractive bluish tinge.

"Now you're ready."

She hardly dared to imagine what for. The virulence of the pegs mingled with her crushing shame and brought about such a feeling of hopeless vulnerability that she wailed piteously. But wasn't this what she had always wanted, to be at the mercy of a cruel Master?

With a dark, hungry regard he considered the exquisite form of the succulent meat before him. Yet even that wasn't enough.

"Turn round. Get up on the platform. Stand looking out through the arch."

Afraid to comply but terrified not to, she stepped onto the platform. He took chains from the bag then climbed up beside her. He drew her attention to metal rings sunk into the sides of the curve of the arch, and it was to these that he attached the chains so they dangled downward. Then he caught her hands, removed the cuffs and replaced them with leather wrist restraints which he buckled tightly before raising her arms above her shoulders. He attached her wrists to clips at the ends of the chains.

Her slender arms were drawn upward, stretched tautly about three feet apart, deepening the hollows of her armpits. He admired her muscles and her veins were visibly and pleasingly stretched.

Never had she known such agony and her eyes stared pleadingly as he stepped off the platform and once more rummaged in the bag. He straightened up and for long moments just stood there, whip in hand. Agitation curdled her innards and her anus tightened in terror. Why was he holding back?

He inched back a couple of steps. His foot shot out and he kicked the platform from beneath her, sending it crashing to the ground some forty feet below.

She flailed her legs wildly as the pain in her arms was increased to a degree she would never have believed possible as her own weight pulled her downward. Her arms felt as if they were being drawn from their sockets. Why the unnecessary cruelty of the delay? She groaned in agony, with her clitoris unaccountably swelling with an urgency that was as painful as the aches in her arms.

"Hurts, does it? Good, it's supposed to." Reaching out one hand to brace himself against the wall, he raised his other arm, narrowing his eyes against the sun, he watched as her legs continued flailing in a desperate bid to find purchase.

A terrifying Swish! cut through the air, followed by a petrifying Crack! A flame of white heat licked the tender flesh between her shoulders. So expert was his delivery that the vicious thongs curled around her quivering body and struck the swell of her tormented breast.

"Five lashes for speaking without permission," he told her

187

as he delivered each with a savage delight. "Five more for getting your stockings dirty."

A blood-curdling yowl followed each loud Crack! as he set about patterning her back, expertly curling the whip, even under circumstances when he could so easily fall, to repeatedly catch her breast with its savagely pegged nipple.

"And another fifteen for theft."

She was mortified. "Theft, M... Master?"

He delivered the first of the fifteen with such ferocity that he had to correct his footing to stop himself from toppling. Again he struck, and again.

"Old Smith wouldn't pay enough for anyone to buy a car like that. I can only assume that either you or your gangster boyfriend stole it. And the clothes, the Cartier..." Swish! Crack! "You must have got them the same way. The bag's obviously stolen because I've been through it and can't find anything with your name on. Unless, of course, Jane Dean is an alias."

He watched her small hands claw at the air as he flayed the skin scorchingly from her provocatively arched back. Hot tears cascaded down her cheeks and snot dripped from her nose. But ah! what a sight she was for any red blooded male as each full-throttled yell was torn from her pale, vulnerable throat. Already she was covered in an attractive sheen of moisture, engendered as much by the blazing sun as by fear.

"Well, I don't care who you are or what you've done," he told her before delivering the next vicious flurry, "you belong to me now and you're going to be broken into submission."

Trusting in the strength and durability of the metal rings which held her captive, she jerked violently under each following, lust-crazed strike. Her piercing screams were snatched away by gusts of wind and it flashed into her mind that they would probably hear her at High Briar.

Still the lash fell with unfettered ferocity as with the accuracy of an expert, he laid each blaze of fire just above or below the last. And as each lash fell and jerked her body, the agony of the nipple pegs to became more acute, the teeth biting more savagely to match the blows.

Even through the agony, shame engulfed her as snot fell from her nose, at the same time as juices began to leak from her rapacious sex. Her inner muscles went into spasm and clutched at emptiness. As he delivered the last and most powerful strike, she let out a shriek and, without permission, her most devastating climax to date ripped through her.

"This time I'll overlook the fact that I withheld my consent since it was a rather fitting end to such a dramatic flogging," he said as he wound the thongs round the whip handle and returned it to the bag. He looked up at her, hanging delicately like choice venison from her chains, then glanced casually at his watch. "My weekend guest should have arrived by now, so I'm afraid I'll have to leave you to it."

The indifference with which he uttered the words skewered her heart, causing pain far greater than the flogging. Desolate, she raised her head and stared with disbelief. A glob of spit fell from her soft, quivering mouth as she opened it to speak, moving her lips wordlessly.

He caught hold of her legs and pulled her towards him. "I'll send someone along for you when I get back." He clamped his mouth, hot and voracious, over her wet pussy and sucked the juice greedily from her channel. When he had taken his fill, he grabbed her ankles, swung them to waist height, then forcibly shoved them away again.

"Aaaarghh!"

No emotion crossed his face as he observed her wildly swinging body. He wiped his mouth on the back of his hand and told her, "The rest of the day will be yours until Alice collects you for dinner." He turned to go, then added, "Jane, or whatever your name is, by now you'll have learnt what to expect from me, as well as what I expect from you… unquestioning obedience. And I don't expect to hear another unauthorised word from you… ever!"

With that, he strode confidently along the ledge and left her hanging while he returned to the house, without looking back. It came to him as something of a shock to realize that he had moved beyond grief for his wife. There would be no time for reminiscing now that he had new flesh to dominate and humiliate. For unlike Saskia, beautiful and submissive though she was, this bitch was everything he could want in a woman, at least she would be, once he had taken her perfect little body and tortured it into complete submission. It was time to live his life to the full and begin to really mistreat the bitch. Moreover, it dawned on him that he had one bitch too many.

***

Unconscious, she was brought back to the house in the back of the Land Rover. She was chained to her bed and left to sleep. Later, she was unexpectedly given the freedom to pamper herself. With her neck encircled by the chain slave collar, she soaked away the raging fire in her shoulder muscles and upper arms along with the pains in her legs, in a long, hot bath. The toiletries provided weren't up to her usual high standard but, she supposed, they did the job just as well.

Remembering that the housekeeper was to collect her for dinner, she assumed she was to join Josh and his guest. With this in mind, she took extra care applying and blending her make-up, using the cosmetics which had suddenly appeared on the dressing table. She would have preferred to use her own as the few items provided consisted entirely of muted colours, but she was nevertheless grateful that her own brand of perfume had been returned to her from her handbag.

Her skin was soft and fragranced and her hair freshly styled into its usual sleek, feathery bob when Alice collected her. Approving her make-up as "tasteful" Alice re-fitted the restraints around her wrists and ankles. Her hands were clipped together behind her and a lead attached to the chain around her neck. Then she was led through the house. With a heady mix of full-throttled lust and lurid horror, her nerve endings bristled

190

with zest for life as she tried to imagine what the evening had in store for her.

***

Alice left her alone in the dining room with Dougie. Standing with her hands linked behind her back and the end of the lead dangling between her firm, heavy breasts, she studied her surroundings while she waited for Dougie to finish whatever it was he was doing behind the drapes along the far wall.

She smiled at the sight of the beautiful old rocking horse. Lovingly restored, it was mounted on a wooden frame. The part of her that had never grown up longed to jump up on its back.

Along one wall was an oak sideboard on which stood a computer, telephone and fax machine, the evidence that Joshua Cordell, whatever else he was, was a professional businessman who was never far from his work. At the far end of the sideboard, the various decanters, bottles and glasses were laid out.

Her eyes were drawn to the odd array of paraphernalia hanging on another wall... one could hardly call them decorations for they resembled more closely instruments of torture. Made of wrought iron and shaped like tongs, they had a curious power which sent a chill along her spine.

There were only two place settings at the table, one at each end, and clearly no evidence of a third party. Her heart beat joyously at the unexpected prospect of an intimate evening alone with her Master. Set with the finest porcelain, crystal glasses and heavy silver cutlery, the centrepiece was an elaborate flower arrangement with eight tall, elegant, red candles.

Having finished his chores, Dougie stepped out from behind the drapes and went to fetch certain items from the sideboard cupboard before dumping them on the table. Summoning Amber to him, he fixed a bright red ball gag in her mouth. He removed her lead and flung it aside, leaving her ankle restraints in place and her slender wrists joined behind her back. Next, he fitted some sort of leather harness around her belly and buckled it in the small of her back.

"Climb on the table, girlie."

She placed her palms down on the top of the aged but highly polished surface, leaning a moment on the long, refectory table with her arms supporting her weight. She was reminded of her how her own history was entwined with this place, and recalled that family archives claimed some of the High Briar furniture had been purloined to furnish the manor house when the estate had been split. Why, this could even be the very table removed from the Grand Hall.

"Stop daydreaming and get on the table."

Amber curled her foot around a chair leg to pull the chair nearer to aid her. She smiled inwardly as she imagined the way her bottom jutted out provocatively as she knelt on the chair and used it to clamber up onto the table.

"Stand up and move the candles."

Whether it was because she was becoming used to obeying or simply because she had no choice in the matter, obediently she kicked the arrangement up the length of the table. Her heart plummeted. Standing in the centre, she realized she had read the signs wrong; the table was set for Josh and his guest, and she was nothing more than an ornament for the table.

Dougie fixed a spreader bar between her feet, joining it to the ankle restrains, then had her bend at the knees. His good eye locked onto the black, pubic bush which frizzed alluringly from her mound before working its lecherous gaze upward.

"Those dangly, misshapen tits of yours look like overripe fruits that escaped the harvest gathering," he jeered, watching as her face flushed.

Her rage bubbled hotly inside. Her boobs weren't dangly! He had maligned her body and she felt an inherent need to defend what she knew to be good, firm breasts, heavy for her size, she knew that, but she had never had any complaints before. Besides, all that really mattered was that Josh liked them. Hadn't he told her only this morning that they were luscious?

"Bend lower! How can I reach your ugly tits up there?"

Compliantly, she crouched with her pussy level with his waist. Burning up with shame, she cast her eyes downward.

"That's right, hang your head in shame. You filthy sluts deserve everything you get." His fingers drove a path straight into her moist tunnel. Agitating roughly, he feasted his eyes on her breasts. Firm and juicy, he could overlook their tendency to hang sideways when it suited him. But one thing he had learned from his employer, he reflected as he withdrew his fingers, was the immense joy it gave a man's cock to humiliate the bitches.

Standing with her legs uncomfortably bent and her feet flat on the tabletop, transfixed, she looked on as Dougie picked up what at first appeared to be a sort of frame. Constructed of two pieces of wood which formed the sides, about six inches long, they were joined top and bottom by metal bolts. He beckoned her closer. She leaned towards him and with a smirk, he fitted the contraption over her right breast.

"It's a tit press," he told her as he turned tiny nuts which caused the wooden sides to move together to imprison her breast, squeezing it horrendously. "I've known Josh most of his life. He started torturing tits when he was at college. You'd be surprised what he can do to a pair of oversized monstrosities like yours."

Her eyes widened in horror, but still he kept tightening the nuts, squashing and flattening her breast at its root until it was several inches thinner. He then repeated the process with her left breast. When both had become agonized pieces of misshapen, discoloured flesh, he pointed out how each press had hooks at the inner corners which linked together to form a savage mockery of a bra. This done, he fitted chains to the four outer corners and had her stretch out on her stomach, still with her hands joined behind her back.

Eagerly, he hurried across the room and pulled back the heavy drapes to reveal a collection of pulley systems and wheels, which he operated with practiced ease. There was a nerve-crunching grinding sound. Amber tilted her head upward to see an assortment of black, heavy linked chains descending from the ceiling above the table.

He locked the mechanism in place and returned to where she lay shivering with fright on the tabletop. Scooping up the four chains connected to the presses, he pulled them up behind her and linked them to one central chain, then hitched a further chain to the belly harness. Yet more chains were fixed to the ends of the spreader bar. Finally, he unclipped her hands and secured her wrist restraints to the two remaining chains, about three feet apart.

When all were secure, he returned to the pulleys and, as her panic button belatedly switched itself on, operated the machinery to raise her slowly. With her heart battering against her ribcage, she was completely helpless as she was slowly lifted free of the table. With her weight supported somewhat by the harness, her arms were pulled backward, so tautly that for the second time that day she feared they were being wrenched from their sockets. Behind the ball gag she screamed at the top of her lungs.

Dougie locked the machinery in place. He drew the heavy drapes across to hide the machinery and returned to the table. He lit the candles and replaced them in the centre of the table. Lastly, he retrieved Amber's lead and left the room.

Suspended from the ceiling with her breasts squeezed until they were almost flat, the pain took her beyond agony to something quite unlike anything she had known before. Slowly, she detached herself from reality and allowed her spirit to soar. It wasn't pain she felt now, nor was it pleasure, it was something quite different, it was... acceptance.

***

Josh escorted his guest to the dining room. The deal was done, contracts signed, and he was set to make a great deal of money. He almost smiled; it had been so easy in the end that it was almost criminal. Reynard Smith's eagerness to get his hands on Saskia had blinded him to the finer details of the deal and the old devil could well find himself out of a job before too long. Beevis and Smetherton were ripe for takeover. Not only that, but he had a new slave into the bargain. Smith's silence on that matter was ensured since to raise the alarm would merely draw attention to his own shady dealings.

Josh opened the door and ushered Smith inside. Leeringly, Smith focussed his attention on Saskia. Naked and sporting the stripes across her torso he had himself delivered with one of Josh's crops, she stood immobile beside the sideboard, ready to pour the drinks. Without looking up, the two men took their seats, one at each end of the table.

As always, Dougie served the meal. Her and Josh exchanged amused glances; the old fool hadn't even noticed the sweetmeats suspended from the ceiling. Josh clicked his fingers and obediently Saskia poured the wine.

"This is all very nice, Cordell, and I enjoyed your woman tremendously, but I understood the privilege was to last the entire weekend."

"And so it shall, I'm a man of my word." He could have added, as you and your company are about to find out, but thought better of it. "But I always think a man wields the whip all the better when he's well fed. Besides, I've something to show you first." With cold detachment, he said, "Dougie. The pulley."

Dougie turned on his heel and headed for the heavy drapes. With the nearest thing to a flourish he could muster, Dougie revealed the pulleys and wheels.

Reynard Smith's mouth dropped open in surprise, revealing the half-chewed smoked trout pate. "What the devil's that?"

Amused by his guest's inability to grasp the significance of

195

the apparatus, he waved his hand dismissively, "Just little a little something I had my man install."

As the machinery started up and the clank-clank of the chains caught his attention, Smith tilted his head towards the ceiling. He watched in open-mouthed disbelief as the suspended slavegirl descended slowly, her head facing towards her former employer.

"Surely that's not the slut who…?"

"The very same."

"You mean… she's agreed to this? I don't believe it! Surely it hurts? Watch for the candles, Cordell!"

"Insignificant details." Josh's smile was faintly vicious as he reassured his guest. Had the man no understanding of SM at all? "Eat up, and enjoy the scenery."

Bulgy-eyed, with her lips framing the red ball, Amber quivered in terror as the candles flickered a mere few feet below her, and still she was descending. Then, just as she felt their warmth fanning her belly, with a jolt Dougie locked the machinery in place.

Josh's throat was parched with lust as he watched the pleasing glow of the candles flicker across her pale, maltreated torso. With stony-hearted curiosity, he watched the conflicting emotions cross Smith's face as he took in the bluey colour of her squeezed tits.

Attracted as he was by her enchanting frailty, Josh only hoped the little bitch had the stamina to last the evening. Drowsy-eyed and horny, he gazed upon her fleshy labia… he would have to come up with a way to hold those elongated lips open… and imagined what further torments his new slave could be made to endure. Still, there was no rush; it wasn't as if he had to give her back.

As on Smith's previous visit, Josh dispatched Saskia to the rocking horse in the corner. Obediently, Saskia draped herself across it in the required manner. While Josh turned his attention back to Amber's dewy quim, Dougie fastened the tall slavegirl in place. Then, taking up a position to one side, he flogged her with the enthusiasm of a man who takes his work seriously.

Accompanied by the Swish! and Crack! as the leather thongs struck Saskia's snake-branded behind, the two men finished the first course, while Reynard Smith tried to imagine the agonies that Amber must surely be suffering. His host, however, paid scant regard to anything, except the pleasures her tortured body had yet to yield.

As the flames heated her flesh, causing rivulets of sweat to run down her belly skin and drip onto the table below, her sense of unreality finally disintegrated. Bullet-like nipples paradoxically tipped her breasts, compressed to little more than thin morsels of tissue. Cruelly suspended and scandalously humiliated, curiously she felt no bitterness towards her torturer. Although the agony was beyond endurance, her pussy juiced freely, and there was such agitation assaulting her sex that if it wasn't attended to soon, she would be screaming against her gag in frustrated delirium.

When the men had finished the first course, Dougie paused in the beating, served the two men with the second course and poured more wine before returning to the flogging. And so the meal continued, until the men were replete. Wearying of the entertainment, they adjourned to an adjoining room for brandy and cigars.

Amber barely had time to massage feeling back into her limbs before Dougie marched her off to join the men in the sitting room. Still gagged and wearing wrist and ankle restraints, her hands were crossed but not joined behind her back.

Josh gestured for Dougie to re-fill their glasses, then dismissed him. For what seemed an intolerably long time to Amber, they ignored her presence as she stood beside the door with her eyes lowered and feet apart.

All she wanted now was to be taken to her Master's bed and fucked. Surely even he couldn't go on playing the game indefinitely? No one really lived this way all the time, did they? Tonight was obviously special because he was entertaining, but things wouldn't always be like this…

"Saskia will be ready to serve your needs again in due course," Josh told his guest. "She'll be waiting for you elsewhere. In the meantime, I thought you might like to see how the training of the girl is progressing."

"I would indeed."

"Good." He clicked his fingers. "Bitch! Down on all fours."

Such was her eagerness to please her Master that her obedience was automatic. She dropped down on hands and knees and crawled across to where the two men sat in armchairs before a fireplace. Josh reached forward and removed her gag.

"I know you've sampled her tits before, but please, feel free to take what's on offer." Josh gave a little laugh before adding with emphasis, "I doubt you'll have another chance." Again he clicked his fingers then, with a nod of his head he indicated Smith's burgeoning cock. "My guest has a pressing problem. See to it, whore."

With her stomach curdling at the prospect, she complied with her Master's wishes and inched along on all fours towards Smith. Her heavy globes, now freed from their nightmarish torture, swayed temptingly, their natural colour not yet fully returned.

She raised a hand to reach for his fly, but was halted by her Master's harsh roar. "No!"

She cast a questioning glance over her shoulder and was stung by his derision-laced answer.

"I can't abide a bitch with no brain. Use your fucking teeth!"

In an effort to hide the tears which welled in her eyes at his stinging reproach, she buried her face against Smith's crotch and, taking the hasp between her teeth, pulled down the zip. Holding her breath so as not to breathe in the smell of stale cigarettes which hung around him like a sickness, she burrowed her nose against his underpants in an effort to find the way in. Thankfully, Smith was too impatient and shoved his hand inside to extract his familiar, beautiful curved cock.

For a moment she simply looked at it. How was it that such a detestable man was blessed with such magnificent equipment? Except she didn't hate this man any more, for without him she would never have met her Master. Her excitement was intense. If it pleased Josh to see her prostitute her mouth, then she would do so willingly.

Opening her pliant lips she took his tool deep into her mouth. Smith's spiny fingers clutched at her sore breasts, manipulating them and squeezing them tightly.

"Quite a pair of udders she's got, eh, Cordell?"

Smith groaned as she licked up and down the length of his shaft. Through half closed eyes he looked along the sweep of her back and gasped at the myriad vivid lines criss-crossing her flesh, taking special note of the broken skin. The slut had really suffered, and it served her right! Panting, he squeezed and twisted her orbs harder.

Sucking and slurping for all she was worth, her cheeks hollowing, she gave herself up to the pleasures of servitude. With her saliva easing the way, she took his prick into her slippery cavity of her mouth and began the to and fro movement that drew deep sighs and shudders before taking as much into her throat as she was able.

Josh's own phallus nudged enthusiastically against his trousers. Regarding her degradation, he felt no shame at having brought her low, just an overwhelming pride. As his slave debased herself, leaning forward to take a good deal of Smith's cock into her throat, he felt no jealousy. She was a thing to be passed around, demeaned, and then punished for that very compliance he demanded of her.

Rising slowly from his chair, he stooped down and fingered the tight pucker of her bottom hole.

She tensed, then drew in a breath as his fingertip pressed its way inside. Please don't let him do it there! She could stand anything but that. She gave a muffled cry of protest against Smith's prick. There was the slightest sensation of cold as Josh's demanding finger applied a thin veneer of gel, then he was pushing, pushing, something hard, something that wasn't made of flesh, into the tiny opening.

Savage with lust, Josh gave a sudden, harsh shove, ramming a dildo past her sphincter. Even with her mouth full she managed a full-blooded scream, almost biting into the wad of hard flesh pistoning her throat. Without care or consideration, Josh continued to push it home; if he ripped her, then he ripped her!

Pleased with his effort, Josh stepped back. He had managed to drive the dildo much further in than he had anticipated, given that hers was a virgin hole. At last her ravished rectum could take no more and with a victorious curl of his lips, he viewed his triumph while she continued to suck. He had succeeded in ramming most of it home, leaving only an inch or so, plus the elaborately carved end sticking out of her defiled little rosebud.

Burning crimson as both men laughed, she continued to suck, with a fire raging up her back passage. She felt dirty, yet so enthusiastic was her fellating of Smith that her whole body moved back and forth as well as her head.

Josh focussed his attention on her as she leant forward. Her back was an aesthetic sweep of female nudity, the network of welts and lacerations which criss-crossed her flesh were a great source of delight, and the lines on her buttocks seemed to draw the eye inward towards the object protruding from her anus... an art deco, carved ivory and bronze ballerina, last used on the night prior to the avalanche in which his wife was lost.

No more reminiscing; he had a new slut now, who was proving to be easier to train than he could ever have hoped. She was a natural, and he saw great things ahead for himself and the slavegirl.

Smith yelled, jerked frenziedly and spurted jet after jet of his acrid sperm down Amber's throat. Almost before he had finished, Josh was behind her, grabbing at her hair with one hand and pulling her head back. As Smith's flaccid prick was torn free, Josh stooped down behind her and thrust his own iron rod into her drizzling channel. Shafting her with frenetic energy, he scrunched his fingers tightly against her scalp, clawing her abused back with his other hand.

It seemed to Amber that long minutes passed before his fierce, war-like cry rang out and she welcomed into her cavern her Master's thick, scalding fluid.

Then, kicked aside like an old used rag with semen dribbling from her mouth and pussy, she was left huddled up on the floor with the dildo sticking out of her bottom, while the two men adjourned to their bedrooms.

"You'll find Saskia tied to your bed," Josh promised. "Flog her, bugger her, do what you want to her. I've no further use for her this weekend, so just return her to me in one piece before you leave on Monday morning."

CHAPTER FOURTEEN

The next morning, Amber's training began in earnest. Stark naked, save for her chain collar and the leather restraints which she rather suspected were permanent, she took breakfast in the kitchen as before. Afterwards, on Josh's orders, Dougie clipped her hands together in front of her. Once outside in the yard, using a chain attached to her wrists, he secured her to the back of the Land Rover, and she was obliged to run behind as he drove around the grounds.

Forced to work in the kitchen until she was chained for the night, Amber didn't see Josh at all that day. Nor did she see him for the next few days.

Slowly, her life took on a kind of routine. After breakfast each morning, taken in the kitchen as usual, she was obliged to run behind the Land Rover. Or occasionally, if it pleased her Master, she accompanied him on his run, carrying a heavy backpack as before, either around the orchard or across the fields.

On her return to the house, she was usually put to work, in a different part of the house to Saskia, to avoid any contact between the two. While her hands were free to enable her to get on with her chores, her right foot was always linked to an eight foot chain secured to some bolt or ring set in the floor. Thus she had enough freedom to enable her to work efficiently while at the same time being unable to escape.

She was completely at the beck and call of her Master. Some days she would be required to spend the whole day in his company, often crawling about on hands and knees while he went about his business. She spent many long hours kneeling at his feet while he worked in his study.

Of course, he disciplined her often. Sometimes it was genuine punishment for some minor misdemeanour or other, though more often it was a flogging or some other cruelty merely for his amusement.

Other days were spent in the stable yard, where Dougie had

rigged up a device which, Josh hoped, would improve her stamina to prepare her for pulling a sulky. The apparatus was, in effect, two gigantic coil springs connected to the wall. Each had a long, wooden handle attached to it, shaped like the shaft of a sulky. Standing with her back to the wall, she gripped the handles, to which Dougie chained her wrists.

Then, under the fascinated gaze of the stable lad, she spent a couple of hours, naked whatever the weather, pitting her strength against the coils. The object of the exercise was to replicate the effort needed to pull a man seated in a sulky behind her. At first, she found it too difficult and she strained her back terribly. Eventually she managed to move an inch or two, then over the following days and weeks, her strength increased. Leaning forward against the resistance of the coils, she made steady progress and, in time, was almost able to reach the other side of the yard.

And so the pattern of her life was set... until the night that she was taken from her bed and delivered to her Master's study.

***

On all fours, with her rectum once again plugged by the dildo, this time fully inserted so that the ballerina appeared to pirouette from her anus, Amber felt stirrings of real fear in her stomach.

Standing behind her and aiming between her thighs, Josh kicked her in that most delicate of places, setting up a painful throbbing. Unable to scream due to four vicious clamps screwed tightly onto her tongue, she slavered like a hungry dog. To make matters worse, metal clips were fitted over two upper and two lower molars. Designed to be held in place, each was fitted with a tiny spring with adjoining chain. In the case of the lower molars the chains were drawn tautly downward either side of her chin where they were connected to her collar. The top set were stretched just as tautly, the

203

chains being drawn up over her cheek bones and fastened to a steel band which fitted snugly round her forehead. Thus her clamped mouth was held open.

"It's for your own good," he told her. "It's a device to help save your voice; you'll be made to scream yourself hoarse tomorrow. I'm taking you and Saskia on a trip to a rather special club for a few days. One of you won't be coming back," his voice had an ominous resonance. "In preparation, tonight you'll learn what torture really is. But now, for the first time, I'm taking you down to the cellar." Again he kicked her. "Lead the way, bitch."

Dutifully, she crawled ahead of him with her scarlet-striped backside swaying erotically, kept on course by Josh's guiding kicks. He piloted her along a narrow hallway, at the end of which was a flight of narrow steps which led down to the cellar. He took the key from the red box on the wall and gave her another kick. On all fours she preceded him, head first down the steps, stopping only for him to unlock the door. Instead of flicking the switch, he set about lighting candles in the wall sconces.

Amber continued her descent. Following behind her, Josh lit more candles. Quiveringly, she reached ground level and cast an uneasy eye around the chilly, damp cellar, lit now by myriad pillar candles which threw eerie shadows across the walls.

Dominating the cold, flagstoned cellar was a collection of black, metal ladders, arranged leaning against each other. Next, her shifting gaze fell on an assortment of whips, canes and other implements of correction. Then horror-struck, she saw Saskia.

Her stomach flipped over and for a moment she felt the tiniest twinge of compassion for her rival. Naked and blindfolded, Saskia lay on her back along a metal bench, her head hanging down over one end and her bottom resting on the other end. Her arms and legs were stretched out over the sides and linked by means of wrist and ankle restraints, coupled to bolts in the floor.

An array of long, shining silver needles stuck out of her breasts at all angles, catching the light and curiously reminding Amber of a dandelion clock. Josh drew her attention to two further candles, strategically angled from wall brackets so that the hot wax dripped onto Saskia's belly and vulva. Lastly, the handle of a small whip protruded from her vagina, its thongs dangling over the end of the bench.

Josh hauled Amber to her feet and marched her across to the ladders. Working quickly, he bound her wrists to the cross beam of the upright, admiring the tautness of her arms. Standing barefoot, she was smaller than Saskia and to his delight he was able to achieve a delicious tautness which was quite impossible to effect with the taller girl. With her back to the ladder, the dildo poked through the rungs without obstruction. Next he secured her feet to the bolts in the floor.

Producing a many-thonged whip, he began to slash mercilessly at her belly and upper thighs, curling the narrow strips of leather with an expertise that extended the pattern around her torso. After some minutes he adjusted his stance and directed his aim across her honey-slicked vulva.

Her brain lit up with multi coloured fireworks as the pain exploded outwards in waves from her sex. Her stifled screams came out as a pathetic, dull sound from deep in her throat. Her crotch was a raging inferno as he set about the flogging with frenzied lust.

Leaving her strapped to the ladder, he went to a cupboard and took out what looked at first sight like part of a suit of armour. There were no arms or legs to the thing, and Amber sooner realized that it was something quite different.

Placing the heavy metal apparel at the foot of the ladder, he released her.

"Stand there!" She came and stood where he pointed. "Hold out your arms." Her obedience was automatic and she held her slender arms out straight in front of her like the stereotypical sleepwalker. "Let me introduce you to the

Girdle."

He raised the horrendous looking metal girdle and placed it against her flesh. He heard her sharp intake of breath as it struck cold against her overheated skin, and took joy in the knowledge that the abrasive inside would chafe her already maltreated body. His eyes shone with sadistic delight as he fitted it in place, delighting in the agony it would engender against the angry red weals.

It was made of overlapping, metal squares held together by wing nuts which, although appearing somewhat cumbersome, allowed adjustment to any part of the garment and thus adaptation for any figure. It fastened at the back by means of special clips which closed with a sharp snapping sound. Her globes were supported but rendered accessible due to the cut away top which ensured they were pushed up and displayed in a most provocative, mouth-watering fashion. At the front it came down to a point at the pelvic bone and followed the upward sweep from thigh to hip and across the back, leaving the buttocks free so one could take a whip to the girl's behind without hindrance.

"Breathe in." Of course, part of the pleasure was in tightening the nuts more than necessary. That way one could contort a girl's form exactly as one wished. With her ponderous globes thrust outward she was even more delectable, and his penis stirred its appreciation. Not only that, but the Girdle would feel as though it were crushing the very life from her. Tightening the nuts one last time, he cinched her waist even tighter.

He clipped her hands together in front of her.

On his command she spread her feet about twelve inches apart. His forehead creased with irritation as, black browed and ruthless, he dragged them further apart until they were separated by a good three feet, then bolted her ankles to the floor. Crossing the room, he operated machinery which, as in the dining room, lowered a heavy chain. He fixed it to her wrists then returned to the machinery, dragging her hands high above her head.

The tension was unbearable as the chain continued to draw her arms upward, stretching her lithe, yielding body almost to the limit while the bolts kept her securely fastened to the floor.

Leaving the dildo in place, he ambled over to the bench where Saskia was bound and stood by her head. He lit a cigar, idly added a few more pins to her breasts and watched the reflection of agony on her face; she was past screaming. Noting how the veins in her long, elegant neck were stretched taut as her head hung downwards, her long hair lying in a black pool at his feet, he clasped his cock in his fist. For something to do while he made Amber wait, he built up a rhythm and wanked over her. He felt no passion, not even contempt… he felt nothing at all as he emptied the contents of his balls over her face. He flicked the last drops from his penis; it was time to resume Amber's torture session.

He strode across to the far side of the cellar and selected a particularly flexible cane from one of the racks. He tested it on the way back, swooshing it through the air so she would be terrified by the sound long before he struck.

Stretched tight as a bow, her body nevertheless jerked as the cane struck across her blatantly presented, peachy-nippled breasts.

"Now you'll learn what a beating really is."

With that, he let fly, wielding the fiendish cane with gusto, bringing its biting edge down with sharp, vicious Thwacks! time after time. Of course, there would be less bruising than with the crop… oh, how he loved the keeper-shaped blotches of black and purple… though the sting would be more virulent. And the faster delivery would ensure that each fiery sting blended with the next to produce a vast wall of pain, giving her no time for recovery between strikes.

No part of her meaty orbs was spared; he brought the cane up beneath them, lashed at the sides, across the swell and near the root. How sweetly her face contorted with pain! Then he changed his target again, slashing at her long, engorged nipples. Slicing the cane this way and that, he emblazoned her tortured breasts with vivid weals of fire.

He was sagging; it had been a long day and his arm was aching. His hand dropped to his side; he couldn't go on. The cane slipped from his fingers and he made a half-hearted grab at her molested breasts. Digging his nails deep into the ravaged flesh, he squeezed and mauled her tiredly. But before he called it a night, there was just one more thing he had to do.

Circling her slowly, he tore the dildo from her with a popping sound. The pain as it was pulled free was excruciating but before she had time to absorb it, there was another pain as his rigid cock penetrated her rectum.

No, no, she pleaded silently as her natural instincts took over and her muscles tried to force him out. This was wrong… dirty… filthy… humiliating. But there was nothing she could do to prevent it. He was her Master and could defile her in any way he pleased. It was what she had always wanted.

With unbridled joy he set about ravishing her backside, content in the knowledge that each thrust would be bringing tears to her eyes as she imagined herself ripped apart. In spite of the way it had been stretched, her hole was still tight and would cause considerable her pain.

With a shout of triumph he pumped spurt after spurt of hot, viscous fluid into her, filling her back passage. If a man was going to own a slave he might as well enjoy himself to the full, he mused, and wrenched free of her while he was still stiff enough for it to hurt.

Breathing jerkily, she wept as creamy semen dribbled from her anus and saliva dribbled from her tortured mouth. While she shivered with anguish, Josh calmly tidied himself. Sore and humiliated, her body was a mass of seething agony, stretched beyond endurance.

"I'll send Alice to release the pair of you," he said casually, adding as an afterthought, "provided she hasn't gone to bed."

***

Amber and Saskia sat side by side on the back seat of Josh's car throughout the journey to Berkshire. Once they arrived, Josh removed their blindfolds and gags, and unfastened their hands, leaving the wrist and ankle restraints in place, as well as their collars.

Entering The Lodge's elegant hall for the first time, Amber couldn't help but feel a kind of other-worldliness about the place, a strange timelessness, along with a fragrance she couldn't quite put a name to. The air was thick with expectancy and cigar smoke. The smells of leather and polish assailed her nostrils but another, overriding fragrance had her flummoxed. She giggled; it reminded her of the bedroom in her dingy, rented flat after a heavy bout of sex.

A man met them in the hall. Not the kind of guy to argue with, Amber thought, taking into account his impressive build and stern expression.

"This is Yuri," Josh told Amber as he handed over Saskia, adding on a whisper, "don't expect him, or his twin, to speak to you… they're both mute."

Watching as the huge man led Saskia away, Amber dared a whispered question.

"Where's he taking her?"

"To the training cellars. Regrettably, I've had to let Saskia go on account of my decision to keep you. I approached John Carpenter, the owner of The Lodge, and he agreed to buy her to serve as one of the Housegirls. Here she'll be safe, happy and will continue to give her body up to pain and degradation."

Amber smiled, her happiness complete. Without Saskia competing for Josh's attention, life would be perfect.

Three men, two smoking cigars, stood in a group at the foot of the wide, sweeping staircase. Despite their hands-in-pockets stance, there was an air of formality about them. Even so, their mood of anticipation was so strong she could almost taste it.

No stranger to opulence, she was nevertheless impressed by her surroundings. It wasn't just the imposing staircase which split in two half way up, nor the carved banisters against which one of the men now leaned, no, it had more to do with the sense of wealth and more particularly, power, which seemed to leak from the very walls. Of course, she was no stranger to money either, and her family had always wielded power.

The formal portraits which graced the staircase made her shiver. One of the things she had always hated about High Briar was being surrounded by pictures of her ancestors.

So, she thought, Josh had brought her to some kind of country club for the mega rich. She wouldn't swear to it, but she thought she caught a glimpse of a rather high-ranking Member of Parliament on the galleried landing, the husband of bloody Millicent Huntley-Watts, no less! Once again she giggled; while Millicent the Dyke hung around the Naismith trying to pick up women, her husband hung around here... doing what, exactly?

"I say, Cordell," the eldest of the three men raised his hand in greeting. "A new toy? Mind if we have a look, old boy?"

With a slight nod of his head, Josh addressed the three men, "Camberwell, Poillerat..." he paused; there was something about the third man which always got his back up... "Masterson." Holding Amber firmly by the elbow, he muttered in her ear as he led her across the hall. "You'll obey all orders, no matter how bizarre or by whom given. Anyone who feels so inclined has a legitimate claim on your body. In short, he can fuck you, flog you or do anything else he has a mind to. You may be wearing a fancy gown but you're still my slave."

She looked exquisite in her new, ruby-coloured, scoop neck, satin gown, its depth of colour serving to emphasise the paleness of her pearly skin, an effect doubled by the jet of her hair. The tight fitting bodice laced up the front, accentuating her meaty orbs and trim waist. The shoes Josh had selected for her added several extra inches to her height, allowing the hem to just clear the floor.

He brought her to a standstill in front of Camberwell. With

her eyes submissively lowered and her hands crossed but not joined behind her back, she stood mutely while Camberwell reached out his hand. He slipped his fingers through the rings of her chain collar to pull her closer, with a "May I?" addressed to Josh, not Amber and unlaced the bodice of her gown to reveal her breasts. He made no comment about her abused state but merely commented, "Big tits for so delicate an object." Manipulating them with a rough hand, he tugged at her nipples. "Long teats, too. Have you thought of having them pierced?"

"All in good time," Josh said phlegmatically. "Would you care to join us in the bar?"

"Love to, old chap," Camberwell's face darkened, "but we're waiting for Madame."

Josh raised a questioning eyebrow. "Trouble?"

"The girl we used," Jean-Paul Poillerat, the thirty-something with male model looks, explained haltingly, "together, last night, in the dungeon, she fainted under torture."

Puzzled, Josh shrugged. "It happens all the time."

"No, no, Monsieur, you don't understand. We had only just started…" he looked at his companions for confirmation.

"Ten minutes," Masterson supplied.

"Three minutes!" the Frenchman continued guiltily. "The standards are slipping, yes?"

At that moment, Madame Stalevsky marched into the hall, her own authoritarian face dark with displeasure. She ruled the girls with an iron will, trained them hard and had virtually guaranteed herself a place in legend. The Housegirls she produced were able to withstand a great deal of torment. But she was also fiercely protective of her charges, and if anyone damaged them, then they would answer to her.

Josh took his leave. He didn't envy the men their run-in with Madame. He had faced her wrath more than once over the accidental damage of a Housegirl!

He headed for the bar with Amber trotting dutifully behind

him.

***

Confused by being permitted to share a table with her Master as if she were his date rather than his slave, Amber thought it judicious to keep her eyes lowered and her hands in her lap.

The opulent furnishings seemed strangely at odds with the behaviour of the club members, she thought. However, she was learning fast; this was no ordinary country club and its members were no ordinary men. They were rich, powerful and dominant... a lethal potion indeed, she smiled secretively.

Josh acknowledged another member, whose hand disappeared up the slit of a Housegirl's gown, before summoning one of the Housegirls himself and ordered her to fetch drinks, brandy for himself and a fruit juice for Amber.

"This club is devoted to SM," he told her, and went on to explain the function of the Housegirls.

Her heart thumped and to her shame, her clitoris throbbed with anticipation. Never had she imagined that such a scandalous, wonderful place could exist. And to think she was really here!

"By the time we leave, you'll have gained valuable experience, Jane. Of course, with Saskia gone, you'll find me even harsher. I might leave you locked away in the cellar for hours, perhaps days. If I take you to my room you'll sleep in a crate at the end of my bed." His look of derision froze her heart and triggered a frisson of anticipation in her belly. "You'll never actually share my bed, unless chained. You'll be moved from the lilac room. Dougie's converting a small room on the other side of the house. You'll have no balcony and no en suite. What you will have are a basin and a jug of cold water, along with a bucket for waste which it will be your job to empty every morning." He laughed at her look of horror. "You'll have a magnificent view across the fields to the grand, Oakley-Dean estate. While you're chained to your bed, you

212

can look out and dream of the kind of luxuries those dull, pampered women over there enjoy. Oh, one word of warning, Jane. You really must learn to control your screaming; it can play havoc with the larynx."

She heard approaching footsteps behind her. Forbidden by Josh's warning look to turn round, she remained seated, with her eyes submissively lowered as the stranger stood behind her.

"Good to see you again, Cordell."

Amber froze. Surely she knew that voice? God, she was in real trouble! She had long ago ceased to worry about her old life, but now the spectre of the press came back to haunt her. If Mummy ever found out what she had become…

Josh acknowledged him with a twisted smile. "You too." There was something about Gascoigne he rather liked. "I believe we have unfinished business in the gaming rooms."

"Indeed we have. I intend to win back every penny you practically stole from me on your last visit."

The two men laughed.

"Can I get you something? Scotch, brandy?"

"I was thinking more along the lines of your plaything." Gascoigne placed his heavy hands on Amber's shoulders. "She seems to be shivering."

"She's nervous; it's her first time here. But she'll be delighted to be of use, won't you, Jane?"

"Yes, Master." Had she really said that? And without hesitation.

"I'd like to blindfold her, if that's okay with you?"

"Of course. I have other plans, so shan't be needing her for the rest of the day. Shall I meet you in the common room later?"

Amber flinched as the blindfold was placed across her eyes and tied at the back. A hand cupped her elbow and helped her to her feet.

"The common room it is, then, after dinner. But I thought I'd pop this little delight along to one of the dungeons."

With that, Gascoigne closed his hands around Amber's neck and guided her from the room. With her heart pounding and her stomach lurching dramatically, cautiously she placed one foot in front of the other.

"You've no idea how delighted I am to find you, Amber."

CHAPTER FIFTEEN

Having heard of the three o'clock display of 'out of service' Housegirls on his previous visit, Josh was eager to see for himself the breast stocks. As one of the other guests had told him, "One can enjoy the services they're still capable of offering." Yet even Josh was unprepared for the joy such degradation of female flesh could bring, and to his mind it was a great addition to Lodge facilities.

It had long been the custom for those girls indisposed by their periods to be kept out of sight of the members, though none of the girls enjoyed their enforced state of abstention. In their minds, their bodies should always be used for the purposes for which they had been trained, namely sexual gratification and abuse, the evidence of which they bore with pride.

But one had to bear in mind the impracticalities of using 'unclean' girls.

And so, those deemed fit enough had always been put to work doing the more mundane chores about the place. This was largely to maintain fitness levels and discipline. Also, it helped the girls to retain pride in their usefulness. They could find themselves scrubbing floors, helping in the kitchen or being shut away in the laundry rooms. In addition, they were expected to help with the preparation and aftercare of those Housegirls still in use, though this caused a degree of resentment among the girls.

However, those unfortunates who suffered painful belly cramps were vigorously exercised behind closed doors. Madame was no believer in bed rest under such circumstances. In her book, the only way to combat the pain was to work it off.

Eventually, after numerous complaints from guests that it really was most tiresome to come all that way only to find that their favourite whore was off limits the new system was introduced, ensuring the membership could still make use of the girls' talents.

Eventually, even Madame agreed that while the girls served a useful purpose doing the household chores it was, after all, only their vaginas which were out of use and therefore a waste of their other talents and charms. She advocated that the old and new systems should run in tandem.

And so the afternoon display system was brought into force. At three o'clock precisely, the girls with periods were put on display along one of the ground floor corridors.

As Josh entered, he selected various items from the racks that were placed in readiness. He walked along the line of girls, with the Frenchman Poillerat some distance ahead of him.

Josh's heart leapt. He had expected to see the girls' breasts imprisoned in devices similar to the tit presses he employed at home, and was delighted by the spectacle which greeted his eyes.

A glorious array of breasts, some a pleasing shade of purple, others merely blue-veined, blossomed from what were, in effect, rather small apertures. Many girls suffer a particularly acute tenderness of the breasts at their time of the month, Josh reflected, and it warmed a man's heart to realize that one could double the suffering so easily, without the onlooker having to lift a finger. Of course, it greatly added to one's pleasure when one applied even more pain, such as the nipple clamps that had been applied by previous visitors to, what he thought of as the Tit Torture Gallery.

Fascinated, he took in the whole, amazing design of the appliances. Consisting of wooden struts and beams, the contraptions were integral to the breast stocks themselves, as was the stool. Comprising a wooden rim on which the girls sat, it obliged their bottoms to hang through. With hinges at the sides, this could be tipped forward to allow access to the back passage.

The girls sat open-legged, revealing the round, metal bases of what appeared to be dildos protruding from their vaginas.

216

Except they weren't dildos at all. Specifically designed to humiliate and punish the girls for what was, after all, a natural bodily function, they were extremely painful when fully inserted. The clever design incorporated a larger than usual, more absorbent tampon. The device was held in place not only by sheer effort but also locking, metal straps round the thighs. Rammed deep into the wearer and clearly visible, it clearly demonstrated the fact that the vagina was out of bounds.

The breast stocks themselves were based on the traditional pillory and stocks, used for centuries for the punishment of criminals… and talkative women, Josh mused, thinking of his quarrelsome new slavegirl. Made up of two wooden boards, tastefully decorated with studs all the way round and with cut-away sections, they could easily be slotted together. Instead of holes for the head and arms, the apertures were for wrists and breasts. The breast holes, smaller than one would have imagined, fitted over the roots of the globes and produced a rather pleasant ballooning effect in the larger girls.

Matching boards with two holes held their feet apart and prevented the girls from escaping. As a further refinement, side struts joined the breasts stocks to those on her feet. Further struts at the front, joined to the edges of the lower boards and angled inward, supported a short, padded bar which ran across in front of the girl. So when one wanted to use her back entrance, one just had to tip the girl forward and she was cleverly supported, thus freeing the members' hands for other purposes.

Perfectly aware of what the vaginas contained, some members got off on raining shame on the girls in the form of lewd comments as they walked along the row. Others stopped to make use of what charms were still on offer. No longer shut away from the guests, the girls were forced to endure the looks of disgust and muttered obscenities from those members who considered women with periods 'unclean.'

After an hour on display, the girls were collected and taken to the drainage room. Here the tampons would be removed and hoses fitted in place.

Josh passed a very pleasant forty-five minutes, puncturing unnaturally blue breasts with the excellent, long needles in use here at The Lodge. Other breasts, some already carrying whip marks, received a thrashing from the crop he had selected. And at least two girls, one of whom he gagged before abusing her breasts terribly, received copious amounts of his sperm up their rectums. As he left the corridor, he realized with regret that he had only taken advantage of the mouth of one girl who already had Poillerat's seed spilling down her chin.

***

After dinner, Josh made his way to the common room.

"Ah, Gascoigne," he said as he approached the little group who surrounded his friend, all the while keeping his eyes focussed on Amber, suspended by her ankles. "I hope she's given you good sport?" It certainly looked like it! Still blindfolded, her face was pleasingly splattered with dried semen, as were her legs. Her upper thighs bore one of Gascoigne's intricate designs.

"My dear Cordell. You have no idea!"

Someone commented, "She's got a good set of lungs on her, Cordell," which was followed by a disgruntled growl from across the room.

"Keep the noise down over there. I can hardly hear this one scream!"

"Thank you for the loan." Gascoigne struck with the lash so forcefully that he set Amber swaying. "I've booked a Housegirl for the rest of the evening, so when I'm done here…"

Grabbing hold of her legs, Josh said apologetically, "I think she's had enough for her first visit." The comment was in no way a consideration for her well-being, but had more to do with the pain in his groin.

With a nod of his head, Gascoigne summoned Ivan to take

218

her down. Turning to Josh, he said quietly, "I wonder, could we meet in the morning? I have some information which you might find interesting."

***

Josh rose late the next morning. After breakfast, he went in search of Gascoigne. Towing an unusually subdued Amber behind him, he spotted him seated on a sofa beneath a pointed archway in the far corner of one of the drawing rooms, behind which was a large alcove. There was a heavy drape across the arch which was pulled back in a flowing line, held in position by a wide black tie back. As far as Josh knew, no one who used the alcove to take pleasure with a girl ever pulled the drape across for privacy; privacy was what the guests' rooms were for! He wasn't altogether sure but it could well be against Lodge rules anyway.

Bent over a trestle with her back to him as Josh approached was Gascoigne's own woman. Her embroidered gown was hoiked up to her waist and fell in exquisite folds which framed her tanned legs and patterned rump. Her bottom hole looked most enticing and her shaven red slit glistened with dew. She was a tall, striking woman with light brown hair and, though surely approaching her mid forties, was a splendid specimen. Josh recalled that on a previous visit, he had given her a rather delightful, though sadly quick, shafting when she had been displayed as she was now.

"Take a seat, Cordell. Coffee? Tea?"

"Coffee will be fine." With a gesture to Amber that she should sit at his feet, Josh settled himself beside his companion.

Gascoigne summoned a Housegirl and two coffees were duly delivered.

"I must say I enjoyed your little piece immensely." Gascoigne nodded in Amber's direction, while she sat quivering. "You really have made the most remarkable find.

219

And she marks up extremely well. Rather nice labials, too."

Glowing with pride, Josh sipped his coffee. "I'm glad you think so."

"How do you feel about a little wager? The youth of your delicate little plaything against the maturity and experience of mine."

"Sounds interesting. What do you have in mind?"

"I thought a contest at the lake." Gascoigne went on to outline his plan. "I must confess that I've already talked the idea over with Masterson. Any objection to his joining us?" he concluded.

Josh could think of no valid reason to object since he had never actually done him any harm. He shrugged. "If he's up for it."

For a while they discussed the idea, until Gascoigne dropped his question casually into the conversation. "You do know who your little toy is, don't you?"

"Her name's Jane." Josh glared at her accusingly.

She shivered at his feet. Her whole world was about to collapse and she could do nothing about it. She turned imploring eyes to Josh, who swerved his gaze away from her.

"Other than her name, there's nothing I care to know."

Gascoigne laughed. "You mean you really don't know? Then it's rather important that I enlighten you. She, my dear chap, is none other than Amber Jane Oakley-Dean."

Josh felt the colour drain from his face. "No, you're mistaken." He had known for some time that she wasn't who she claimed to be and was only too aware that she had a secret. But he had thought she was a thief… in a way, that would have been preferable. Now he shook his head disbelievingly and gave a little laugh. "This slut?" He kicked her, but his confusion prevented his usual enjoyment of the way her face flushed with shame.

"I'm sorry, old boy, no mistake."

There was a terrible certainty in Gascoigne's voice. Even so, Josh wasn't entirely convinced.

"How can you be so sure?"

"Because, dear chap, I'm married to her mother. And this…" Lawrence Gascoigne struck out at the delicious rump of the woman over the trestle, "is my whore wife. Penelope, introduce yourself."

The woman straightened up and turned round. Smiling down at a horrified Amber, she said haughtily, "Say hello to your mother."

"H… hello, Mummy."

***

How dare the bitch lie to him! She had made a fool of him and no punishment would be too harsh.

Josh ordered her to strip. When she stood naked before him, save for restraints and collar, he told her, "This is a fully equipped dungeon, just right for teaching lying whores a lesson."

Amber had never seen him so angry. Terrified, she cast her eyes around at the terrible apparatus, like the rack which stood malevolently awaiting its victim. Ropes and chains hung from the ceiling as well as from huge metal rings set in the walls. She daren't even begin to imagine what indignities and cruelties he would be able to inflict upon her here. This was worse than the cellar back at his place, worse even than the small dungeon Lawrence had taken her to last night.

"So, Amber," he called her by her real name and made it sound like an insult, "what've you got to say for yourself?"

"I… I… I'm sorry, Master. I… I tried to t… tell you, but…"

"You didn't try hard enough! Now you'll pay for it."

Forgetting herself she rounded on him, flinging the words at him, daring him to hurt her.

"Then make me pay! Teach me a lesson and make it sting."

"A lashing's too good for you!"

"Punish me as you will, but afterward, please, Master, take

me home."

"Home?" So far he had refrained from the use of the kind of language frowned upon by The Lodge, where one should always remember that one was a Gentleman. But all that was about to change. "To that fucking estate bordering mine? The one you neglected to tell me belongs to your family? You stupid, posh-arsed slut! Do you realize how humiliated I feel? What will the other members think when they find out that you've played me for a fool? I'll never be able to hold my head up high again, you brainless daughter of a whore!"

"And what about me? Don't you think I feel humiliated? My own mother… a whore! And to see her like that, bent over a trestle…"

"Your humiliation is one of my greatest joys, and entirely appropriate for a slave. But my shame is another matter entirely. Don't you realize that I've had your fucking mother over a trestle? And a bloody good fuck she was, too."

Yes, that hurt, he saw it in her face. However, what he didn't see was the moistening of her quim as her arousal was heightened by shame and fear.

Having already decided on the appropriate torture, he grasped her arm and marched her across the room. Despite everything, he couldn't help but smirk as he thought of her undergoing the terrible pain and indignity of the Rod.

***

With Amber suspended by her ankles, Josh operated the machinery until she hung at the correct distance from the floor, her legs held achingly far apart. Her head hung level with his waist and the flush of arousal was on her cheeks.

"Meet The Rod."

This was a particular favourite of his and being something of an expert in its use, he relished the idea of introducing her to it. The poor bitch had no idea, he laughed. He depressed a button. There was a low-toned grating noise as a panel in the

222

ceiling was drawn back. Then, at a painfully slow rate, a steel rod descended like a stalactite from the ceiling. With the girth of a slender woman's wrist, it tapered at the end like a giant dildo.

Unable to see what was happening and alarmed by the sound, she began a futile struggle which set the chains jangling and her body swaying jerkily. Slowly, the rod descended, and Josh came to stand in front of her to hold her still. Then, guiding the rod into position, he used both hands to open her pussy. With a chilling smile, he watched as the cold, fearsome rod was lowered deep into her vagina.

"Aaarghh!"

"Stretching you, is it?"

Her screams were deafening as it probed deeper, she was terrified that not only would it stretch her but that it would go in far too deep and spear her insides on its journey through to her chest. However, the safety mechanism ensured it would cut out when it was fully inserted, though Josh saw no reason to allay her fears. It was about time she learned that a woman's body was nothing but an instrument with which men took their pleasure, and if it pleased a man to torture it, then it was her place to submit.

Again she screamed. It felt as though it were burrowing a path right through her body.

When The Rod was fully extended as it was now, the girl impaled on it always put Josh in mind of a horse on a fairground carousel.

But the awesome rod had yet more secrets. At the flick of one of several switches on the wall, it could be either vibrated as a conventional, multi-speed vibrator, cooled or heated. On this occasion, he decided to turn up the heat.

With her vagina stretched and impaled, she shrieked in agony as the hellish device warmed up. This wasn't mere pain, this was pain and fear mingled and she screamed at the top of her lungs, feeling as if she were being burnt from the inside out. Terrified that she would sustain permanent damage, she

223

knew she was about to faint.

Josh grinned as he watched her body curl and twist in desperate efforts to escape from the device. He knew exactly how terrified she was. But he also knew that a thermostat controlled the temperature it would reach. No harm could possibly be done; but of course she didn't know that. All she would feel was the alien steel deep inside her, relentlessly heating up. And her own imagination would do all that was required.

"Not yet," he grabbed one of the buckets set aside for such purposes. "I want you conscious!" With that, he drenched her face in icy water and his rigid phallus tried to bulldoze its way through his trousers as she wailed.

He flicked another switch to turn the heat off. The rod would start to cool now, but very slowly.

Her screams subsided to be replaced by sobs. Working his way around her cruelly impaled body, he listened for a moment to the altered sound of her ragged breathing. He shrugged; best give her a few moments to recover herself. Leaving the still warm rod in place, again he reminded himself he was no barbarian but the sight of her pathetic, tortured form, naked and covered with a sheen of sweat, was more than flesh and blood could stand. At last he took out his cock. Holding it tightly in his fist, he worked it with long, slow movements, gradually building up speed. He took aim as he began a frenzied pumping. Spurt after spurt of glutinous fluid shot up over her tear-stained face and ebony hair. Wiping his hand clean on her breasts he couldn't resist the temptation of giving her nipples a savage twist.

"When I take you down, I'm going to fuck you senseless."

***

On the appointed day, the group gathered on the shore of lake for Gascoigne's contest. In all there were five competitors, and the girls, of course, plus two umpires.

Josh ran his eyes over his fellow competitors. Alan Masterson, who had unsurprisingly elected to race the lovely Marietta, stood beside him. Also present was Camberwell, who had chosen the leggy blonde Housegirl who had good, muscular arms. Poillerat had picked the chestnut haired beauty, Elke whose name Josh rarely remembered, while Lawrence Gascoigne was racing Penelope, Amber's tall, delightfully experienced mother.

The umpires checked the rowing boats. Once satisfied, they gave a command and the five naked females took up their positions, one behind each boat.

The Housegirls were favourites to win, of course. The very embodiment of courage, each possessed a strong back that was well used to prolonged sessions of beatings, as well as strong forearms and thighs. In addition, thanks to Madame Stalevsky's training methods, they were all able to withstand a high degree of pain. And there would be pain today… plenty of it.

Even Josh doubted Amber's ability, though the sight of her suffering would be reward in itself. With his habitual sombre expression, he regarded her as she stood with her back towards him. Sensuously curved with narrow shoulders and slender waist, sinuous and yielding, the strength in her limbs had been greatly enhanced by her training. And the scarlet stripes which adorned her body bore testimony to her ability to withstand a good flogging.

"Get ready…" The umpire raised the starting pistol.

The shot rang out and the five competitors made a dash toward their respective boats. They set to tethering their own girl to the sterns by means of a rope slung round her waist. Then the men leapt into the boats while the girls were left on shore to launch them.

Once in the water, the men began to row furiously, with the girls swimming behind. The umpires also began their journey across to ensure fair play.

So far so good, Amber thought with growing optimism.

Although Josh was a powerful oarsman, she could easily keep up. She had always been a strong swimmer, having been introduced to the pool at High Briar before she could walk. At least she was a better swimmer than Mummy, who preferred to sit on the side rather than get her toes wet. She glanced across to her... oh dear, she had gone under again!

They were about half way across the lake, with Marietta in the lead, followed closely by Elke. Amber wasn't far behind. Camberwell and his blonde Housegirl seemed to have given up... Amber was later to find out that the girl had suffered a bout of cramp. Penelope was having a dreadful time of it. Lawrence was too strong for her and she couldn't keep up at all.

From somewhere, Josh seemed to find some extra power and Amber had to make a special effort. They reached the shore level with Masterson and Marietta, though the Housegirl was ahead again when it came to pulling the boat ashore. The men weren't permitted to help and instead, after untying the girls, ran off to a nearby group of trees. It went without saying that the first man, in this case Masterson, picked the best tree.

Everything the men required had been provided, including ropes, whips, and ladders. It didn't take long for the leading girls to shin up the trees and attach the ropes themselves. Once again, Marietta was first, but when it came to the suspension itself, Josh had Amber actually suspended before his rival. It seemed one of the rungs of Masterson's ladder had given way, thankfully slowing him down.

Hanging by her wrists from a branch, Amber braced herself as Josh set about flaying her back. The girls were required to count the strokes aloud so they could be clearly heard by the umpires. Josh and Masterson were both well experienced and it was neck and neck. But Poillerat didn't seem to have the knack for rapid strokes and by the time Amber and Marietta shouted, "Fifteen!" in perfect unison, Elke called out, "Nine!"

Amber saw her mother suspended by her wrists and a shiver ran through her. She couldn't quite come to terms with the way Lawrence was laying into Penelope's shapely body. She was quite a looker, Amber allowed, adding a whispered "for her age!"

"Count, you stupid bitch!"

Her last five lashes hadn't counted towards the total due to her lapse, and Masterson was heading back to the lake as Amber shouted, "Sixteen!"

Such a dark hopelessness came over her as Josh cut her loose after the required twenty-five lashes, and she fell in a heap. What she wouldn't have given to call the whole thing off. But that, of course, wasn't allowed; she had no choice. Except it wasn't only for herself she worried.

Greater than her own humiliation was the disgrace she would bring upon Josh if she failed him, especially if she was beaten by her own mother, who was even now having her ropes cut. As Amber picked herself up and ran for the boat, the fear of failing was replaced by sheer bloody-mindedness; no way was she going to let that bitch Marietta beat her!

Re-tied to the boat, the difference on the way back was that she had to tow it. The men weren't permitted to row nor, to Josh's disgust, allowed to whip the girls to urge them on. The umpires had been adamant that any man caught, either punishing or encouraging with the whip while the girl was in the water, would be penalised by being held on the shore for five minutes.

The strength in Amber's arms had been greatly increased by the sessions with the springs in the stable yard, and she called on hidden reserves from somewhere, finding it easier to tow the boat than to swim behind it. She was catching the leading boat fast!

By the time they were three quarters of the way across the lake, the two girls were neck and neck. Josh took his eyes off Amber and flashed a black regard in the direction of his rival. Masterson, however, was too interested in winning to respond, and urged Marietta on with words of encouragement.

Josh did likewise with Amber. "Put your fucking back into

it, you lazy little bitch!"

It was Amber who reached the shore first. As the rules dictated, Josh stayed inside the boat until she had hauled it onto the shore.

Now there was only the course to run! Start and finish lines had been set up with a distance of some two hundred yards between them. The object was for the girls to run the course without falling. The winner of the entire contest was the girl who crossed the finish line first.

Amber rated her chances as pretty good. The other two women hadn't even come ashore yet and, tough as her opponent was, Amber's daily run following the Land Rover had soon helped her recover some of her former ability.

As she set off, with Marietta in hot pursuit, she imagined that day all those years ago when she had won the prestigious Battenburg Cup for her school. Now, with her feet pounding against the grass she knew, as she had known then, that the prize was hers. Except in this case, her prize would probably be something far more painful than the victory 'bumps' she had undergone in the school dorm.

The end was in sight. Marietta was on her heels. Just one last ditch effort…

She raised her arms aloft as she broke through the tape. Whooping with delight, she spun round as Marietta crossed the line. To everyone's surprise, Amber threw her arms around Marietta and hugged the girl who had given her such sport. Was this what the life of a Housegirl entailed? Tonight, Marietta would probably be found in the common room, undergoing some kind of punishment. And yet Amber envied her, and for a moment she almost wished it was she, and not Saskia, who would be left behind.

But then her Master was walking towards her, and she knew she was wrong; she didn't want anything but to be his slave for the rest of her days. But her heart dropped to her feet as she watched Josh claim his prize, namely fucking the loser… her mother!

***

The long, blistering summer was drawing to a close, yet the next morning was as bright and clear as Josh had ever known. As he set off with his pony, he couldn't help but enjoy the feeling of freedom it always gave him, even with a new pony between the shafts. There was nothing quite like enjoying The Lodge grounds from a sulky.

He cracked the horsewhip viciously across the girl's shoulders.

"Come on, Amber. You can do better than that!"

Again the whip struck, lighting a path of fire across her shoulders and causing a blaze between her legs. Damn the man! Did he know he was keeping her in a state of perpetual arousal? She smiled. Of course he did!

Once again her lips curved into a smile. Life was good… perfect. But who would have guessed it of Mummy? Was that the reason behind all the marriages, had she merely been searching for the harshest Master? It was hard to believe that she had managed to keep her slavery a secret for so long, for in private she was every bit as much a slave to Lawrence as Amber was, and would continue to be, to Josh. And the best of it was, Amber realized, that here at The Lodge no one would think ill of her if her mother's husband whipped and fucked her. After all, wasn't that why Josh had brought her here, to share her with his associates? And he would bring her here again, often, just as he had done his wife.

She was a victim, yes, an abused victim of Josh's insatiable lust. Could she really face again such vile indignities as he had put her through, to go on like this day after day? Could she stand the agonizing cruelty and mortifying humiliation? The whip Cracked! across her shoulders and she knew that she could. Though she had no idea to what level of depravity he would take her, she didn't care. All that mattered now was that he was thrashing her.

And now for the opening of next month's title "Linda's Master" by Nicole Dere

CHAPTER 1

'Hey up, slag! There's your lordship calling for you! Go and get your legs round that big throbbing engine of his!'

Linda Hammond tried to halt the blush she could feel rising through her features, tried to hold a pose of calm dignity as she crossed the few yards which separated her from the drumming motor cycle and the black leathered figure of Alan Harding sitting astride it and waiting with that easy, possessive grin of his. Deeply aware of it, and of his dark eyes which seemed to slide familiarly over her, she was also uncomfortably conscious of all those other eyes, glinting with aggression and contempt, fastened on her slim back view as she swung herself onto the narrow pillion seat and settled herself behind him, her arms slipping round his waist, after tugging at the short grey skirt which had ridden up to display an embarrassing amount of her pale thigh. Her own eyes stung with tears, and she prayed for him to pull away and take her far from her fellow pupils.

She felt the Kawasaki 500's power transmit itself through her thighs, through the base of her belly like a deep stirring sexual caress, and then they were moving, the hem of her skirt flapping even higher, her bare legs caught and chilled in the rush of the wind, despite the fine summer day. She bent forward, nestled into the shape of the figure in front of her, bending her head and turning it to shelter behind the glistening shoulders, feeling the rub of the smooth cold leather on her cheek.

Why were her schoolmates so bitchy towards her, she wondered, with a trace of bitterness. She thought of how in the past they had taunted her, made her the butt of so many snide jokes and insults, and all because of the prudery and old fashioned shyness she had so spectacularly abandoned since meeting Al again. 'Linda Loveless' they had named her, from way back in year nine, when boys had loomed as almost the sole topic of conversation between the girls in her form. And then the graphic descriptions of sex, doing it, having it off, shagging, and all the other unlovely terminology involved with their first serious

231

explorations into the fascinating subject which occupied their every waking minute — and half their sleeping ones, too, if the vividly erotic accounts of their dreams were anything to go by.

She had always been "one of the quiet ones" as she progressed through her secondary schooling. Shy and pretty, in an unspectacular kind of way, the lurid accounts of her school fellows frequently embarrassed and worried her, stirring deep seated fears along with the other more turbulent sensations her adolescent body subjected her to. 'Bet you haven't done it, yet, have you, Hammond?' they would tease her, their scorn becoming more apparent as they advanced through year ten, and then eleven. 'Sweet sixteen and never been screwed!' Blushing, trying to hide the threat of tears, she would refuse to say anything, to rise to their baiting, but it didn't help.

To her own private dismay, she had found herself dreading the idea of going out with boys of her age. They seemed so crude to her, so insensitive, though her attractiveness meant that plenty of them tried. She went out with a few, but their clumsy or brutal gropings, and the slobbering smother of their kisses, open mouthed, on her lips or her neck, made her shiver with distaste. 'Maybe there's something wrong with me?' she tormented herself. When she first heard the cruel jibe which changed her nickname to 'Lezzy Linda', she *was* reduced to stinging tears, much to the delight of her tormentors. From then on, the cruel mockery increased tenfold. Even the boys joined in, and she became something of a social outcast.

Things scarcely seemed much better when she moved up to year twelve, among the elite studying for A levels, though by then she was getting used to her situation. By quietly refusing to rise to their taunts, she took the edge off some of the more virulent of her aggressors, blunting their anger to an almost good-natured contempt for her prissiness. But then had come the cataclysm of her fall from grace.

And what a fall! Al Harding had been one of the tearaways at school, couldn't wait to get away as soon as he was sixteen. Linda had been secretly a little afraid of him, though he wasn't the only one, of course. Most boys made her nervous, though she did her best to hide the fact. And Al had never directly bothered her. Had hardly spoken to her, in fact, or seemed to notice her. Which had made it even more of a surprise when, a few months ago, returning unexpectedly to an open evening at school, he had made a beeline for her and made it abundantly plain that he was interested in her. Her blushing, stammering gaucheness had only intrigued him even more, and to her reeling bewilderment, Linda found herself being chatted up, and, even more shocking, responding to it. 'You're not like the other slags,' he told her, with that steady, dark eyed look that felt like he was touching her. 'You're far too decent for this lot. And you're a real looker, too. You turn me on.'

Since that fateful meeting, the last two months had been unreal for Linda. At times she was frightened of the transformation which had overtaken her, the way in which both her body and her mind had been so drastically made over. But then, as was happening right now as she clung to him and felt the rush of wind carrying her along, her thoughts fused into that trembling ecstasy of want and need that made every nerve quiver, made her thigh and belly muscles tauten, and other, hidden muscles beat, too, and cause the moist film of desire to make itself felt against the thin cotton which pressed tightly against the swell of her most intimate flesh.

The bike slowed, the engine snarling as they climbed the narrowing, curving road that led up to Falling Woods. They bounced and juddered as Al competently steered the machine off the road, on through the tufty, leaf strewn undulations of the woodland, until they were well hidden from the road, and other prying eyes.

Their favourite trysting place. Linda blushed anew as she climbed from the pillion, and shook down her skirt, removed the helmet and smoothed her wildly tangled, honey coloured hair. This was where it had first happened. That terrifying, shaming, and finally wonderful experience of giving her body for the first time. It had hurt, she had cried, shocked at the ferocity of new sensations tearing through her, just as that fearful, hard column of his flesh had driven into her softness, taking, demanding, burning through her surrendered virginity. But then, when her sobs had quietened, and she had thought it was at last over, all the torture

233

wondering and speculation, he had taken her again, opened up her sore and trembling body to her own dazed senses, revealed a fierce torrent of passion she had never dreamed of, until she was lost, twisting and threshing under him, knotted to him, unaware of anything save for the floods of release soaring through her, possessing her utterly, so that she could never be the same girl again. Goodbye Linda Loveless, hello Linda Lovelost.

'Come here, you sexy thing! I can't wait another minute —'

'Please, Al! Somebody might see us!' she gasped, in that soft, quavering protest that rose instinctively, and uselessly, to her lips. He grabbed her round her waist, bore her against the thick, seamed, scaly trunk of the stout old chestnut, half lifting her as her heels slid and scuffed against the unevenness of the roots at her feet.

'Get those sodding school knicks off!' he grunted, his rough hands already moving, sweeping up under the grey skirt, the hardness of his searching fingers scratching at her skin as he hooked them in the waistband of her white cotton briefs and dragged them down off her loins, on over thighs and knees, to wrestle them over the white ankle socks and the solid, ugly, sensible school shoes.

She felt her own shiver of distaste at those outward badges of her schoolgirl status, even as she moved awkwardly to assist in the final removal of her knickers. At eighteen years old, and the participant in such passionate loving, she felt the stigma of the neat uniform which tied her to her adolescence. She squirmed at the teasing quality of Al's knowing grin, his oft repeated comments. 'I love you in that school uniform. I can't wait to get you out of it.'

But now he literally couldn't wait, and, suddenly, neither could she. He clawed at his own shining loins and there, thrusting exotically from the leather clad crotch, jutted his erect penis, the swell of the huge dome inviting but intimidating. His hands moved again, lifting the scrap of her skirt about her waist, parting her thighs to expose the small triangle of her brown pubis, the eagerly beating cleft of her vulva. His thumbs peeled back the soft furls of her sex lips, to reveal the gleaming inner surfaces, wet with urgent desire for him, and he jerked, slammed his cold belly

234

against hers, and drove into her, the tightness of her closing and spasming about his thrusting column. She felt the roughened bark press and scrape brutally on the base of her spine, and the clenched rounds of her buttocks as she in turn thrust forward clashingly to yield him even deeper possession of her. It was all part of the savage ecstasy, the pain of it, her pulsing tightness about him, and the start of the merciless potency of the orgasm rippling, then rushing through her, so that she screamed out, a sharp yelp of pure sensation, and bit deep into the leather smoothness of his shoulder, jerking and jerking against him, impaling herself, sobbing with fulfilment while he battered her against the thick trunk. He pounded on and on, deeper and deeper, until she was all burning pain and only dimly aware of the mighty final thrust and the shuddering impact of his own climax and the softening of his engorged prick deep within her.

It was inevitably a terrible moment for her when, dizzily returning to consciousness of her surroundings, she felt all the physical discomfort of such violent love making; the cold withdrawal, and the obscene reality of her own gaping, livid wet rawness, the slickly gleaming helm of his hanging prick. What minutes ago had seemed such intensely passionate love was all at once reduced to the rutting blind instinct of two animals. She could scarcely hold the tears as the crumpled skirt tumbled back over her shame, and the feel of her under the grey cloth merely added to that animal sense of nakedness.

'I want to be in bed with you,' she whispered to him. 'To fall asleep in your arms, to wake up slowly beside you and make love again.'

They *had* been to bed before, at a shabby terraced house which was the home of a friend of his. But she had felt tense and afraid in the strange untidiness of the dark bedroom, too conscious of the furtiveness of their coupling to relax. Ashamed yet unable to help herself, she had been revolted at the faint body smells of the stale sheets. Al had spread a clean, rough towel under them, had stripped her fully naked for the first time, and feverishly begun to arouse her with his lips and his hands, sucking at her nipples, letting his fingers play and prise into every intimate orifice, until she had been moistly brought to a throbbing excitement. She had opened herself wide, raising her legs, splaying herself in blatant pleading to be taken. But afterwards she had felt sullied and ashamed at her own depravity, glad to be covered by her own clothing once more and out in the clean cold of the open air.

Yet she had to admit that he had revealed a shocking, hitherto unknown facet of her personality to her by his unsubtle sexual approach. As the weather grew warmer, they spent most of their time out in the open, up here in Falling Wood. She had never done anything like the things he made her do, never dreamt that she could. She was helpless to prevent him, or, rather, incapable of summoning up any vestige of will to stop him. From the beginning, that was part of the shameful thrill of sex, to be taken there, under the trees and the sky, that dark sense of her immodesty at being naked, of making love outside, breaking all the moral taboos that she had been brought up with.

She felt it now, even though it had happened so many times before. She thought, having satisfied himself so hastily, and her, too, that might be enough for him. But no. She acknowledged the inner quiver of arousal, in spite of the power of the climax she had so recently experienced, when he smiled, in that easy, conquering way of his, having cleaned himself and reaching for her.

'Hey, not so fast, baby,' he crooned, at the signs she had given of being prepared to leave, the pulling of her comb through her tangled fair hair, the straightening of her clothes. 'We can't leave you in that schoolgirlie outfit, can we? Even though it *is* so cute. Besides, that was just for starters. I just couldn't wait. I'm such a greedy sod, aren't I? I know it was far too quick for you, babe.'

She blushed. 'No, Al. It was... great,' she sighed, but she was completely powerless to resist as he reached for her again, gently this time, and pulled her into him. He kissed her, long and hard, his tongue slowly inserting itself and filling her mouth, holding the embrace until her senses swam dizzily and she was panting when he released her. His fingers moved with masterful deliberation now, unlike his former furious tugging. He loosened the knot of the maroon and blue striped tie, undid the buttons of the white, short sleeved blouse, unhooked the waistband of the skirt. It fell about her feet, and she stepped out of it, deeply aware

236

of the pale nudity below her midriff, the small wiry bush of her fleece against the creamy conflux of thighs and belly, the smooth rounds of her haunches, over which his hands played hypnotically until the cheeks clenched, the deep hollows appearing in the symmetrical curves.

'Such a sweet little arse,' he whispered, his lips brushing her neck. She shivered. Already, his hands were plucking at her open blouse, slipping it off her shoulders, drawing it down her arms, to let it drop onto the grass on top of her skirt. She felt briefly ridiculous, standing there in the white, lace trimmed bra, and the white ankle socks and shoes, but then his fingers expertly unfastened the bra, eased the cups off her breasts, and she felt the cool of the air, felt her nipples bud and harden, felt the tingling response to his light, cupping caresses, and she shivered deeply.

'Oh, Al!' she murmured, the tears trembling in her voice. 'What if someone comes? There's kids around.'

'Won't they be the lucky ones?' he answered, his deep voice stirring her rapidly resurrecting hunger. 'You're a sight for anyone's eyes. I'd like the whole world to get a look at you.' He pulled her down into his arms, folding her into him as they nestled at the foot of the tree. 'In fact, I'm going to make sure people *do* get a good look at you, babe,' he whispered, his lips moving over her warm, satin soft breast, and nibbling at the pale little teat which crowned it.

The words registered, sent tiny shivers of alarm bells ringing at the edge of her consciousness, but his fingers were now sliding with assuredness between her thighs, seeking out the still damp furrow of her vulva, claiming the pulsing narrowness of the cleft he had so lately possessed, and her senses swam, centred to that awesome physical need and pleasure. She no longer thought of words, or of the weird spectacle she must present, curled up under a tree under the summer dappled sky, naked except for white socks and shoes, aware only of the throbbing desire at her very centre that his skilful fingers were fanning. She surrendered entirely to it, and to him, gladly, letting her thighs fall slackly open, lifting her body to him, in willingly slavish abandonment to his domination.

...to be continued

The cover photograph for this book and many others are
available as limited edition prints.
Write to:-

Viewfinders Photography
PO Box 200,
Reepham
Norfolk
NR10 4SY

for details, or see,

www.viewfinders.org.uk

TITLES IN PRINT

Silver Mink

UK £5.99 except *£4.99

All titles, both in print and out of print, are available as electronic downloads at:

http://www.adultbookshops.com

e-mail submissions to: Editor@electronicbookshops.com

Silver Moon

UK £5.99 except *£6.99